Deadman

Also by Jon A. Jackson

The Diehard

The Blind Pig

Grootka

Hit on the House

Dead Folks

Man with an Axe

La Donna Detroit

Deadman

Jon A. Jackson

GROVE PRESS
New York

Published simultaneously in Canada
Printed in the United States of America

FIRST GROVE PRESS EDITION

Library of Congress Cataloging-in-Publication Data

Jackson, Jon A.
    Deadman / Jon A. Jackson.
    ISBN 0-8021-3771-7
    I. Title.
PS3560.A2161D4   1994   813'.54—dc20   93-31521

Design by Laura Hammond Hough

Grove Press
841 Broadway
New York, NY 10003

01 02 03 04   10 9 8 7 6 5 4 3 2 1

For Jean Allison

Thanks: to my ballistics guru, Mike Gouse, and Bitterroot Valley gunsmiths Bruce Scott and Don Allen . . . to Hill Blackett, Jr., for information on cleansing filthy lucre . . . to Father Dusan Koprivica of Holy Trinity Serbian Orthodox Church, in Butte . . . and Barry Axtell, ditch rider . . . and especially to Jocko Jemmings of the Butte–Silver Bow Sheriff's Department.

Deadman

1

Roadkill

Some mornings are not just wonderful but nearly miraculous. A September morning in Montana can be like that. As far as Joe Service was concerned, this was one of them, a morning to remember. Driving east on the interstate between Deer Lodge and Butte, there was still a bite in the air at ten o'clock in the morning, and the air tasted delicious, as after a thunderstorm. But there had been no storm and there were no clouds, just a deep blue sky over the mountains and the broad valley floor, a degree bluer than Joe could ever remember seeing. The blinding sun of summer had gone. September's sun had declined to the south to create a mellower golden effect. The magpies swooped and swung along through the yellowing alders lining the creek bottom, deer lifted their heads out in the range, and high overhead the rough-legged hawk flexed his long primaries in the thin air and scanned the sparse grass for rabbits and mice.

It was a wonderful morning, a miracle, and Joe felt terrific. He was almost bouncing on the seat of a brand-new four-wheel-drive pickup. He was on his way home to his cabin in the mountains above Tinstar, a dusty little forgotten crossroads south of Butte. Helen would be there. She ought to be glad to see him, he thought. He'd been away for a few days, on business, and he knew she got bored and lonely in his absence. He had made some nice arrangements for them to take a little "toot," as he called it. He had finally resigned himself to the the fact that she was a city woman. The mountains didn't seem to interest her for long. She liked the country, but it was just a place to visit, to enjoy for a while. Now, he figured, a trip to Hawaii would cheer her up. His business was doing fine, she would be glad to know, although he really had no business except to "rinse funds," as he joked, and then find places to invest them, which he did very judiciously, very conservatively. She would be happy. Especially when she saw the truck, a present for her, a toy, just like one she had admired a couple of weeks ago. And if all that didn't cheer her up, to hell with her. He wasn't going to let it bother him, not on a morning like this.

He wasn't so much thinking about Helen as thinking around her. He was doing something he would have liked to call mind juggling, except that he didn't like the word "juggling." He liked the concept, the notion of many disparate things whirling around his head, being touched and propelled, directed, released, then touched again. It was better than holding something, clutching it and pondering it. That was too static for Joe Service. He much preferred juggling . . . if only the word weren't so dumb, so clumsy sounding. How did such an oafish word become attached to such an airy art? He wanted something nimbler. Helen was nimble. Like him she was small, lithe, and quick.

On his left as he traveled toward Anaconda, he noticed again a huge berm, or mass of freshly piled earth, with a number of yellow machines grooming it. He kept meaning to inquire about this project; he was interested in everything that was going on around him. But he hadn't pursued it. Some kind of Superfund cleanup site, someone had said. It had something to do with a century of mining in the Butte area, plus the residue of the Anaconda smelter. The mining had stopped in the early eighties and only recently started up again, on a reduced scale. The smelter was gone now, but both processes had apparently left plenty of heavy metals and other toxic minerals in the river system that made up the headwaters of the Clark Fork River. Joe made a note, mentally, to drive back here soon and check it all out. He didn't like the thought of poison in this paradise.

The road swung to the east now, headed toward Butte. The brown hills of September were dotted with sagebrush and then many strange-looking evergreens that stood about in isolation, like little green monuments—they seemed vaguely funereal. Ground juniper? He didn't think so: They didn't spread out, but were quite vertical, like sentries. He'd have to ask someone, or look it up in his little field guide to Western trees.

The road rose up, nearly empty of traffic, until beyond the near horizon he glimpsed the first jagged tops of the Continental Divide beyond Butte. In a little notch on the ridge he could make out a white figure. That was Our Lady of the Rockies, an immense statue of the Virgin that was lit up at night. It was a little kinky, Joe thought, but . . . what the heck. You could pull anything in Butte, it was a real joint.

At approximately the same moment, he saw the hitchhikers, a quarter of a mile ahead. Two men, one of them seated on a pile of duffel bags and the other standing with his arm outstretched. Joe didn't ordinarily pick up hitchhikers. In fact, he'd just left a zone around the town of Deer Lodge where stern highway signs advised motorists not to stop for hitchhikers because of the nearby Montana State Prison. But it was a beautiful day, Joe felt great, and as he approached he got the impression that these guys were dead beat—the seated one was slumped down like a man at the end of a long run, and the stander had that hand-on-cocked-hip look of someone who would prefer to be sitting.

He pulled over onto the shoulder and backed up to save them

the effort of lugging their bags. There really wasn't room for both guys in the cab of the pickup, but he figured one of them could ride on the bags in the back.

The thumber was a lean fellow with long black hair flowing out from under a new cowboy hat with a tall crown. All of his Western garb looked brand new—the hat, a leather vest, a fancy fringed leather jacket, jeans, and tooled cowboy boots. He stepped up on the passenger side and peered in the lowered window. "How far you going?" he asked, smiling.

"The other side of Butte," Joe said, "over the pass. Where you going?"

"That'd be great," the man said. His face was narrow and dark, he needed a shave, but he looked okay, just a long-haired cowboy wannabe—not an unfamiliar sight in these parts. Joe himself was rigged out in a variation of this wardrobe, only more working class. This guy didn't look crazy or criminal, just temporarily afoot. Joe hadn't noticed any vehicle broken down, but the east- and westbound lanes were widely separated out here; possibly the man's car was westbound and hidden behind one of the rises of land that sometimes shielded the lanes from one another.

Joe started to ask the fellow if he'd had car trouble, when the man said, "I need a little help with my buddy. He's not feeling too good."

Joe suppressed a sigh of annoyance. It was always like this, he told himself. You go to do someone a simple favor and it turns out to be more complicated. Chances were he'd end up taking these guys into Butte, maybe even to the hospital. But it was too nice a day to complain. He turned off the ignition and set the parking brake before getting out and coming around the pickup to where the other man sat, still slumped on the duffel bags.

"What's the trouble?" Joe asked. A quiet breeze whisked roadside dust. Joe put his hand on the crown of his own Western hat. He looked at the seated man. He was bigger, heavier than the thumber and not so well dressed. He had a sweat-stained cowboy hat pulled down over his brow and he was bearded. He wore an old military overcoat that could have used a cleaning, a year ago.

"I don't know," the thumber said, "he won't tell me. Won't talk at all."

Joe squatted down and peered up into the seated man's face. The mouth hung open. Joe reached up and lifted the man's hat brim slightly. The man's eyes were closed. Joe glanced down at the man's hands, folded in his lap. Joe looked up. The thumber was smiling slightly.

"The problem is," Joe said, "this man is dead."

"No shit," the man said. He held a .32-caliber automatic in his right hand, and he motioned with the barrel toward the corpse. "Better give me a hand with this dude."

Joe glanced around him briefly. There wasn't a single vehicle in sight, except for a distant semi, at least three, possibly four miles back, glittering silver in the sun, laboring up the grade. Joe estimated it would take at least four minutes to reach them.

The sun was shining brightly, the magpies were yakking in the fields, but the delicious Montana air had a metallic taste to it now. Joe sighed and stood up. He tried to hoist the dead man by his armpits, but he was very heavy. The other man lowered the tailgate of the new truck. There was a black vinyl cover over the box, fastened with snaps. The man wrenched it back, still covering Joe with the .32, then came to help him. He glanced down the highway. The truck was no longer in sight. It had apparently dipped down into an intervening depression.

"Move it," the man ordered, taking one of the dead man's arms. Between the two of them they managed to flop the heavy man onto the extended tailgate, and Joe shoved him into the bed of the truck, under the unsnapped portion of the vinyl cover.

"Throw that stuff in there," the man ordered. Joe piled the bags in behind and around the corpse and the other man flipped the vinyl cover back as the truck rumbled by them in a little flurry of dust. The gunman smiled, standing on the far side of the pickup as the semi passed, the .32 held down along his leg. Joe grasped the tailgate with both hands and slammed it upward to close it. He looked over at the gunman while he snapped the vinyl cover down securely.

"Let's go," the man said. "You drive." He moved along the ditch side of the pickup, watching carefully as Joe moved along the road side. When the gunman reached the passenger door he opened it with his left hand, which meant he had to turn awkwardly to his right. Joe opened the driver's door and brought up his own snub-nosed .38 with his right hand.

"No!" the man shouted, and his automatic erupted with a flat bark, firing across the bucket seats of the pickup cab.

The velocity of a bullet varies greatly, depending on the weight of the bullet and the load of the propellant, but in this case it was less than a thousand feet per second. As Joe was standing little more than six feet from the muzzle of the gun, he had about two hundredths of a second before impact. This is a very small period of time, but it is measurable, and time, as everybody knows now, is relative. Subjectively, it seemed a near eternity. Joe squeezed the trigger of his own pistol once. He did not see if his bullet had hit his assailant, for his head was suddenly smashed as if he'd taken a direct blow in the face from a sledgehammer. And that was it for Joe Service.

He fell backward, sprawling on his back on the paved road, his pistol still clutched in his right hand, his mouth open, his Western hat rolling away under the pickup. The bullet wound in Joe's forehead was small, almost unnoticeable, except that blood was welling out of it. His assailant raced around the front of the pickup and kicked the door shut, his pistol at the ready. He stared at Joe in disbelief, then stepped closer. He looked around wildly. The semi was gone down the highway, tires singing now as it picked up speed. No other vehicles had passed or were approaching. The blood was now trickling down the side of Joe's head, soaking into his thick black hair.

Hurriedly, the man jammed the .32 into his waistband and knelt to pry the .38 from Joe's hand. He tossed that into the front seat of the truck, through the open driver's window, then stooped to grasp the limp body under the arms. He dragged it to the other side of the pickup truck, off the road, and then rolled it down the embankment into the ditch. The body lay there, face down. The gunman looked around. Still no traffic, but the chrome of a car glinted to the west, approaching rapidly. The man drew out the .32 and emptied the magazine at the body. He stuffed the gun in his waistband again, then slammed the door on the passenger side. He got into the driver's seat and was reaching for the key in the ignition when he realized he was sitting on Joe's pistol. He extracted it and stuck it into the glove compartment as the car whistled by him. Then he paused. He reached under the dash and pulled the hood release. He got out and lifted the hood, then looked around. A westbound car crested the hill and whisked by, some hundred yards or so away. A couple more cars could be seen back to the west, miles away, but approaching.

Quickly, the gunman scuttled down to Joe's body and turned it. There was an awful lot of blood. He riffled through the pockets, taking everything that was on the body. He could hear the cars approaching. He stood and with his back to the road, shoulders hunched, held his right hand to his crotch, as if he were urinating. The cars sped by and one of them honked. He laughed. He looked down at the body and was tempted to piss on the body for real, but the urge wasn't there. He found a piece of paper in his shirt pocket and searched for a pencil. He knelt to the body again and quickly stood up.

By the side of the pickup he glanced around. There was a splatter of blood on the pavement. He saw the brim of Joe's hat jutting out from under the pickup. He bent and drew out the hat, then sailed it down into the ditch. It landed nowhere near Joe. The body lay at the bottom of the ditch, hardly visible to a passing car, or even a truck driver. A magpie sailed down the side of the hill and landed on a post of the interstate fence, its long tail swaying in the breeze. The magpie waited for the man to go.

"Joe Service, himself," the man said. "Who'da thought?" He shook his head with disbelief, then grinned broadly and got into the pickup.

It was two hours before the body was discovered. A passenger on the eastbound Rimrock Stage bus happened to glance up from the novel she was reading, and her eye was attracted by a party of magpies and a couple of ravens in the ditch alongside the interstate highway. The bus was already past the scene when she realized that the object of their attentions was not a roadkill deer, but a man. She cried out and stood up. The driver glanced into the overhead mirror and caught her eye. She signaled at him, waving her hand, then quickly made her way to the front and told him what she'd seen.

The driver instantly slowed and then braked to a halt. He tried not to swear in her presence—she was a nice-looking young woman, on her way to college in Bozeman—but a bus driver never likes an unscheduled stop. But out here you didn't not stop, even if you were confident that the passenger must have just seen a dead deer. He pulled over as quickly as possible and radioed ahead to the Butte–Silver Bow sheriff's department, informing them that a passenger thought she had seen a man down, in a ditch. He was going back to check, he said. He gave them a rough estimate of his location, about two or three miles west of the junction of I-15. He hadn't noticed the last mile marker. The dispatcher said a vehicle would respond.

The driver started to inform the passengers over the P.A. system, but then he stood up and assured the folks in the coach that nothing was amiss, just that he had to check out the report of a passenger—he'd be right back. He jogged back down the road in the cool midday sun. He didn't see anything, and by the time he had walked over the crest of the hill, out of sight of the bus, he slowed down and lit up a cigarette. It was very pleasant out here, he decided. He saw the ravens first. And then he spotted the body. As the jacket was brown, he thought at first that it might be a deer, but he hadn't approached much closer before he saw the blue jeans.

The magpies flew up reluctantly as the driver neared, and they didn't go far, but landed optimistically on the interstate fence, a few yards away. The two ravens had mounted well up into the sky, croaking. The driver knelt beside the man. There was a lot of dried blood, and there was birdshit all over the back of the man's canvas "tin coat." He turned the man and winced at the bloody face. He'd been shot at close range. The thick black hair was stiff with blood and the face was a bloody mask. But it didn't make any difference, for clearly the man was dead. He could detect no pulse, and the gravel was soaked with what looked like enough blood for two or three men.

He stood up and took a deep breath, then moved away and lit another cigarette. To his relief, he could see a police car, a Butte–Silver Bow County sheriff's Blazer, approaching in the westbound lane. He waved and the blue flickering lights on the roofbar went on. The vehicle slowed, then cruised a few hundred feet until the cop found a more conveniently negotiable section of the median. The Blazer swayed and bounced through the swale then turned onto the eastbound lanes and came rapidly forward.

The sheriff's deputy was a thickset man in his early thirties with a huge square face. He was evidently an Indian, but not evidently a Montana Indian. This was an Olmec, or a Toltec face. The bus driver had seen a face like this in a *National Geographic* magazine article about Central American ruins of the pre-Columbian era: massive stone heads, weighing hundreds of tons, sitting on the earth and veiled by jungle overgrowth. The brassy-looking nameplate on the deputy's tight, starched tan gabardine shirt was engraved "DEPUTY SHERIFF JACQUES LEE."

Deputy Lee nodded at the driver and stared down at the body. He put his huge hands on his narrow hips and pursed his thick lips.

Lee had a very large upper body but almost no buttocks and relatively short, slender legs. Still, he was over six feet tall. Seated behind a desk, or in a car, he would look even larger. Now he squatted down beside the body and picked up the limp wrist. He peeled back one of the man's eyelids and peered into the iris. The eye was glassy, but the iris shrank. Lee got to his feet with a huff and straightened his gabardine slacks, stooping to adjust the trouser legs over his dark and deeply polished boots.

Without a word he strode back to the car and reached inside for the microphone. "Three-nine-six, four-twelve. Mile marker one-thirty-six, got a man down. Ambulance. Tell 'em to bring blood, lots of it."

"Ambulance?" the bus driver said, incredulously. "Better call a hearse."

Lee didn't respond to this. He opened the back of the Blazer and got out a blanket, which he spread over the body. Then he turned to the driver, drew a notebook and a ballpoint pen out of his breast pocket, clicked the pen to expose the point, and said, "Name?"

The driver gave his name and the few details he could provide. "I've gotta be getting on," he said, "I got a bus full of folks."

"You're stopping in Butte, right?" Lee said.

"For fifteen minutes, less if I can get 'em to move," the driver said.

"If I'm not there, go ahead," Lee told him, "but get the girl's name and address and a phone number and leave it for me."

The driver jogged off down the road, and Lee returned to the body and carefully searched it for information. There was no wallet or personal effects at all—strong evidence of robbery, given the victim's generally well-appareled appearance. The boots alone were worth a few hundred, and Lee wondered that the killer/thief hadn't taken them. Thrust into the half-closed, inert left hand, however, he found a card, just a piece of heavy manila paper that appeared to have been cut out of a larger sheet with not very neat scissor-work. The card, about the size of a business card, was smeared with blood on both sides, and someone had scrawled with a #3 pencil two names, one above the other, in childish lettering. The writer had not pressed down very hard, and the lead was not very dark. Later, on closer examination, Lee would see that the first name was actually "CAR-MINES," but that the S had been obscured by blood and dirt. For now, he read it as "CARMINE," and the name below it as "DEAD-MAN."

Lee held the card by the edges and found a plastic evidence bag in the car for it. By that time the ambulance had arrived.

"Oh dear," said Sally Gradovich when she saw the body. "Is he dead?"

"Oughta be," Lee said, "but he's still winkin' . . . just. You better give him blood, he's about out." He didn't exactly smile, but there was a faint easing of the heaviness about Lee's face. Sally appreciated it.

"Okay, Jacky," she said, "we've got him." She and her colleague, Tom, eased the body onto a stretcher, and Lee helped Tom wheel it to the ambulance while Sally ran to radio in for full crash preparedness on arrival.

After they left, Lee began his methodical examination of the area. He found an expensive Stetson cowboy hat, boot prints, bloodstains on the road, and six empty .32-caliber cartridge casings. That was about it. He went on into Butte, to the St. James Hospital.

2

Jack the Bear

Jacky Lee was said to be taciturn, but he didn't see it that way. He could talk fine when he had something to say. It was just that he never saw the need for casual talk. Who knew, for instance, that his real name was Jacques LeBruyn? The last name had proved too difficult for most people, so when he went into the marines, he dropped the "Bruyn." It was just too much of a pain in the butt to explain time and again—to people who didn't really care—what the name was, how to pronounce it.

Too many people talked before they knew what to say, Jacky felt, before they actually knew anything. For instance, he knew nothing about the man he'd found on the highway, so when the admitting people at St. James asked for a name, Lee told them, "Carmine Deadman." And when doctors and nurses or other cops asked him about Deadman, Jacky just shrugged. What was there to say?

Within twenty-four hours, Deadman's condition had stabilized. But he was in a coma, and Dr. Morehouse, the emergency-room leader, was not optimistic about the man's chances.

"The man's got a bullet in his head," Morehouse said. "We could operate, but CAT scans and X rays cost money, and anyway, the prognosis is in the garbage can. I don't know if I'd recommend surgery at this moment if it was my favorite uncle. Who is he? Who will pay for it? The county? The bullet is antiseptic. It can stay there for now. Can't you find out who he is?"

"How come he's alive?" Jacky wanted to know. "A man takes a bullet in the middle of the forehead, he ought to be dead."

"Oh, *that* bullet," Morehouse said. "That's nothing. That bullet struck at a funny angle, I guess. It fractured the skull, but it didn't penetrate. It traveled along the surface, subcutaneously. Here it is." He held out a misshapen chunk of silvery metal. "Found it in his hair, actually."

"You mean there's another bullet in his head?" Jacky asked.

"Yeah, and four in the body. One in the shoulder was fragmented, the others were buried in the flesh of the back. You know, I'm gonna get me one of those 'tin coats.' I think that the low power of the bullet, plus the resistance of that heavy duck material, a shirt, an undershirt . . . it might be what saved his life—if he lives."

"What about the other head shot?"

"It might have deflected, but it entered behind and below the ear. The X rays show it, with some destroyed brain tissue, probably. I probed but not too extensively. It's lodged in there. We really need better pix. And Dr. Wilder. He can pick a brain. I can't."

Deadman looked like his putative name. His face was swathed in bandages, but it was about the size of a large pumpkin. He was wreathed in tubes and wires. The machines said he was functioning all right, heart beating strong and respiration regular, steady brain waves. He had a body like a god, tan and muscled. Morehouse pointed to this as the key reason for the man's startling physical recovery.

"The guy's got a hell of a lot going for him," Morehouse said. "Anybody else lost that much blood he'd look like a deflated balloon.

But this guy . . . hell, we hooked him up and he started cooking right away. Good brain waves, too. Who knows what's going on in that blown-up noggin?"

Dr. Wilder, the brain surgeon, had by now examined the patient extensively. He was more reserved in his estimates than Dr. Morehouse. "I think he is thinking," the doctor said, "but who knows what thoughts? Bullet in the left lower cranium . . . I don't know." He shook his own closely clipped skull mournfully. "One thing for sure: Mr. Deadman won't think like he used to think."

Jacky had taken the fingerprints and transmitted them to the FBI, but nothing had come back as yet. The name Carmine Deadman didn't mean anything to the National Crime Net. Jacky had not given that as the victim's name, simply as a name found on him. They did come back with the name Dante "Carmine" Busoni, a well-known mobster who had been shot in Detroit six months earlier. Jacky Lee didn't make anything of this, but he entered it into the file.

Two days after Deadman was picked up, an anonymous woman called St. James hospital. Presumably she'd read a press report, for she inquired after the condition of "Mr. Deadman." She also inquired about the medical expenses. She was referred to billing, where Mrs. McCoy rattled off a figure that she said was growing by the minute and informed the caller that if they were unable to identify Deadman and if he had no insurance, then the county would have to assume the burden. The following day, ten cashier's checks totaling nearly $30,000 arrived at St. James, via Federal Express. They were drawn on ten different banks, or bank branches, in Salt Lake City and were accompanied by instructions that the amount was to be applied to the medical expenses of "the patient known as Carmine Deadman." Further funds would be available, the instructions said.

With that the doctors proceeded. The patient's condition had improved considerably and surgery seemed a good bet. The bullet was removed and the patient responded well. He was young, healthy, and not just stable but improving. He did not regain consciousness, however, and the doctors weren't sure that he ever would. In subsequent days, more cashier's checks arrived via regular mail, each one in the amount of $2,995, and dedicated "for the recovery of Mr. Deadman." At first the checks were all from Salt Lake City, but then checks appeared, usually in groups of ten or more, from Los Angeles, Reno, Denver, and again, Salt Lake City.

When Jacky Lee heard of this development, he contacted the banks. It was a dead end: In every case, a woman had simply purchased a cashier's check with cash. The bank people remembered her, however, and generally described the purchaser as small and dark, about twenty-eight to thirty-four years of age, abundant black hair with a silver or white streak running back from the right temple. In a couple of cases, the woman wore a scarf, and then no mention was made of the hair, but she was always described as attractive. She never gave a name. One bank officer in Salt Lake City noted that she was suspicious of the woman, who had carried an expensive piece of luggage in which there was, she estimated, more than $50,000 in cash. But as the woman only purchased a check for $2,995, there was nothing to be said about that.

The Federal Express people remembered the woman, who had given the name "Alice Williams" and a Main Street address in Salt Lake City. The phone number belonged to a realtor's office. They told Lee that they'd never heard of any "Alice Williams." Subsequent letters didn't even have this information.

The next interesting development came when Deadman regained consciousness. He couldn't talk. His jaw on the left side had been shattered by the bullet, and part of his tongue was macerated by bone splinters. But his blue eyes were open and he seemed mentally alert. He made some preliminary sounds, not much more than groans, then he lapsed into silence. But his eyes began to move around, to register what was happening.

His nurse was Cathleen Yoder—Cateyo (or "Katie-Yo") to her friends. She was delighted with her patient's partial recovery. She'd been washing his body for several days, and she was impressed. "This is no dead man," she told her fellow nurses, with a little smile.

Dr. Wilder, the brain surgeon, told Jacky Lee that until Deadman chose to communicate, there was no way of knowing if the man remembered anything of the shooting, but he would be surprised if he did. "Usually a trauma of this sort blanks out the incident. It can be recovered, sometimes, in part, but rarely completely. We just have to wait and hope. For all I know, he doesn't remember anything at all." Too much of the brain had been destroyed, the doctor suspected. The injuries to the jaw and tongue could be repaired. The man would need speech therapy, no doubt, but it seemed likely that he would talk again, though it wasn't clear just how all this would come about. For the time being, Deadman was a ward of the county. Assuming that his anonymous benefactor continued to provide assistance, the hospital would provide the best of care.

In the meantime, Jacky Lee attempted to reconstruct the scenario of the crime. It had happened in broad daylight, practically high noon, but no one had witnessed it. Newspaper accounts had included a plea from the police for witnesses, but the only ones to come forward had said that they had noticed a pair of men hitchhiking in that area, about that time. An abandoned vehicle had been found some fifty miles west, on the same interstate highway, stolen in Missoula and out of gas. Had the hitchhikers been in this vehicle? Had another good samaritan picked the two men up? If so, why would they be let out at such an odd place, nowhere near another road? Was Deadman one of the hitchhikers, or was he someone who had picked up the other two, who then shot him and left him out on the highway? There seemed no way to tell.

The story soon disappeared from the news, the patient made progress, and Jacky Lee turned his attention to a series of arson fires that were plaguing the Butte area.

3

Ditch Bitch

Blood is thicker than water, they say . . . but not in Montana. Ask Grace Garland.

"Red" Garland was a reasonable woman, a kindly woman, in fact. She tolerated pheasant hunters and elk hunters on her land, if they asked first and closed the gates behind them (if they didn't close the gates, they could ask with their last breath, next time, and it wouldn't matter). She didn't mind trout fisherfolk at all, as they absorbedly drifted or waded through the Ruby River where it flowed across her property, or even crawled on their hands and knees up the twisty but trout-rich Tinstar Creek, which fed down from the mountains behind her spread. She had even welcomed over the years a dozen or so graduate students from the state university in Bozeman who were compiling an exhaustive census of fish, fowl, and mammal life on the Tinstar. But this amiable woman's eyes developed a reddish tint when the basic question of water rights was mentioned. In this she was one with every rancher or farmer in the West. Water is life. You don't mess with a rancher's right to water.

Garland ran a few hundred head of red cattle and cut a few hundred acres of hay on her spread up on the north end of the valley. She was sixty-three, a widow with an accountant son in Seattle who had recently told her he had AIDS, and a daughter who had become a wildlife biologist in Yellowstone Park (she had initiated the Tinstar Research Project while in graduate school). Red's late husband's father and his grandfather had done pretty much what Red was doing on this same land, although they'd possessed a bit more of it. A few years ago, Garland had sold an entire section to a fast-talking, cheerful young man from somewhere else, Canada he'd said. This fellow, Joseph Humann, had purchased the land above Garland's, on Garland Butte, that abutted on the National Forest and Bureau of Land Management lands that were being considered for inclusion in the Tinstar Wilderness Area. Tinstar Creek arose on that small mountain and trickled down to the Ruby River. All the water rights belonged to Garland, although she had conceded a few miner's inches to Humann for domestic purposes. There was also a lovely little hot springs on the mountain, on Humann's property.

Joseph Humann had been a good neighbor, so far. He kept to himself except for a few times when he'd dropped in at the ranch and shared a bottle of whiskey with Red, talking about the West and how it had been. Red had liked him. You couldn't ask for a better neighbor, although Red was a little uneasy about all the shooting that went on up there. . . . Well, not uneasy—it's certainly no sin for a man to shoot a gun on his own property, particularly out in the West—but a little curious, anyway, although she never said a word about it to the man. He wasn't a hunter, she knew that, somehow, but he sure was a shooter. It wasn't really a problem, it was a distant sound—Red figured he must be doing most of the shooting on the other side of the butte—but every time you hear a shot, even if you know it must be just sport, it kind of nags at your attention. After a while, of course, you ignore it, more or less.

Red tended to think of Humann as a temporary resident, a renter. For one thing, Humann had purchased the land with a provision that Garland (or her heirs—not likely, she feared, although her daughter might still prove out) could buy it back at the purchase price if Humann died or decided to sell before death. He had also agreed that Garland could pasture cattle on the meadowland, though not more than usual, for no fee. It was almost as if Garland still owned the property.

But a few months earlier, Humann had returned from one of his periodic prolonged absences with a young woman, whom he had introduced as Helen. He hadn't described her as his wife, and Red hadn't inquired further. This Helen was a pretty woman, about Joe's age. She looked as if she could be his sister: small, dark, athletic, with a lot of black hair that featured what Red considered an overly dramatic streak of silver in it—at first Red had been almost certain that it was a wig, but later she wasn't sure. The woman wasn't as cheerful and friendly as Humann. She and Red hadn't really hit it off. Red had been a little annoyed by a remark that Helen had passed, something about it must be difficult for a woman to run a big ranch like this, and didn't she get lonely? Red had simply said, no, it wasn't particularly hard and she'd never been lonely that she knew of. She'd been working on the land all her life; it seemed like a reasonable thing to do, something *worth* doing.

Now Humann had been gone for a month or more and his woman for about as long. They had a separate access road and a gate, which they kept locked. Red didn't see much of them, ever, though she always had a sense of their presence or absence, somehow—if nothing else, several days would go by without any shooting.

The problem was that the flow of water on Garland's land, below the Humann property, had noticeably declined. Part of this could be attributed to a dry summer. But Red Garland was beginning to think that there was more to it. She had ridden on horseback along her entire ditching system and the trout stream itself, but she hadn't ventured onto Humann's property. Because of the drought, water levels were generally down so much that even the most avid anglers were not traipsing up into this usually productive creek. There was minimal flow, and the trout were either hiding out in the pools or had fled to the Ruby. So it was likely just low water, but in low water the rancher measures each cupful, and Red was thinking that Humann, being an ignorant flatlander, might have left a sprinkler running on a garden or something while he was away, or even left the water running in the bathtub, or maybe the pipes broke, or . . . well anyway, it was being lost somehow, 'cause there ought to be more water than this.

Garland tried to call Humann, but there was no answer, just some dumb goddamn machine that she refused to speak into because she was damned if she was going to talk to a machine. She rode up there on horseback the first afternoon she could spare a half hour, and the gate was locked. There was no sign that a car had passed that way since the last rain, which was a couple weeks, which confirmed her feeling that he'd been gone a while and his streaky-haired whore not long after. Finally, Garland called the water judge and complained. The judge notified the ditch rider, Sally McIntyre, and asked her to check it out.

A ditch rider works for the irrigation district. They don't ordinarily ride along a ditch. Once upon a time they did, of course, patrolling on horseback the miles of irrigation ditches that make modern agriculture possible in the West. Nowadays, he or she cruises along the dusty access roads in four-wheel-drive pickup trucks, looking for violations. These violations occur at the headgates, usually, where some crafty farmer or rancher has tinkered with the inflow to gain a little more precious water. But sometimes there are problems that aren't visible from the road, such as when a blowout occurs. Say, for instance, that a badger has undermined a ditch, and it finally caves in, and the water flows out into a field, causing considerable loss of water for the downstream users. In mountainous country, such as this was, there could be a rock slide, or a fallen tree, perhaps beaver dams, that create ponds and little rills that run off into the woods. The ditch rider drives out along the system, looking for the break. Often enough they become ditch walkers. In this case, Tinstar Creek was itself a part of the ditch system.

That was what Sally McIntyre was doing in the lower Ruby Valley that morning. She'd been able to drive her truck along a good deal of Tinstar Creek on Garland's land, but she'd found nothing to account for the loss of water. She came at last to the fence that marked off the Humann property. The upper section was inaccessible by truck.

Sally McIntyre was a lean, rugged-looking woman. She was square-faced, handsome rather than pretty, and tended to dress in jeans and boots, a man's shirt, a sweat-stained cowboy hat crushed on her billowing red hair. She was in her thirties. She'd been a ditch rider for some fifteen years. It was a job she loved. From early spring, before the runoff started, until early winter when the snow and ice closed off the flow of water, she was empowered to roam this entire country, walk onto anybody's land without notice, and look at water. She called it playing with water. Like many people, Sally had loved to fool around with water, especially running water, from the first day she had toddled out into the sunshine—in her case, into a wonderfully muddy and reeking barnyard that was skirted by an irrigation ditch. She wasn't allowed near the ditch, but she could make puddles, divert rivulets, dig channels, and best of all, do all this in the bright sunlight or in the sweetly falling rain. She loved it. Nowadays, she still marveled that she was paid to play with water, to stroll along streams, to watch prairie dogs and badgers and coyotes, to pick flowers and dig river banks.

There was a little metal sign on Joseph Humann's fence, warning that it was electrified, but as she expected it didn't react when she tapped it with a screwdriver. Just about every electric fence she encountered was off ninety percent of the time. She didn't hesitate to climb over it in her jeans and rubber boots and go tramping up the meadow, a trash fork over her shoulder. It was a beautiful day in late

September. Her job was almost done for the year. The sky was so blue it broke your heart. You could see stars in mid-morning. The huge golden eagles were wheeling about the sky, the Clark's nutcrackers clacking away in the tall ponderosa pines. She saw three antelope beyond the ridge, bouncing away down the meadow. A fox drifted along the tree line, its red tail like a Chinese windsock. The last meadowlarks sprang up and twittered away, the white panels of their tail feathers declaring their identity.

Now and then she stopped to clear some debris from the trickle of the stream with her trash fork. She climbed on, up the hillside, appreciating the warm sun on her back. The stream wound around the shoulder of the hill, deepened into a gorge by untold centuries and lined with alder and willow that were turning a bright red. A few aspen were shedding their golden leaves, rattling brittlely in the breeze.

She walked the stream until she was up near the trees, mostly bull pine and ponderosa. Eventually she came to a diversion. She bent and felt the water. It was noticeably warmer than the main body of the creek. She had long heard that there was a hot springs up here—Garland Hot Springs, the old-timers called it, and complained that some flatlander had fenced it off—but she'd never visited it. Now she set off up the warm trickle until she came to a little glade where some-one had rearranged a few rocks to form a simple dam. A little digging had been all that was needed to deepen and enlarge what had proba-bly once been a small pool, perhaps no more than a hot mud bath, into a pretty little pond, maybe a hundred feet long and thirty or forty feet wide. The pond backed up against a low wall, or cliff, of granite outcrop and miscellaneous rock, the broken edges softened by wet, steaming moss. Obviously, the springs welled out of the rock, though probably there were many bubble holes, because she could see that there was a partially sandy bottom, which was probably a deposit from the upwelling water.

The pond was completely surrounded with giant old ponderosa

pines, and their long brown needles lay scattered on the surface and collected against the flat rocks that formed the dam. The water was steaming in the cool September day.

Without hesitation, Sally laid aside her trash fork and sat down on a large flat rock that seemed to have been placed there for that purpose and shucked off her boots. She stood up and unbuttoned her denim shirt, tossing it onto the rock. She unhooked her bra and tossed it onto the shirt, then slid off her jeans and socks and her panties. With hardly a glance around, she stepped down into the pool. It was hot, easily ninety degrees or more. With a great sigh she sank down onto the gravelly bottom of the shallow pool. She lay there, her legs outspread, feeling this wonderful heat penetrate her body. She thought about a cowboy she knew, named Gary. She wished he were here right now. She slipped down into the water until only her brows and cheeks were exposed and stared blissfully up into the deep blue sky.

The lofty pines surrounding the pool created a great blue window eighty feet or more above her. Festoons of waving gossamer wove a threadbare canopy into which an occasional Clark's nutcracker or a Steller's jay flitted, calling down raucous comments at her pale pinkening body. Her red hair soaked and fanned out into the hot water as she gazed upward. This was the time of gossamer, the goose summer, when thousands of tiny, nearly invisible spiders spun out these long filaments of silk and then cast off in the autumnal breezes, sailing away to fetch up on pines and sagebrush. She thought about the cowboy's lean body, and her hand crept down between her thighs.

After a while she sighed and crept through the shallow water, drawing herself along with her hands, her body floating, into the deeper water at the head of the pool, against the low cliff. Several little siphons, or outlets, in the sandy bed of the pool kept the sand gently fluttering and soft. Suddenly, her hand fell upon something hard and alien. At first she thought it was a rock. She grasped it and drew up her knees, her shoulders rising out of the warm water. She looked at the object that she raised through the water. It was a shiny, chromed revolver.

Sally stood up. She felt a little weak, but the feeling was delicious, despite the oddly menacing effect of finding a .38 under one's hand, in a secluded hot pool. With one hand she slicked the water off her body. A gentle breeze chilled her and she stepped into the warm sunlight to hasten her drying. She laid the pistol down on the large rock, next to her trash fork. When she was dry in the sun, she dressed and stood for a moment considering the gun. She left it there with the trash fork and walked up the path toward where she thought Humann's house might be. It was just over the ridge a short ways. But it was soon clear that no one was home, just as Red Garland had told her.

The path came out next to a shedlike garage on the edge of the clearing, in which the low log cabin stood. There were two motorcycles draped with blue plastic tarp, parked against the back wall of the simple, open-fronted structure. A late model Ford Escort was parked in one of its two gravel-floored bays. The other bay was empty.

The gate on the driveway to the clearing was a hundred yards away, but Sally could see that it was chained and locked. She went up on the porch of the cabin and knocked, although she knew there was no one there. There was no answer at the door. Not a sound but the soughing of the wind in the ponderosas that stood back from the cabin.

Sally walked around to the rear of the cabin, skirting a latticework structure of weathered cedar that concealed a propane tank which presumably fueled the range and/or the hot water heater, and stepped up onto a low deck supplied with a picnic table and some wooden lawn chairs. Someone had forgotten to take the cushions off the chairs and they were covered with pine needles and bird stains. There was a sliding patio door and she cupped her hands against the glass, trying to see inside. The drapes on the door were nearly, but not quite, pulled shut and all she could make out in the dark interior was the end of a brass bed and a view through an open door into a room beyond, presumably the living room, where a portion of a couch was visible. She shrugged and went back along the path, up the ridge and down past the pool, where she stopped to pick up her fork and the gun she'd found. She continued on along the warm trickle of runoff, the spill from the pond, until she came to Tinstar Creek.

She headed upstream. She had walked perhaps a quarter of a mile when she came upon a huge wet spill that spread down the mountainside. Under the water the grass was still a pale glistening green, flattened. Many little rills trickled off into the meadow and were lost among the rocks. The grass was deep green there.

A hundred feet farther up the creek she found the reason. Debris had jammed among the rocks, creating a dam. At first she thought it was just a mass of branches and possibly a chunk of rotted cottonwood. She set the pistol down on the ground and prodded among the debris with her fork. It was well-packed and oddly yielding. Then she saw a glint of paleness, and she thought it might be a dead fish, a pretty good-sized one, at that. She had heard there were some surprisingly large trout up these creeks, but in this dry season they would surely have fled down into the river. Maybe it had been spawning. She didn't know enough about trout to be sure, but she thought there was a fall spawning run and the spawning would take place in the feeder streams, rather than in the river.

This was interesting. She dagged at the white spot again with the fork. It had considerably more heft to it than she had initially thought. Much more than a fish. No fish could be that big in this creek. So what could it be? A sheep? Red Garland didn't run sheep. A calf? A white calf? Fallen into the creek? She raked away the debris and tossed it up on the opposite bank. She worked at this preliminary task methodically, like the earnest child she had once been, digging and poking, engrossed and unheeding a mother's tentatively anxious calls. She exposed more and more of what she began to think of, abstractly, as a waxy-looking bundle, when suddenly she realized that she was looking at the back of a human being. That tapering part of it led to a shoulder and an arm thrust into a mass of old black branches. And then she could see the back of the head—longish black hair tangled among the brush. And still the significance of it didn't strike her, so intent was she on her task. She was about to poke the major bulk of it with the fork again, when the enormity blossomed in her consciousness.

She gave a cry of dismay and stepped back, flinging the fork from her. She stood on the bank above this temporary dam for several long minutes, gawking down on this fleshy mass partially engulfed and obscured by debris, willing herself not to run. She breathed deeply and checked her watch. It was 2:30. She looked around. There was nothing of any interest, except for the eagles soaring and the distant view of a road, miles and miles away. A red fuel truck was driving down the road, trailing a plume of dust. Then she turned and searched in the grass for her fork and the pistol, found them, and walked back down the mountain.

At her truck she flipped on the CB radio. "Base, one-seven," she said. When they answered, she said, "I'm up on Garland Butte, Doris. I found something odd. You better call Carrie, get her out here. Ten-four."

Doris wanted to know what "odd" meant, but Sally said only, "Real odd. Too odd. Call Carrie, Doris. In fact"—she sighed—"you might as well call the sheriff's office, in Butte. But call Carrie, first. I'm on the service road above Garland's place. They'll have to come through the gate. I'll be waiting."

Then she sat down. She felt a little ill, a little queasy, but not bad. The magpies were still sailing around. "Hey! Indian woodpecker!" she called out at the magpies, a name she'd heard old-timers use. "You're no woodpecker," she said, as the long-tailed birds swirled about and glided up across the meadow to inspect the thing in the ditch, "you're a dead-skunkpecker and deer-hit-by-car-pecker. Call you the deathpecker." She frowned, thinking of the implications of a phrase like "dead-skunkpecker," then laughed. Why are you laughing? she asked herself. Well, why not? I'm not going to cry for this . . . this whoever it is, or was. She wanted to go back up and do something about the corpse, but what was there to do?

Carrie Conlin, the sheriff's deputy who lived and worked in the Tinstar area, arrived in her fancy county Blazer. She was a woman much like Sally. They had been to school together. They had both run off men who couldn't treat them right. But they were not friends, for some reason. Carrie Conlin was just too—what? Too cool, too distant?—for Sally's taste. Sally didn't think that Carrie liked her, or approved of her. Sally didn't fret about it, but there it was. It got in the way. Still, they got along, in a careful, gingerly fashion.

The two women hiked up the stream to the site. Sally fell back and waited a few yards downstream. She had no need to see the body. When Carrie had stooped and hunkered and looked to her heart's content, she walked on back, and the two of them descended the meadow in silence.

Jacky Lee arrived shortly afterward, with Deputy Kenny Dukes riding in the passenger seat. They got out and talked to Carrie for a few minutes, then Jacky came over to Sally. She liked Jacky. Once upon a time she had liked him too much, and then he had gotten married. She told him how and why she had found the body and then they all hiked up to the creek.

"Well, he's not going anywhere," Jacky said, after he'd viewed the body. They had not attempted to move it. "Kenny, go back down and call. We'll need the coroner and the wagon, and make sure they bring a body bag, for a drowning."

When Kenny had gone down, Jacky turned to Sally. "How did you happen to find this?" he asked. Carrie Conlin stood off to one side, listening but not part of the conversation; she might be guarding the body.

Sally told him again, the longer version now: about Grace Garland, declining water flows. Then she remembered about the gun. For some reason she had forgotten all about it, hadn't even mentioned it to Carrie. It was lying on the seat of her pickup, down on the road.

Jacky frowned when she told about finding it in the hot springs. "What were you doing up there?" he asked.

"I thought it might be closer, to call," she lied. "It was just lying there in the shallows. You couldn't miss it." For the life of her she couldn't imagine why she had made up this awkward version. It wasn't like her. Shock? Embarrassment? She didn't know, but it was too late to backtrack and it wouldn't make any difference. She would just tough it through.

"Nobody home up there?" Jacky asked.

Sally shook her head. "Didn't look like anybody'd been there in a while. There was dust and pine needles on the porch, in front of the door. No car tracks, no footprints."

Jacky listened attentively to these observations, but said nothing. He looked at her carefully. She looked all right, a little upset, a little nervous, but okay. In fact, she looked pretty good—fresh, clean, her hair a little frizzled from the wind, he guessed. "How are you?" he asked.

"I'm fine," she responded, returning his gaze frankly. She didn't say, How's your wife?

"Whose house is up there? Didn't Grace sell to some guy from California or something? A new house?"

Sally related the story she'd heard from Grace Garland, adding, "Red says the guy—Joe Humann—is some kind of gun nut. Target practice every day, when he's home. Maybe this gun didn't shoot straight and he tossed it." She pointed off beyond the trees where the hot springs was. "The cabin is just beyond the ridge."

Jacky asked Carrie if she'd mind sticking around, then he asked Sally to show him where she'd found the gun. They set off for the woods. When they got to the springs, she pointed and said, "Out there."

Jacky hadn't said a word on the walk up there and he didn't say anything now, just looked at the pool. Finally he asked, "Out in the middle?" When Sally nodded, he said, "You must have waded out to get it, eh?"

"Deeper'n it looks," Sally said. "I had to take off my boots."

Jacky glanced at her dry jeans. The faintest of smiles softened his large Indian face. "Pants too?"

Sally laughed. "Pants too," she said.

Jacky looked away, up the path, as if to hide his smile. "This the way to the house?" She nodded and they walked on. He walked about the place, much as she had, even peering in the window and lifting the lid on the lattice-work frame that concealed the large white propane tank to find out who serviced it. He jotted some notes in a little book. Finally he said, "I think you're right, nobody's been here for at least a coupla weeks, or more. Well, a body was found on the property and a gun in the pond. I think we could get a warrant to go in. I'll have to check it out. We better go on down, talk to Mickey"—the coroner—"he'll be here by now. If I need you later, I guess I can find you."

"Oh, really? You remember where I live?" She stalked away.

4
Dirty D

It was overcast, cool but not unusual for October. Jimmy Marshall found a parking place among the abandoned autos interspersed with the occasional late-model Chevy on the narrow street. This wasn't a neighborhood where you could find a lot of parking during business hours because not so many people were actually at work, not in the daytime, anyway. It was the east side of Detroit. The houses were brick multifamily flats, massive and unpretentious, though undoubtedly quite prosperous and encouraging, once upon a time. That was a long time ago, however. Now at least a third of the large front windows wore plywood glazing, and there was no grass, no flowers planted on the little yards in front of their front-wide porches. Here and there a wrought-iron fence was bent and battered ruthlessly, the gate always missing, though sometimes it could be seen nailed over a window.

Mulheisen and Jimmy Marshall stood on the street for a moment, neither of them feeling very cheerful under this gray but no doubt rainless sky. A little rain would have been better, Mulheisen thought. Rain was natural, it was something happening, falling out of the sky and collecting on sidewalks and washing some of this dirt down into the gutters. But it didn't rain as much as one always thought that it did, when one remembered the long parade of dull, gray, overcast skies.

The Big 4 cruiser was parked around the corner, a large sedan with wings painted on the doors and the words DETROIT POLICE. Dennis "The Menace" Noell leaned back against the hood of the cruiser, all six feet and eight inches of him, with his arms folded across his chest and a sour look on his handsome face. "Okay, Mul," he said, "you got ten minutes, then we're coming in."

By "we," he meant the other three members of the team of special detectives, all of them over six-four, all of them white. They stood out in this neighborhood like statues on a mountain. The only black man in the whole group was Jimmy Marshall.

"Better make it fifteen," Mulheisen said.

"It's my collar, Mul," Dennis insisted. "I saw him first."

"It's your collar," Mulheisen conceded. "I just want to make sure he gets to jail alive." He and Marshall set off around the corner.

The steps of the house were gritty with broken glass and dirt. The door in the center that led up to the second floor was gone. There was a tattered piece of paper that said PINCKNEY in a faded ballpoint script with an arrow pointing upward. They trudged up the stairs. It smelled pretty bad. Moldy plaster, Mulheisen thought, but the awful odor was compounded of many things: garbage, cat piss and cat shit, rotting clothes, beans cooked too long, cabbage cooked to perdition, vomit. Huge chunks of plaster were hacked or smashed out of the walls of the stairwell. There was scribbling all over the walls, idle obscenities in crayon or spray paint, an exhausted litany of rage and despair. The stairs themselves were littered with garbage and broken things. One couldn't always tell what the things had been—toys? Smashed pieces of plastic or pot metal. Things were actually jammed into the wall—curious pieces of wire, or the broken-off barrel of a cap pistol—as if someone had casually stabbed the house just in passing.

At the top of the stairs was a dirty sash window, the bottom pane knocked out. On either side were doors to the two opposing flats. On the right was the sibling of the note downstairs, saying PINCKNEY. Mulheisen stepped to one side of the door and pulled his raincoat back, laying his hand on the butt of the pistol in his hip grip. Jimmy Marshall actually took his gun out of his shoulder harness and held it in his left hand, then knocked on the door.

They were both good-sized men, Marshall a bit leaner and ten years younger, dark with a widow's peak on his closely cut black and curly hair. Mulheisen was older, fortyish, and his pale face had a much sadder look. It was the eyes, light blue and slightly protruding with the beginning of bags under them. When he smiled, or tried to, however, he revealed the long, somewhat spaced teeth that had given him the street name "Fang."

The door opened and a young black girl looked out. She could see they were cops. She was only about fourteen but had unusually large breasts. She wore a too-small yellow sweater that didn't reach the waistband of her very short leather skirt. Her mouth was open, slack, and her thick lips were heavily smeared with dark red lipstick. Her eyes were sharp, however, and intelligent.

"What are you looking for?" she said, directing her question at the black detective.

Jimmy Marshall didn't answer her. He pushed the door open and stepped past her into the incredibly cluttered and filthy kitchen. The sink was full of dishes and scummy water with oily crust; rings surrounded the utensils and dishes that broke the cold but molten-looking surface.

"Hey!" the girl said, but not loudly, really a hoarse whisper, as if not to wake a sleeper. There was loud but muffled music coming from an interior room.

Mulheisen moved past her looking to the left, his gun out. Jimmy went directly for the front of the house, shoulder to the jamb of the entries, then slipping through, looking to either side, sweeping his pistol smoothly, carefully, not extending it so that a hidden person could strike at his hand.

Mulheisen had checked the back porch and came on behind and to the left of Jimmy. The house was very cluttered with furniture and clothing thrown here and there, trampled underfoot, and many cardboard boxes. It looked like someone was moving in or out. A cat lounged placidly, its fur matted and yellow. They moved swiftly through the dining room and into what had once been a parlor. Doors opened off to the left, into bedrooms. The first door was open, and inside appeared to be the girl's bedroom, for it was neat and orderly, the bed made and no clothes strewn about. Mulheisen caught glimpses of posters stapled to the walls: Whitney Houston, was it? Michael Jackson? He wasn't sure.

The second bedroom door was closed, however, and this was the room where the music was playing. Jimmy Marshall barreled through the door low, his shoulder at knob level. He dropped to his knees, gun ready.

This was a good thing, for a fusillade of nine-millimeter bullets rattled through the opening at about the chest level of a man. The boy on the bed, his back against the headboard, was shucking out the clip when Jimmy hit him, sprawling across him, pinning him to the far wall. The Cobray submachine gun flew, smacking against the wall and bouncing back on the bed. The boy cried out, but his cry was stifled as Jimmy rolled across him.

Mulheisen stayed in the doorway, looking into the other rooms as available to line of sight. A middle-aged woman, perhaps no older than himself, sat frozen on a couch in the front room, surrounded with junk and clothing, her head, wrapped in a colorful cloth, turned slightly, eyes staring.

When Mulheisen was sure that the boy was subdued and Jimmy was in control, he moved cautiously into the front room and looked about. The television was going. Oprah was raising an eyebrow sarcastically at some women who were gesticulating wildly and

talking all at once. There was nobody else in the room. Mulheisen
nodded and backed away, looking behind him. The girl was glowering
in the doorway, her hands at her sides.

"David Pinckney," Jimmy said, hauling the boy to his feet,
"you're under arrest for the murder of Scott Willard. You have the
right to remain silent, you have the right . . ." His voice recited precisely. The boy was slender and handsome, about sixteen years old,
wearing sexy briefs and a tank top, his hair cut in topiary fashion. His
eyes were large and expressive. He wore no other clothing. He said
not a word as Jimmy cuffed his hands behind his back.

"You know what I like about the Cobray?" Jimmy said to Mulheisen as he brought the boy forward.

"It's not very accurate," Mulheisen said.

"And it gets empty real fast, especially when you're excited and
just hang on the trigger," Jimmy said.

Mulheisen stepped back into the front room. "Mrs. Pinckney,"
he said, "we're arresting your boy, David, for killing Scott Willard.
You probably want to call a lawyer. We're taking him downtown, to
Homicide. Thirteen hundred Beaubien. Jimmy," he called into the
room, "get some pants and shoes on him. A jacket."

He looked back at the woman. She had that dull, resigned look
he had come to dread. "You can't come in here like this," she said, but
with no great energy.

"Well, yes. Yes, I can," Mulheisen told her. He waved a legal
document. He looked around, taking in the disorder, smelling the
decay, the disgrace of this wretched place.

"I'm sorry the house is a mess," she said.

Mulheisen shrugged. "You didn't know I was coming."

"We was gonna move soon," she said. "Davey was gonna buy
us a house. In Warren."

"Well," Mulheisen sighed. "It would have been a good idea, I
guess." He wanted to say that the girl, the daughter, had kept her
room nice. She had tried to make a life for herself, something that

wasn't just a hell. He looked at the girl. She looked grim, her arms folded under her extraordinary breasts. Then she went into her room and slammed the door.

Afterward, they stood on the street as the cruiser took the kid away. It was really awful out. Dreary, smelly—smoke in the air, as usual, but not something nice like burning leaves, an odor suitable to October and one which Mulheisen remembered well. . . . Nor was it wood smoke, romantic and intriguing. This was the usual wet, noxious smell of smoldering garbage, of wet mattresses and sodden auto wrecks. It pervaded the air of Detroit these days. Mulheisen lit a cigar to defeat it, and he paced slowly back to the car with Jimmy.

"Sixteen," Jimmy was saying. "I don't know how you get to be a seasoned killer by sixteen."

"It's not young," Mulheisen said.

"Not young? Sixteen is not young? My Kirby is twelve, a child. He won't be grown up in four years."

"Knights were probably only teenagers," Mulheisen said. "In most North American Indian tribes you had to prove yourself a man by that age. An old man would be . . ." He paused, looking around at the wreckage of this venerable city, ". . . say, thirty. A sage, a very wise old man would be my age."

Jimmy regarded him with good-humored sarcasm: "You feeling sage, old man?"

"No, but I knew a lot at sixteen. I knew a lot more than people—my parents—gave me credit for. They kept thinking I was only a child. But I was more than a child. We underrate kids. This guy has some growing up to do—too bad he'll be doing it in prison. He'll be pretty grown up when we see him again. But my point is, a hundred years ago he would have been considered a man at his age."

"David Pinckney isn't a man," Jimmy said. "I doubt they'll try him as a man. And Scott Willard wasn't a man. He was only fifteen. He wanted to join the gang, but David just used him for target practice."

"Sometimes, you know, Jimmy, you just fall into your life. And sometimes . . ."

"Fall into your life?"

"Your life falls together," Mulheisen amended. "But then it never holds together, does it? Every once in a while it kind of falls apart, or sags awry . . . and all at once you find you can walk through gaping holes. The fabric is torn."

"You're not feeling sage," Jimmy noted.

Mulheisen shook his head. "I feel strange. I'm thinking I should become a . . ." he hesitated, looking shyly at Jimmy.

"What?" Jimmy looked over the top of the car, unlocking the door.

"A disc jockey," Mulheisen said.

They got in the car and drove, dodging in and out of spaces to let opposing cars by. "A disc jockey," Jimmy said, thoughtfully. "Like on the back of a matchbook cover. 'Big Money in Broadcasting.' "

"I'd just play jazz. Older jazz," Mulheisen said, "from the fifties and sixties. Coltrane . . . Cannonball . . . Horace Silver."

"Forties, too," Jimmy suggested. "Ben Webster, Benny Carter . . . maybe the John Kirby Sextet."

"Or a pilot," Mulheisen said. "I always wanted to fly."

"You'd be a terrible deejay," Jimmy said. "You don't have the personality for it."

"I don't?"

"You're too . . . I don't know . . . quiet. Too thoughty."

"Thoughty?" Mulheisen smiled.

"A deejay has to be more upbeat."

"Believe me, Jimmy, if I had nothing to do but play jazz and talk about it, I'd be more upbeat."

Mulheisen was in one of those periodic moods, not quite depression—no, no, not that—but still, a little gloomy, where he was wondering what the hell he was doing in the cop business. Most of the time he was quite happy in this business, engaged, intrigued, fascinated even. But often enough, more often lately, the sheer caseload had begun to wear him down. An endless task from the very beginning, it had become a monumental task, a job for mythic heroes.

He wasn't one of those who actually believed that cases are solved, but generally he expected to see an end to a case, a moment when there was little more to do. The murderer would be apprehended, the evidence gathered, the case gone to trial, the murderer locked away. In reality it rarely happened in just such a fashion, but occasionally it did. And anyway, he sort of expected it to happen pretty much along those lines. Sometimes a case would be shunted aside until a more favorable moment, but then he'd come across some interesting new lead and it would all spring back to life. Anymore, however, that didn't seem to be the usual way of it at all.

Instead, the new way was that he'd barely get started, and he'd be called away for something more pressing, some murder more bizarre, more spectacular, the victim more important, the press more interested. This had something to do with the burgeoning of violent crime in America's large cities, particularly in Detroit, where he was the mainstay of the Ninth Precinct, on the east side. For a long time, out of some peculiar sense of loyalty to his hometown, he had denied that Detroit was any worse than other large cities. Or at least he would insist that they were turning the corner, digging out of the hole. But lately he just didn't find it in himself to say that, even to himself.

When they got to the precinct, there was a message. A body had been found in Montana. There were some indications that the body belonged to Detroit. It belonged to the mob. Homicide thought it might be a link to a persistent case that involved Mulheisen. The case concerned the death of a well-known mob figure in Detroit.

Some lawman in Montana had asked if Mulheisen was interested. There was a phone number. A Mr. G. Antoni, county prosecutor, Silver Bow County.

Mulheisen sat in his tiny cube of an office and mused about Silver Bow County. He had a kind of Charles M. Russell vision of plains with snowy mountains in the distance, an encampment of Sioux by a winding river, the smoke from campfires rising silently into the Big Sky . . . perhaps a file of blue-coated soldiers on horseback, approaching the camp.

"What's it like in Montana?" Mulheisen asked the man on the other end of the line.

"It's great, Mul!" the man said, surprisingly familiar. "The aspen are all gold, the sun is shining, the trout are biting." Then, when Mulheisen didn't respond, the man said, "Hey Mul! It's Gianni! Gianni Antoni! Remember me?"

The name was faintly familiar. Mulheisen had a momentary flash of rows of double-decker bunks in an air force training camp in Texas. Footlockers. Uniforms hung up with the left sleeve exposed.

"An-*tony*," he said, emphasizing the second syllable.

"An-toni," the voice corrected, accenting the first syllable.

"Antoni," Mulheisen agreed. His heart lifted. This was a good memory. A good guy. They'd been in boot camp together. The drill instructor had always said "An-*tony*," and the other troops had insisted on this pronunciation, despite Antoni's constant corrections.

"Antoni," Mulheisen said again. "What the hell. Are you the guy behind this mob thing? They have the mob in Montana? Where is Silver Bow?"

"It's Butte. Mul, I'm so glad to get hold of you," Antoni said. "What are you, still a cop? You know anything about this guy?"

The questions tumbled back and forth. The sheriff had found a body. Some identification checked through the FBI said it was a man named Mario Soper, reputed to be a hit man out of New York, but with a reference to slain Detroit mob boss Carmine Busoni. Could this be Busoni's killer? And why would he be in Montana? Could Mulheisen come out?

Mulheisen was astounded. This was the breakthrough, he thought. The murder of Carmine had been on his lap for months. He had so many questions to ask Antoni, but they seemed too many for the telephone. Gone were all thoughts of becoming a disc jockey.

The dead man, Mario Soper, had been found on property belonging to a man named Joseph Humann, who had moved into the area a few years earlier, presumably from Canada. Humann had been missing for more than a month, along with a young woman named Helen, who had been living with him since earlier in the year.

"Tell me about the woman," Mulheisen demanded.

The local cops had come up with a description. She was about thirty, small and dark, a city woman. She'd appeared with this man Humann about six months before, after Humann had been away for a few weeks, as apparently he was wont to do (some of the locals were of the opinion that he had a job, or a business, in California, and had to return there from time to time). The woman had impressed everyone. Very attractive. A mane of black hair, with a silver streak in it. She might be the man's sister; they were both small and dark.

Mulheisen was puzzled about Soper. He knew who Soper was, but he had never connected him to Carmine's murder. He had no idea why a notation on Soper's FBI file would mention Carmine. Perhaps Carmine had employed Soper at some time, or the mob employed him to track down Helen, and an informant had passed it on to the FBI. Mulheisen had never heard anything about it. Still, it was interesting. He told Antoni that he would have to check it out with his superiors. It might be worth sending an investigator.

Mulheisen called Laddy McClain, the chief of Homicide. "We've got a lead on Helen Sedlacek," he said. "She may have been in Montana, just a few weeks ago. Apparently, one of the mob boys tracked her down. But she—or someone—got him first." This concatenation had occurred to Mulheisen just in the act of relating it to McClain.

McClain was just as interested. "Maybe you better go out there," he said.

5

No-Fat

Humphrey DiEbola was reflecting on how quickly things change. Truly, nothing was permanent in this ephemeral world. The old priest from his father's hometown, not so far from Salerno, had told him this when DiEbola took his father's body home for burial. DiEbola had only been in this little sunny village once before, not long after World War II. In those days Humphrey was Umberto to his family, but no American kid was ever called Umberto by his friends. Among his friends he was called not after the tough guy Bogart, but a character who appeared in the "Joe Palooka" comic strip. This Humphrey was a huge, cheerful blimp of a guy who rode around on a tricycle that carried his house, although one could never see how the character could have squeezed into the house, which resembled a hillbilly outhouse on wheels. This nickname was a very painful thing for young Humphrey, but he learned to take it cheerfully. There was no question that he did in fact much resemble the cartoon Humphrey.

When Umberto/Humphrey returned to Italy in 1972, to bury his father, the village was no longer a village. It had survived the invasion of the Eighth Army, but not the automobile, television, and prosperity. "Only the Church endures," the old priest had assured him, but Umberto DiEbola thought that another durable institution, La Cosa Nostra, might rival the Church. He was no longer so sure of this.

Even the name Humphrey hadn't lasted for long. As young and clever DiEbola rose in the mob hierarchy in Detroit, he had come to be known simply as Fat, or the Fat Man. That was the doing of his best friend, Carmine. If Carmine called you Fat, everybody else called you Fat. In time this cruel epithet had taken on a kind of dignity, even respect, because of the man behind it and the man behind him. Then one day, in the space of an hour, Fat became Humphrey again. And now, since no one remembered the ridiculous comic-strip character, the name had even more dignity and respect than Carmine. Because it was soon apparent to all but a few disappointed Carmine followers that Humphrey was the man who should have been running things all along.

Yes, it was just one day, a matter of seconds. Carmine was riding in the backseat of his dark brown Cadillac, on his way to work, when the unthinkable happened. The regular driver was sick, so Guiliano Valentia was told to drive. He had recently immigrated and didn't know the city at all, had hardly been out of the compound at the Krispee Chips factory where he was living in the dormitory with the other young immigrants, but he was reputed to be a good driver. The street on which the factory was located was narrow, with parking on both sides, which meant that the Cadillac traveled a narrow single lane. The block was very long, and they had barely entered and started down this narrow lane when a van pulled out at the last minute and Guiliano swerved to crash into a parked car. They weren't going very fast, of course, and the damage was not significant, nobody was hurt, but when Carlo, the bodyguard, angrily leaped out of the front seat, he was immediately cut down by a shotgun blast.

Guiliano tried to scramble out his door, but the Cadillac was too close to the car it had struck, and he couldn't get the door open far enough. Someone fired a shotgun into the front seat, hitting

Guiliano, literally blowing him off the seat so that he fell down and was jammed between the partially opened door and the front seat. Then another blast was fired into the backseat, and someone actually got into the car and leaned over the seat to shoot poor Carmine again and again, the car rocking and thundering from the blasts. Then the assailant ran away.

Guiliano survived. Having instinctively raised his right arm and then falling half out of the car and into a kind of protective crevice where the killer couldn't easily get another shot at him was what had saved him, although he lost his right eye and the hearing in his right ear, and his right arm was practically useless. He insisted that the killer was a rat, a small man wearing a rat mask and a hat. At first he said that it was the rat from Carmine's office, which was a cunning man-sized steel sculpture of a shotgun-toting rat—a piece of modern art that was at once humorous and mocking and strangely powerful. Carmine's wife had bought it for him from a well-known artist, a man who went by a single name: Jabe.

Guiliano's confusion was understandable, in a way. He was not a sophisticated young man. He had seen killers in the old country who carried shotguns on slings, bodyguards actually. And he had seen the rat statue on his single visit to the boss's office. It had frightened him, or at least had caught his imagination. Where he came from, statues were sometimes reputed to have magical, or religious, powers; they wept, bled, and performed miracles. Another witness on the street, however, had told the police that he thought the killer was a woman, wearing a Mickey Mouse mask and a fedora. "Ran like a girl," said the witness, one Markis Belgravy, a resident of a house close to the scene. "She run and jump in another van, headed in the other direction, toward Jefferson. Then they hauled ass." The van that had caused the accident was abandoned, of course, and it had been stolen just an hour earlier, not a mile away.

Carmine had been dead for twenty minutes when the Fat Man was told. One of the secretaries at Krispee Chips had called him. The men who should have called him, Carmine's other bodyguards and assistants, were being questioned by the police and otherwise too rattled to act with judicious dispatch. Fat heard the news on the phone in the breakfast room of his home in Grosse Pointe. He was having a kind of second breakfast, a midmorning snack, of menudo and crusty Italian bread. His cook, Chef Pepe, made a very good menudo, although he disapproved of his employer's instruction that he must use the various chilies sparingly. Fat was very fond of doctoring the menudo himself, with bottled sauces. Currently, he liked a piquin sauce from Mexico, called Salsa Picante de la Viuda, which he referred to as "the Widow," his soft baritone lingering on the final syllable in a whispery mock horror-movie style while he widened his eyes theatrically. He also liked a habanero sauce that came from Costa Rica, a small bottle with a humble brown paper label and a tiny opening—a surefire sign of volatility in the Fat Man's estimation: "They don't dare let you put too much on; they could be sued." This sauce was undeniably more flavorful and much hotter than "the Widow," but Fat was a man of loyalty, and he wasn't going to drop his old flame, as it were, overnight.

Many of his associates had remarked on DiEbola's taste for Mexican and/or Latin American cuisine, seeing it as a kind of betrayal of their native Italian cuisine, but here the Fat Man's loyalty divided. Like many otherwise intelligent people, he had an irrational fear of doctors and medical practice generally, and he had developed his own complex theories, almost a philosophy about his body and his health. The principal focus in this theory was the war on fat, a war that he reasonably saw as handicapped by the ingestion of pasta, not to mention olive oil. Spices were good, because they were not in themselves fattening and could satisfy the appetite. Italian cuisine was spicy, but not spicy enough. But most important, he deeply believed, deep down in the lardy nucleus of his being, that chili peppers burned off fat. He had read it in a women's magazine in the checkout line of the Wrigley's supermarket. Just the mere ingestion of vegetable fire consumed calories. The Latin American cuisines were heavily dependent on the chili, and so now was Señor Fat (yet another nickname, never used to his face). Since he loathed exercise and had never in his life actually performed anything that could even remotely be called labor, the chili was his only faithful ally in the war on his own relentlessly multiplying flesh.

The secretary from Krispee Chips had addressed him as Mr. DiEbola when she gave him the bad news about Carmine. She had always previously called him Fat, in a cheery familiar way, but for some reason she had adopted the formal usage now. He immediately countered by saying, "Thank you, Miss Gardino. As soon as Mr. Rossamani is available, will you ask him to call Humphrey?"

"Humphrey?" Miss Gardino said. He visualized her eyebrows lifting straight up.

"Me," he said, and he went back to his menudo. It was a very good menudo, the tripe particularly meaty and the sauce thick rather than watery. It took the habanero sauce well. He, the man who feared pasta, slathered butter onto the Italian bread and soaked up the juice after he had eaten all the chewy stomach lining and the nutty garbanzos. It was very good, and he felt exhilarated and not too stuffed, though he was a little sad about his old friend Carmine.

But he was philosophical. It had been a long time since Carmine had actually run the show. Basically, what Carmine had done of late was alter and delay Fat's schemes and machinations, thereby creating a worse situation than if he'd made his own decisions and plans. Whenever Carmine had moved against DiEbola's advice, it had gotten him in trouble. A significant instance was the matter of Big Sid Sedlacek. Several years back, Big Sid had skimmed a quarter of a million dollars off the mob's take on numbers, loans, women, and so forth. Carmine had wanted to knock Big Sid, but he had allowed himself to be convinced by the Fat Man simply to slap him around a bit and put him out to work his way back into favor. DiEbola still believed that this had been good policy. Big Sid had been a useful, amiable man; he projected a positive image for the mob, and his theft had not been major. Why alienate a lot of Big Sid's many friends and dependents, if not in fact fire them with revenge, by hitting this friendly goof? Really likable people were more than a little thin on the ground in the mob. A man like Sid, who brought a smile to the faces of everyone from shoeshine boys to hardened whores the minute he hove into sight, was worth a lot to the mob.

What Humphrey had not approved of was Carmine's putting Big Sid in charge of the street drug scene, once he had seemingly rehabilitated himself. In fact, Humphrey had not approved of going back into the street drug trade once they had pulled out. He hadn't approved of pulling out in the first place, either, but that had been argued to death on higher levels, councils where Humphrey DiEbola hadn't been heard, yet. The council had decided to abandon the street trade, at least on the retail level, because they foresaw huge amounts of federal money being spent on eradicating this trade, and they wanted to avoid damage. But, of course, on every local scene, the mobsters began to sneak back in. The sneakback in Detroit, however, was Carmine's idea, as was the idea of using Big Sid. Carmine's angle was that it could be done without the council knowing ("Hell, they're doing it themselves, Fat! You know they are!"), and if they found out, it could all be blamed on Big Sid, who was a known backdoor man anyway.

Well, Carmine had been almost right—a condition which Humphrey considered as fatal as macaroni and cheese. Big Sid had skimmed, or rather shoveled away, millions this time, but the councils had not learned that it had been Carmine's doing. (Or had they? Could they be behind this hit? DiEbola didn't think so, but he didn't rule it out either.)

A key player in the Big Sid matter had been a freelance mob investigator named Joe Service. He worked on contract for everybody, across the country. Humphrey had a lot of respect for Joe. The young man was, in his eyes, smart, efficient, amoral, and, most important of all, avaricious to a wise and judicious degree. He was also loyal to a gaugeable degree: i.e, if you didn't screw over him he would not screw over you. Carmine, the consummate cynic, did not believe this and had systematically tried to cheat Joe on every single contract he had taken on for them over the years. Service had complained, as had the Fat Man—who thought it was stupid to hire good help and then when they did their job to try to renege on the contract—but he had faithfully carried out Carmine's wishes in this as in all things, once he saw that his counsel couldn't sway the boss. Service, for his part, as Humphrey saw it, stayed more or less loyal because he always foresaw that he would have a subsequent chance to mend his fortunes. Well, Joe Service was right. Humphrey knew that he would definitely be needing Joe's services now.

When Rossamani, one of Carmine's more useful minions, called DiEbola shortly after the secretary had, he hesitantly said, "Humphrey? Rossie. You heard about Carmine? What do you think?"

DiEbola was gratified. By this simple statement he knew two important things: The guys had instinctively assumed that he, Humphrey DiEbola, was the boss now; and he knew he would never be called Fat again. Who knows? It might even help him lose weight. A positive state of mind is essential for great undertakings. But these were fleeting thoughts.

His first order was for Rossie to get hold of Joe Service. They were both under the impression that Joe was still in Detroit, still working on cleaning up the Big Sid mess, but no one had seen him in days. They would have to contact him in the usual way, through an answering service in San Francisco. Joe always called back within hours, or no more than a day. DiEbola believed this service passed the message to another service, which passed it to another service and that to another. How long this chain was, he didn't know, but it was normally efficient. Only this time nothing happened.

What could this mean? Was Joe Service involved in the murder of Carmine? Was he acting at the behest of other bosses, perhaps annoyed at Carmine's disregard of the council ukase on the street trade? DiEbola's first impulse was to call his confidential contacts in the other mob satrapies around the country, feel it out. He might be able to get a hint that one or more of the other bosses were behind this. But then he decided no. It wouldn't do, in these first few days in office, to betray this kind of alarm. No one in Detroit had argued against DiEbola's assumption of power, but this was not necessarily true elsewhere.

Instead, he called in the man whom Guiliano had replaced as driver, one Peter Merino, a middle-aged man who had driven for Carmine for many years. He was a cousin of Carmine's wife.

The interview took place in Carmine's old office, at Krispee Chips, under the eye of the rat. Peter was very nervous. He had called in sick the morning of the killing, he said, because he *was* sick. Not only that, his whole family was sick—his wife and his two kids. They were sick to their stomachs.

"What is this, food poisoning?" Humphrey asked with horror. In his mind nothing could be more evil than food poisoning. If you couldn't trust your food, what could you trust?

"Bad milk," Peter said. "I'm sure it was the milk. The kids was throwin' up, the old lady was throwin' up, I was heavin' my guts—an' all I did was put a little in my coffee! The kids had it in their Froot Loops! It coulda killed 'em!"

"What did you do with the milk?" Humphrey wanted to know.

"The old lady threw it out," Peter said. "I was mad as hell, I was gonna sue the dairy, the store, everybody. But she's that way, she poured it down the drain before anyone used any more of it. Hell, the fuckin' cat threw up and shit all over the house!"

This was ominous. Humphrey called on the widow of Carlo, the bodyguard. Had Carlo been ill that morning? No, she said, but maybe he was a little sleepier than usual. She had been sleepy too, even though they'd had coffee together, as usual. She'd gone back to bed, which she never did.

Humphrey visited Carmine's widow, the beauteous art collector Annamaria. She said she had noticed that Carlo seemed a bit slow when he came by with Guiliano that morning. When Carmine asked why Guiliano was driving, Carlo had just yawned and said he didn't know. Carmine was annoyed but that was all.

Humphrey didn't find out any more than that, but it was enough. Someone had been diabolically clever, he saw. A faithful, competent driver is sick; a bodyguard is a bit slow; not enough to raise the alarm, but enough to lower the defenses and increase the odds for a successful hit. A very daring and flamboyant hit, practically on the boss's threshold.

So, a clever killer and at least one accomplice to drive. A small person. A very smart person, bold and ruthless. If you knew Joe Service at all, you knew he was small, very clever, bold, and ruthless. When Humphrey didn't hear from Joe Service in the next few days, he was forced to make a reluctant connection.

This information had to be passed to the rest of the leadership around the country. It was a little sticky at first. But Humphrey was able subtly to communicate the idea that it was the fault of Carmine, who had evidently alienated Joe Service and then enlisted him in some unknown enterprise—Humphrey hadn't known a thing about it, or so he said. Mitch, from New York, was helpful. He reported that Carmine had asked for a hitter to take out Service just a week or so before Service had done the number on Carmine. Then Carmine had put the hitter on hold. Now, if Humphrey liked, Mitch would gladly supply the hitter. Humphrey liked. He had liked Joe too, once, but that was once. A guy who would poison food . . . who would have thought?

Mitch's hitter he didn't like, not even for a minute. He was a prick. He called himself Mario Soper. Self-important—you couldn't tell him anything—and he didn't talk. He just sat and looked at you with dull eyes and a slack mouth, like he wanted to pull the trigger on you, too. Maybe he thought that was a good tactic; it kept everybody on their toes. But Humphrey thought it was bullshit. Now, Joe, he was arrogant too, in his way, but he was funny, he was human. This turd . . . Humphrey couldn't stand him. He was perversely pleased when the jerk didn't find anything. Everybody in Detroit was glad when the prick left after a few days. He'd managed to piss everybody off.

And then, of course, just when everything was settling down and business was back to normal, Humphrey's least favorite cop, Mulheisen from the Ninth, started nosing around.

Mulheisen didn't look so tough at first glance. He wasn't a big man, but big enough. He might be known on the street as "Sergeant Fang," but he really wasn't unattractive; many women liked him, some of them quite a bit. His friends didn't just like him, they were devoted to him. But he had enemies and they loathed him. It didn't seem to bother Mulheisen, one way or the other. He wasn't one of those men who cares what others think of him.

One afternoon, not long after Carmine's death, Mulheisen had dropped into Humphrey's office at Krispee Chips, accompanied by his young assistant, Jimmy Marshall. Tall, dark brown, sometimes wearing glasses, sometimes wearing contact lenses, Sgt. Marshall was in some ways more menacing than Mulheisen. As Marshall had gotten older (he was about thirty), he had filled out a little, he looked stronger, and he was. He cultivated a kind of Malcolm X clean-cut look, complete with enigmatic smiles. He could make one believe he was looking right through one and didn't like what he saw.

Mulheisen gazed about the office and said, "I see you've still got Carmine's rat. Mind if I smoke?"

"Go right ahead, Mul. The rat belongs to Carmine's wife, but she hasn't come for it. Sit down, sit down. Can I get you a drink? Anything?"

"No," Mulheisen said, lighting up a No. 4 La Regenta. "Well, coffee. Do you do good coffee, Fat?"

Humphrey lurched forward, his great belly pressing against the desk, to poke at a teak name board on which was mounted what looked like, but surely wasn't, a solid gold plate. It was engraved, MR. DIEBOLA. "Call me Humphrey, Mul," he said.

Mulheisen's pale brows shot up. "Humphrey? You mean like Hubert H.? Or would it be the old Smollett character, Humphry Clinker?"

"Smollett?" Humphrey was surprised and pleased by this reference. As a teenager he had struggled through Smollett's strange eighteenth-century novel about an amiable and competent servant of a country squire, hoping in some sympathetically magic way that it would help to inform him about who he was. It hadn't, but he had found it amusing. He had never told anyone, of course, that he had read such arcane stuff, just as he had never let it out that he had read Jane Austen. But it was curiously gratifying to know that Mulheisen knew about Humphry Clinker.

Humphrey punched a button and told Miss Gardino to please bring in a tray of coffee. Then he heaved himself to his feet and made his way with swinging arms to a handsome cabinet, from which he extracted an old bottle of calvados. He wheezed his way back and set it on the edge of the desk just as Miss Gardino arrived with a chromed vacuum carafe of coffee, accompanied by a bone china creamer and sugar bowl to match the three cups and saucers. She poured. They all declined cream and sugar, so she left. Humphrey poured calvados into three tiny flutelike shot glasses. He carried his own coffee and calvados behind the desk and the two men helped themselves.

Mulheisen sipped the calvados with pleasure and drank the coffee. He cocked his head slightly and said, "Very good. Colombian?"

"Sumatra Blue Lintong," said Humphrey.

"So, Humphrey," Mulheisen said, "life is good? You're the king of the castle now. I imagine it's rather like Harry Truman found after the old man died—a lot more trouble than pleasure, eh?"

Humphrey smiled benignly, nodding his head in seeming assent. "What can I do for you, Mulheisen?" he asked. "How can I help you?" He spread his pudgy hands.

"I don't know if you can help me," Mulheisen said. "I guess you don't know who killed Carmine? I didn't think so. I just thought I'd drop by for a visit, see how you were getting along and to ask if you knew anything about Helen Sedlacek."

"Big Sid's girl? No. What should I know? We aren't very close. Although she used to like me. But when her dad died . . . well, she was a little angry. Grief, I guess, or shock. I could understand that. By the way, Mul, you did a fine job tracking down Sid's killer. I'm sure you will find Carmine's killer, as well. If I hear of anything that would help, I'll sure . . ."

"She's disappeared," Mulheisen said. "Sold out her business and left, not a word to anyone."

Humphrey was surprised. Big Sid's beautiful and fiery daughter was a successful businesswoman who ran some kind of consultant firm in Southfield. She had been outspoken about her father's death, recklessly blaming Carmine. Some said she was cooperating with the police. Well, of course, it had been a hit. The whole world could see it was a professional hit. Humphrey had hired the hitter himself, a man named Hal Good. But it wasn't as if Helen hadn't grown up knowing her father was a big man in the mob. There is a kind of discipline expected in these circumstances. But Helen, this crazy little girl— Humphrey remembered her as tiny and lively, a kind of black-haired Tinker Bell—she couldn't shut her mouth.

On Humphrey's advice Carmine had ignored her. So now she had sold out her partnership in her firm and had disappeared. This was not good.

"Just like that?" he said to Mulheisen.

Mulheisen shrugged. "Packed up and moved, bag and baggage," he said, "except that she didn't really move. She put everything in storage. Her mother hasn't heard from her, her friends have no idea where she went. They say she had a new boyfriend, but none of them met him, and she didn't mention a name. So . . . I just thought, since her dad used to work for you, you might have some idea. No?"

"Mul, if I could help . . ." Humphrey spread his arms and his hands helplessly. "I'll certainly ask around, and if I hear anything . . ."

"I know," Mulheisen said, standing. "Thanks for the coffee, Fat . . . er, Humphrey. You know, Humphrey suits you. I like it. And thanks for the calvados."

They had not cleared the lobby of Krispee Chips before Humphrey was on the phone to Rossie. "Get me the Yak," he said.

Roman Yakovich had been a lifelong associate of the late Sid Sedlacek. He still lived in an apartment in the garage behind Sedlacek's home, looking after Mrs. Sid, as he called her. He was a good man, Humphrey knew. He had him brought in, and from him he learned that Helen had been visited by Joe Service just a couple of weeks before she had disappeared.

"I didden think nothin' of it," the Yak said. "They played racquetball in Sid's gym, in the basement."

"Did he come around again?" Humphrey asked.

"I didden see him," the Yak said. "Joe's a good guy. Liddle Helen was mad at him, at first—she thought he was one of Carmine's boys—but then she seemed to think he was all right."

"Well, don't worry about it, old friend," Humphrey said, patting the burly Yak on his shoulder. "But if you hear anything . . . By the way, how does Mrs. Sid take this? She must be going crazy. She loved that girl."

The Yak shook his head grimly. "It ain't right, Mr. DiEbola. First Sid . . . dies . . . which she almost died herself from grief. Then Liddle Helen just runs off."

"Kids," Humphrey said, despairingly, "they break our hearts." He, of course, had no children. He had never married. He hadn't been interested in the opposite sex since he was about seventeen. He was quite comfortable about this by now. He had a benign if obscured view of women: He didn't really see them, in a way, but they seemed to be all right. Still, he had seen Helen since she was a baby—he had gone to her christening, in fact—so he didn't think of her the way he thought of women. She was more like a niece, a favorite niece. She used to bounce on his knee and make him give her horsey-back rides. She used to call him Uncle Umberto—"Unca Umby," at first. He had seen her grow up and become considerably less interested in him, but he hadn't minded. They were still pals, at least up until the time that her father was killed. In fact, she had called him a few weeks after, tearful and outraged. He had tried to console her, but it was impossible. She wanted him to do something about Carmine.

"What can I do, honey?" he'd said. "It's the way things are. Your daddy knew that."

No, no, she insisted, it wasn't the way things were. He must know that. He must do something about Carmine.

"You can do something," he'd said, quietly. He had surprised himself by saying it and he didn't really know what he meant by it, but perhaps Helen had known.

Humphrey suppressed this thought now, this whole conversation. He hadn't really said any such thing to her, he decided. But now Helen had done something, he knew it in his bones. Helen and Joe. It bothered him that Helen would make herself so . . . well, how could you put it? So like a man. It wasn't right and it bothered him.

"Is Mrs. Sid all right for money?" he asked the Yak.

"Oh, sure," the Yak said. "We got the household account. There's plenty. Sid allus had plentya money."

"That's good, that's good," Humphrey said, "but if you need anything, don't forget who to call."

This information too went to the councils, and soon the loathsome Mario was back in town. He poked around and this time he got poked around, by the Yak. Roman had caught him nosing around the house, actually in the house. For this he got some loose teeth and some deep bruises. But no hard feelings, he just took off and business went back to normal.

And then one day in October, Humphrey's inside man in the police department called: Mario Soper had been identified in Montana. He'd been found, shot to death, in an irrigation ditch. Mulheisen was investigating.

Not long after, the Yak called. He was not eager to talk about the family, but he trusted Humphrey. Mrs. Sid had received a postcard. All it said was, "Ma, I'm so sorry I haven't written. It wasn't possible. I'm all right. I'm fine. I'm very happy. But I can't bear for you to be unhappy. Are you all right? I'll contact you again, soon. Love, Nelly."

"Nelly?" Humphrey said.

"Mrs. Sid allus called her Nelly," the Yak explained.

"Oh yeah." Humphrey remembered. "So what's the return address?"

"Liddle Helen didn't put no return address," the Yak said. "It's got a pitcher of the Holy Mother, standin' on a mountain. It says it's Our Lady of the Rockies, Butte, Montana." He pronounced it "Butt-tee."

"Butt-tee?" Humphrey got him to spell it. "And it's postmarked when?" The Yak didn't know about postmarks, but Humphrey told him about the little circle stamped on the card. When the Yak finally figured out that it had been mailed in Montana on September 5, Humphrey wanted to know how it had taken so long to get to Detroit, and why was he telling him about it in October?

"I didden see it," Roman said. "Mrs. Sid had it under her pillow. I don't know how come she didden tell me about it. So, I don't know, maybe I shoulden even of told you."

"No, no, you should tell me," Humphrey said. "You should always tell me."

6

Helen

She'd be just as happy if he never came back. Not true, really. It was a way of punishing him, in her mind, for going away. Of course, he had to come back, he would come back, she wanted him to come back. She couldn't live without him, but . . . she had begun to enjoy the time when he wasn't around.

Oh god, what a miserable thing. She asked herself why women let themselves be trapped into these situations. But then she refused to feel trapped. This was a situation of her own making.

She had gone to Joe for help, she couldn't deny it. And then he had invited her to come with him. The trouble was that having done what she had wanted to do, and having gone with Joe voluntarily, she had begun not to like it here. Who in the hell wanted to lie around Montana for the rest of their lives? She had things to do. She was a young woman.

Joe had things to do. He went off and did them. He didn't tell her about them, not really, just little jokes. He called it his Gogol Scam and then, because she'd misunderstood and said "Go-go?" he'd laughed and taken that up. For a time she had been convinced it had something to do with girls, that he had another woman somewhere whom he went to see. What was the big secret? No secret, he insisted, it was just too complicated to get into. He'd tell her all about it one of these days, if it worked out.

Helen hated that kind of talk. She was stuck here, waiting. That was the way it always was. She wanted to call her mother. No, says Joe. She wanted to send her mother a note. No. Don't contact your friends, he had warned. When you took out Carmine, you said good-bye to friends, to family. Sorry, but that's the way it is. Those guys get a lead on you, we're dead. They never quit. So, here we are. This is where we live now. Don't you like it?

She liked it plenty, for a while. They went fishing, they floated on rafts, they hiked. They bought matching Harleys and roared up to White Sulphur Springs, careening down empty highways through the mountains and over Missouri River bridges and dodging antelope, lights out, driving by moonlight. But soon enough, they roared home. It wasn't as if they had nowhere else to go. On a whim, they flew to Vancouver Island, to take high tea at The Empress Hotel in Victoria, then dinner in Seattle and the sweet ride on Amtrak's "Coast Starlite" to San Francisco to shop for a few days. They drove down to Flaming Gorge to make love on a mountainside, ignoring the cars winding up the road. But always back to the cabin.

She liked it here, basically. The house was terrific. She'd bought some nice things like dishes and a good sound system, hundreds of CDs, some great clothes. It was a lot of fun. They spent money sometimes like there was no end to it, and of course, there was no end to it, practically speaking. Boxes and boxes of money.

On a normal day they would get up late, loaf around over breakfast—which they made themselves, since Joe refused to have servants of any kind. This was a point of contention. Helen argued that since they couldn't very well go out for breakfast, they ought to have someone in to cook and do the housecleaning. Joe laughed long and hard at this. "You can't make your own breakfast? Hell, I'll make it." And he did. And he cleaned house, too, though it was not an arduous task, after all.

After breakfast was shooting. Usually it was just Joe, but Helen frequently went with him. She didn't really enjoy shooting, not as much as Joe did, but she knew that he liked her to come along. They would walk up through the trees and back into the canyon. Some days they shot pistols as they walked—snap shots, Joe called it (he alternated right-hand days and left-hand days, quick drawing)—but usually they took the AK-47s, or the Uzi, and always a few handguns. After shooting, one of them ran down to town for the paper and to check the mail. Later they might fish, or go to Butte for dinner, or even to Bozeman or Livingston. There were some good restaurants over that way.

The one thing she loved without reservation was the hot springs, just over the ridge from the house. The hot springs almost made Montana a good deal. It was a sacred place, she'd decided. Lately she had come to resent Joe's presence in the hot springs, and Joe had seemed to recognize that. He liked her to do things on her own. He didn't mind if she traipsed off, naked as a jaybird, walking the four or five hundred yards over the ridge to the hot springs by herself.

He was almost unobjectionable. He acceded to everything. But so what? The gritty little basic thing was that she had grown up in Detroit, in the city. She liked people. Joe didn't give a damn if he never saw another human being in his life. It wasn't true, of course; he was very outgoing and gregarious at times. But at other times he seemed totally indifferent to, or even hostile toward, people. Helen found this unbearable. She needed people, particularly other women. She couldn't live without friends. If he knew that she had been to Holy Trinity, the Serbian church in Butte, he would flip.

As for Tinstar—well, it wasn't even a town, it was just appalling. A bar, a gas station that was also a post office, and a kind of convenience store that wasn't conveniently open—the hours depended on how the trout were hitting. And there was more poverty than she had expected: so many of the people on welfare, on some kind of assistance, living in shabby trailers. It didn't have the abject misery of Detroit, but misery was there just the same.

And she couldn't go by her own name. At first she had found it amusing to ask Shawna in the Tinstar Saloon to call her "Buddy." But lately she had found it disagreeable. She wanted Shawna to call her Helen. She wanted to be friends with Shawna, but Shawna was an awful hick, it turned out. She was also on aid, even though she was employed. Conversation with Shawna was like, "Did you watch Sally Jessy Raphael yesterday, she had a guy on there who admitted that he'd raped two hundred women, whyn't they cut his balls off?"

Well, what did she expect from a bartender? The women available to her weren't equals, they were hairdressers and ranch wives, waitresses and unwed teenaged mothers. The milieu did not include upscale career women, lawyers and go-getters. About as close as it got was Milly, a realtor in the Ruby Valley, who sometimes came into the Tinstar Saloon. But Milly was in love with some redneck rancher and had a couple of kids. There were also a lady sheriff, whom Helen necessarily avoided, and a kind of interesting but somewhat aloof (or at least cool) single woman who had some kind of job with the irrigation district. And the old gal who ran the Garland Ranch, the XOX, who had sold Joe the property—she was not to be believed, a raw-boned, wind-rubbed cowgirl who evidently preferred the conversation of red cattle.

Butte wasn't a hell of a lot better. A raggedy old falling down city, a kind of Flint-in-the-Rockies or maybe some time-warped decrepit burg from the Depression. She didn't find it nearly as interesting as Joe did. It looked trashy to Helen. She had been stunned to discover a Serbian Orthodox church there, of all places. Evidently, the Serbs had come to work the mines, and they made up one of the largest Serbian communities in the West, but it was incongruous, and anyway, she'd never been much for church.

Bozeman was a college town, deadly boring. Livingston was campy, tanned oldsters wearing Gucci bandannas. Missoula was also a college town; it had a couple of rock joints and some cultural offerings, but it was too far away and annoyingly self-important. Helena, the state capital, was the most boring of all: a political town in a state where the legislature only met for ninety days every other year. This was not the year.

Montana was not a bad place, she conceded. Their little mountain, their house, their pine trees, the view down the valley. But after all, what was it? Take away her hot springs and it was just okay, but it wasn't anything, really. Joe liked it. Joe loved it. He kept talking about how great it was, the air, no people . . . a man could piss off his front porch without checking on the neighbors. Big deal. Fine for him. But what was there for a dynamic young woman to do? Pissing on the front lawn didn't get it.

After a while she couldn't stand it. The day she discovered Holy Trinity in Butte, she felt so blue that she couldn't resist sending a card to her mother, mailed it from Butte. Big deal. What was the use of being infinitely rich if you couldn't live like a rich person, or even send a stupid postcard, like a poor person? Her idea of being rich was that they should live in, say, San Francisco, in the Palace Hotel. They would buy a boat. They'd have a small crew, and they'd sail to Mexico when they wanted to, or perhaps to Panama or Peru. But Joe didn't like the idea. Instead he'd suggest a float trip on the Madison, or maybe on the Missouri. Big deal.

The other part, the part that she didn't discuss with Joe, was that she had begun to have dreams about Carmine. Not so much Carmine, as it turned out, but the bodyguard. She had shot the man, after all. The guy was looking at her, and she just swung up the shotgun and blasted him. Then crawling into the car and blasting Carmine, with the little shit screaming and whining, "Don't kill me" . . . Well, she'd wanted to kill Carmine, but she'd never considered the bodyguard. She kept seeing his big dumb face, before she'd blown it away. He'd looked like a guy she knew. She thought she did know him. His name was Carlo, or something. She couldn't remember. And then in her dreams she kept trying to remember. She'd see his stupid face and he'd say, "Do you know me?" like some fool in an American Express ad. And then she'd raise her hand and his face would slide off his face, in a way, in a bloody slide, and she would have to think very hard about who he was. But she couldn't think of his name.

It was Joe's fault. She knew that wasn't fair, but there wasn't anything she could do about it. It was Joe's fault. He knew she wanted to kill Carmine and so he made it possible. He had coached her. He had said, This is how it goes. You hold the gun like this. The kick is fierce, but brace yourself. Once you squeeze the trigger, don't stop. Keep shooting. Keep going. And he'd said, If you don't succeed, if it goes wrong, don't look for me. I'll be waiting if you do it all. If you don't do it, I'm gone. It's your show.

Well, it was her show, and she'd done it, and she'd been proud. She'd been beside herself. She'd loved Joe for making it possible, but now . . . well, it *was* his fault, wasn't it?

Had she ever meant to kill anyone? She had to wonder about that. Of course, she had harbored and nurtured the idea that as her father's son—well, only child—it was her duty to avenge him. She was clear on this. But what is vengeance, here in America? Is it really the same thing? Couldn't she have defended her father's honor in some less violent manner? Mightn't she have found some way, eventually, to humiliate Carmine? To show others that he was slime?

Killing is such a crude, brutal thing. She hated killing. Animals kill. Well, she had killed, but it was just Carmine, or should have been just Carmine. Anybody would kill Carmine. What slime. The proper way to kill Carmine would have been to step on him and then scrape your shoe off on the curb. She couldn't help feeling that, left to herself, her violent feelings toward Carmine would eventually have dissipated. But then she had met Joe. He was used to killing. Killing meant nothing to a man like Joe, she felt. And in the sway of his casual attitude, and given her perfectly normal passion for the guy, she had fallen in with his idea that she should kill Carmine. A responsible man would have loved her and convinced her that she didn't need vengeance, that their love was enough. If Joe had really loved her, he would have gone to any lengths, even have left her, to prevent her from doing something so horrible. But, instead, he had helped her. He had in a way encouraged her to kill Carmine (and that other unfortunate man). So, really, *Joe* had killed Carmine. She was simply the method, the weapon, the tool. Was that the act of a man who loved? Did love say kill? She could hardly think so. No, Joe didn't really love her. He couldn't love her.

She couldn't get it out of her mind. Killed a man? No. She hadn't killed anybody. Of course, a guy like Carmine, anybody would kill that son of a bitch. The other guy, she couldn't think of his name, and now she couldn't think of his face. It wasn't like killing.

The simple fact was this: She had to get out of here. She loved Joe. He was the greatest man she'd ever met, but who needed a man, anyway?

Joe had gone to do his business. Another "go-go" trip. What crap. Why should she put up with this? She decided to go soak in the sacred pool.

As usual, she stripped completely naked and walked out the back door. It was a cool day in October, but the pool would be hot. She wanted to be chilled by the time she got there, walking through the pines, walking on the bed of needles on the path, barefoot.

She carried a large, fluffy towel. Her head was no longer shaven, as she had worn it when she was preparing to avenge her father. Joe had wanted her to keep it shaven—he liked the small silky patch that she'd retained, a kind of reverse tonsure—but she had let her thick black hair grow out, with its single silver stripe running from her right brow. There was no hair on her body except for this black mane. Her breasts were tiny and the nipples were tight from the chill.

When she got to the sacred pool she breathed deeply, inhaling the odor of the pines, and then she stepped down on the flat rocks into the hottest part. She lay back and looked upward through hooded lids at the tops of the huge Douglas firs and ponderosas. The gossamer was out. Joe had told her about the gossamer. It drifted through the incredibly deep blue sky and caught on the tops and the branches of the firs in such profusion that she felt like a houri in an ancient Arab pool, a silken canopy waving gently over her. She lay back in the hot pool feeling energy seep out of her as she scissored her legs slowly, feeling the warm water seep into her.

She rested her head on a rock and let her body float out, staring upward. A jay flew across the pool. Then a raven drifted from the top of one great tree to the top of another. Neither called, but both looked down at her nakedness.

Yes, this was a sacred pool, a place sacred to women, probably sacred to countless tribal women who had come here. She wished she had been here then, that they were here now to talk to her, in soft, musical voices. They would talk about what was proper to women, about children. This was a place where even the mention of men was banished. She was so relaxed, so calm, she almost forgot about Joe.

Despite the mood of softness, of weakness even, she paradoxically felt strong lying in this pool. This is why she had come to prefer being here without Joe. All the foolish craziness of wanting to be a son to her father, to avenge him, was erased here. The strength and vitality she felt in this blessed pool seemed to her a kind of energy that emanated from all the tribal women who had doubtless soaked here in days gone by.

And while she lay in this pool, her eyes nearly closed in ecstasy and release, she did not see Mario Soper, who came along the path and stood on the little cliff above her. The jay flew. The raven whacked his wings to rise upward and bend away. A squirrel chattered with alarm, but she had never paid any attention to the squirrels and birds and did not now heed this alarm.

Mario gazed down at the woman below him. She waved her arms and her legs indolently to keep herself afloat. Her black hair spread out around her head. He was aroused by her lack of pubic hair. He laid down the two pistols that he carried and stripped off all his clothes. Then with a joyous roar he leapt out over the rocks to fall nearly on top of her.

The shock of his entry into the water stunned them both. But before she could recover he was upon her.

Mario seized her by the shoulders, shouting crazily, "Oh yeah, you fucking pussy!"

He forced her back against the rocks, their sharp edges biting into her shoulders and buttocks. He thrust his knees between hers and levered her legs apart. His cock was large and stiff. He immediately, though fruitlessly, began to thrust his pelvis against hers, his stiff cock blindly stabbing at her stomach and thighs.

Helen gasped and gawped. She struck at the man with her small fists. He grabbed her head with both hands, his fingers locked in her hair and forced it under the hot water. With one hand he pressed her head down against the sandy bottom, then he seized his cock with his right hand and tried to direct it between her spread thighs, into her.

She wrenched her head free of his single hand and threw a wild punch that struck the man in the chest, her little fist as hard as a rock and momentarily stunning him. She twisted and escaped, her face surfacing. She gasped for breath. But he yanked her back again by her hair. He laughed wildly.

Helen could feel his nasty cock poking at her flesh, and revulsion and fear surged in her. So this was rape. This is what rape was, this smashing and forcing and heedless wrenching at her bones and ligaments and flesh. He would rape her and kill her, she knew. She threw her knotted fist against his face and was pleased when it struck his throat and made him gag violently. Then she thrust her knee upward but the water slowed the movement and her knee slid harmlessly along his inner thigh, not reaching its target.

She felt strong, however, a surge of determination. This was *her* pool. She sensed that he was enervated by the heat, whereas she was invigorated. She clasped her legs about his hips, ignoring the already wilting cock thrusting impotently at her, and flung herself over so that she rose astride him, his arms flailing out to the sides, thrashing to prevent himself from sinking under.

With both hands she grasped his head and smashed it against the rocks, digging her thumbs into his eyes, trying to gouge his eyeballs out of their sockets. She rode him down, under the surface. His hands quit searching her body and scrabbled furiously at her thumbs. She smashed his head against the rocks again, and sensed a kind of relaxation in his body. In a panic she pressed down against his chest, literally mounting it on her knees. She reared her streaming head into the delicious air, gasping but still bouncing on the man's chest on her knees and shoving his head against the rocks as hard as she could. She pushed. She thrust. She bounced. His arms lay out on either side.

And then she leapt off his body and scrambled through the splashing water, which slowed her. Glancing back over her shoulder, flinging her wet hair out of her eyes, she saw him rise slowly to a sitting position. He lurched to his knees and then stood. The water was only to his knees in this spot, whereas it still came to her pelvis. She waded frantically, conscious that he could simply step after her, not having to drag his legs through the water. He reached out and grasped her shoulder just as she attained the rocky edge. His hand slid off her slippery skin and he tumbled sideways, flopping on his butt on the gravelly bottom. Incredibly, he laughed.

The laugh infuriated Helen. She seized a large rock and spun about, bringing it down heavily on the man's head. It made a horrible, soft cracking noise. The man groaned and fell backward, his head not quite submerged in the shallow water here. Helen danced out of the water, frantically hopping about and uttering little noises. Then she turned and started to run toward the cabin.

She saw the two guns lying on his clothes, by the path. A handy little .32 automatic and a familiar looking .38 revolver. She stooped to pick up the automatic and racked the slide back as Joe had showed her. It was loaded, cocked and ready to fire. She picked up the revolver in her left hand and walked purposefully back toward the pool.

She stood on the little rocky cliff above the pool, from which the man had leaped upon her, and aimed the .32 automatic at arm's length. The first shot smacked into the water to the right of the man. She adjusted and fired again. The bullet hit the water first, but then his left thigh. The man yelled and sat bolt upright. She fired again and again, not counting the shots, aiming at his chest. She must have hit him, for he groaned and fell back into the water. Then the gun was empty. She threw it at him and it splashed into the water near him.

To her horror, he rose from the shallows, sitting up with his hands on the bottom. He brought his left hand to his face to sweep his dripping hair from his vision, then heaved himself to his feet and clambered out of the water. He stumbled up the path toward her. Helen stared in horror. She started to run, then realized that she still had the revolver. She switched it to her right hand and took aim.

The first shot hit him in the chest and he staggered sideways, teetering on the edge of the rocks. She fired again. She didn't see where it hit, but he toppled backward and fell with a great splash onto his head and shoulders in the pond. Standing above him, she carefully aimed and fired the remaining three shots into his body. When the hammer clicked on an empty chamber she heaved the gun at the man's sprawling body.

The noise in the little enclosed space was too loud to really be heard, just a great roaring noise, then ringing. Finally, it faded to silence and then, after a long, still moment, one could hear the tiny *yank-yank* of a nuthatch.

"Oh yeah," Helen gasped. She stood on the ledge, bent at the waist, hands on her thighs, breathing heavily. "Oh yeah." Oh, what a fine thing. Yes, yes—yes indeed. She made no connection between this miraculous victory and what she had done before, against Carmine. Oh, it was fine, now. She had won.

The man floated in the pool in a cloudy corona of pink water, his arms outstretched. When she regained her composure, she stood erect, and with a grim face she turned and walked rapidly back up the trail toward the house.

Fifteen minutes later she reappeared, dressed in jeans and a sweater and boots, pushing a red wheelbarrow. She sat down by the pool and took off her boots and socks, then waded in and grabbed the naked man by his hair, towing him to the edge of the rocks. He trailed a pinkish slick that drifted slowly toward the bottom end of the pool.

Helen strained to pull the man onto the rocks that lined the pool, and with a great effort she got his upper torso onto the wheelbarrow. Then she sat down and tugged on her boots. The barrow tilted and balked as she struggled to push it up the hill toward the house. Twice the body slipped out of the barrow and sprawled against the rocks. Needles and dirt became plastered on it. She hauled it back onto the barrow each time, but finally she gave it up and turned about. With much less difficulty she was able to guide it down the path toward the meadow below, toward Tinstar Creek.

She had thought of carrying the body off and dumping it a long ways from home, perhaps in another state, but now she reckoned that she herself was long gone for another state and the body could stay in this one. She was not, however, inclined to let it rest in the sacred pool. Indeed, the pool had been violated, not only with the would-be rapist's blood, but with the violence that had been expended there. From the creek it would wash down into the irrigation ditch, she supposed. She hoped that the flow of the springs and the rains would purify the sacred pool.

On her way back to the house, trundling the empty wheelbar-

row, she picked up the man's clothes and tossed them into it. At the
house again, she recognized that Joe's vaunted security had been
breached. She had noticed the new yellow pickup truck standing
before the house when she'd run back for her clothes. Now she
searched the cab. The paperwork for this vehicle was lying on the
front seat. It declared that it had been bought the day before, in Missoula, in her name. So this was what Joe had been up to, she thought.
The yellow pickup, a fancy four-wheel-drive affair, was supposed to be
a present for her. She had seen one like it in Butte a few days earlier
and had told Joe that she had to have it. No doubt the killer had used
the address on the forms to find where they lived.

No tears came to her eyes with the realization that Joe was
dead. That was clear. This man with two guns, one of which was
Joe's—she had recognized the special small grips (Joe had small
hands, like hers)—obviously had killed Joe and had come here. This
was the way Joe did life, she knew; now it had done for him. So be it.

There was a fancy black tonneau cover on the box of the new
pickup truck. Helen undid several of the snaps that held it down and
peeled it back to discover a pile of strange gear in the back of the
truck. She started to empty it out before she realized that the biggest
bundle was a dead man in an old army coat.

Helen was stunned. To be sure, she had just survived a shocking attack and had mustered the strength and will to dispose of a
man's naked corpse, but this . . . What could this be all about? Perhaps
Joe had killed this man, but had been overcome by the other. It was a
mystery that she couldn't begin to fathom. She sat down on the narrow rear bumper of the truck, groaning softly. It was too much, too
much. She felt close to tears, but suppressed them with anger. If she
had refused to mourn Joe a moment earlier, now she cursed him.

But after a minute to regain her strength, she sighed and stood
up. Now the problem was to get rid of this body. She wasn't going to
drive with this grisly load in the back. She let down the tailgate and
dragged the dead man out on it until he sprawled in the sunlight. A

stained cowboy hat lay among the gear. She looked down on a bearded face that was dirty with many broken vesicles in the cheeks and nose, the hair filthy and long. The flesh was weathered but pallid and old, dried blood was caked around the throat. Now she realized that the throat had been cut. Surprisingly, there wasn't a lot of blood on the layers of flannel shirts the body wore. Apparently, he had lain for some time on his face, which had dirt embedded in it, and most of the body's blood had drained away. He was about average height and heavy, perhaps as young as twenty-five or as old as forty, she couldn't tell. He looked like a derelict, an alcoholic. She had no idea how long he had been dead. He didn't smell so good, but then he must never have smelled very fresh. At any rate, he wasn't obviously rotting.

It was too mysterious for her. She dragged the body off the extended tailgate and let it fall to the pine-needled floor of the drive. Then she jumped up into the box, unsnapping the cover and rolling it back. She tossed all the alien gear out onto the hard-packed yard. There was no blood in the truck box, she was glad to see.

She packed all her gear and carried it out to the truck. Then she took the wheelbarrow and walked up above the house to a path that led around the side of the mountain to Joe's cache. This was an old abandoned mine adit, once framed by timbers, which Joe had removed when he discovered this entrance hidden behind brush. To one side was a large ponderosa. But the pine had been struck by lightning a few years earlier and had finally died, along with the parasitical mistletoe that had helped to obscure the opening. Joe had explored and developed this disused mine long before Helen had come to join him here. She thought it was crazy and spooky, poking around in an old and surely dangerous mine, but it was part of Joe's obsession with security.

He had cleared away the debris for some fifteen feet inside the opening and provided a slatted floor of rough planks on logs. On this platform he had constructed a studded and raftered frame and sheathed it with rough cedar. The cavity was dry and cool, and if someone should stumble on the well-concealed opening, guarded by brush and seemingly fallen branches, they would encounter a solid metal door mounted in the recessed frame. One would have to be looking for this opening to detect it. Here Joe kept the boxes of cash he had taken from Eugene Lande, a thief who had stolen the money from a mob money-laundering operation in Detroit. There were also various other valuable papers and some guns stored here.

This door was kept securely locked, but Helen knew where the key was kept under a nearby rock. She pried up the rock and found the key, then opened the tomblike cavity. Carrying two boxes at a time on the wheelbarrow, she transported the money down the path to the truck. She didn't bother the boxes of Joe's private papers and records, nor his guns—a carefully oiled and wrapped Stoner rifle, a Browning automatic shotgun, a Cobray automatic, and a couple of revolvers.

It took her a good hour to haul the money down to the yard. The yellow pickup truck accepted ten boxes of cash in its box. She had to rearrange the boxes so that the tonneau could fasten down, but it was easy to do. There were a few boxes of money left up at the cache, but Helen didn't care. She had already loaded the truck with at least ten million dollars, perhaps more. One box that she couldn't quite fit in she regretfully tossed aside. There was no telling how much it contained. Some of the boxes held small bills, fives, tens, and twenties, and probably contained as little as $500,000. Others, with larger bills, could hold nearly a million. It wasn't worth opening them; there was a world of money in the back of the truck.

She actually backed up over the dead man as she was leaving. Ordinarily that bump and the realization of what she'd done would have appalled her, even made her physically ill. Not any more. It was just another dead body, and she didn't even know who it was or what it meant. She drove forward, passing over the body again on her way out the gate.

She was halfway down the long road that served as their drive when she slammed on the brakes and the yellow pickup skidded to a halt. What, she asked herself, was she thinking about? What was the use of hauling a naked rapist halfway down the mountain to dispose of him in an out-of-the-way irrigation ditch if she was going to leave another corpse lying in the drive in front of the house?

Cursing, she turned the truck around and roared back up the road. Despite her feverish haste and anxiety she couldn't help noticing and appreciating the responsiveness of the truck. What a terrific gift! Then she put it out of her mind. Where to stash this new body, so an idle passerby—say, the UPS delivery woman—wouldn't see it and immediately call the cops? She needed at least a little time, a day or two, to get out of this country.

Once again she got out the wheelbarrow and loaded the body into it with great effort. No point in going up the ridge and down to where she'd disposed of the rapist. The answer was obvious. She pushed the wheelbarrow up the small trail to the cache. It was an agonizing effort, but this body was clothed in a heavy coat and it didn't slip as much as the rapist's naked corpse. She dumped it unceremoniously into the cache, among the guns and the remaining boxes of money. She went back for two more loads, piling the bags and odd gear about the body that she had dumped against one wall of the cache, where it sprawled leaning slightly to one side, propped up by gear. The legs extended straight out before it, the soles of the cowboy boots splayed to either side. She slapped the corpse's greasy cowboy hat onto the lank and tangled hair and left, carefully locking the door and rearranging the debris to mask it. Then she put the key back under the rock. With any luck the body would never be found. It was an ideal tomb. Joe had often explained to her that the mine was so well drained and ventilated that the money and the guns would not be subject to damp, even in the spring runoff. The last thing he wanted was to come back from a trip and discover that rain or melted snow had seeped into his cache and mildew had ruined all his goods. Well, now it would serve a more solemn purpose.

Somehow she couldn't be grateful to Joe for his foresight. She was angry instead. She had graduated from Michigan State University with honors; why should she have been brought to such a terrible place, to have to dispose of bodies that had nothing to do with her? For some time she had resented the way that Joe, a man with no formal education, had assumed a superior manner. Well, now his stupidity had done him in and she had successfully applied her own ability to think and plan in order to save herself and their goods. Angrily she wheeled the empty wheelbarrow down the path and parked it in the little shedlike garage where it belonged.

She returned to the cabin and went to Joe's little alcove, where he kept his current bills and paperwork—nothing incriminating here, you could be sure—along with a couple of properly purchased guns, and selected one she'd always liked. It was a Dan Wesson revolver, a .357 magnum, and it came with several interchangeable barrels. She took three of the barrels and tossed them in a bag with a couple of boxes of ammunition. Then she went around and closed and locked the iron-barred shutters—more of Joe's security—and finally pulled all the shades and locked the back door. Everything was turned off, no lights, no burners on. She locked the front door and left, this time for good. She even stopped to lock the gate.

An hour and a half later, having cruised effortlessly through some spectacular high-range country along Interstate 15, she crossed into Idaho at Monida Pass. According to her map, Salt Lake City was less than three hundred miles south. She would feel much safer there, two states away from Joe's cabin and two dead bodies, anonymous in a large city. She could check into a nice hotel and rest and assess the situation.

7

Dream Kill

Does everybody dream of murder? Joe Service did. Not constantly; that might have driven him completely crazy. But he had a long time to dream, although a coma is not precisely like being asleep and, anyway, not everyone agrees on what a dream is. For the first few hours of his unconsciousness, the brain was doing many things, and there was a kind of shock period in which the semiconscious functions flickered in and out. There were terrible dreams in this period: jumbled, hectic replays of a bullet smashing into one's face, of the hand flying up in a futile gesture, looking over and over again at the hand of the killer, the bullet issuing from the barrel, the bullet spinning toward the face. The eye did see all of that and the brain is certainly capable of breaking down these images and replaying them in slow, slower, and dead slow motion, but it is more probable that Joe Service was more or less willfully creating this horrifying video punishment for himself. Why? Who can say? Perhaps it helped him, steeled him for the work ahead, the need to overcome this trauma.

The real terror was to come, in the long dreamy days and weeks of coma. These were the dreams of murder. There were several, but one was prime: A child is swinging on a playground swing, usually a little girl of five or six, but sometimes it is a little boy. Another child appears, or rather doesn't quite appear, since he is the dreamer, and he looks out past his own blurry nose at the swinging child. The dreamer is eight and he carries a shotgun. Sometimes he stands behind the swinger, sometimes before. But in each case he raises the shotgun and fires.

The immediate aftermath is never clear. This isn't one of those modern movies (nor even like the bullet dream) where one is shown in slow motion the impact of the shotgun pellets, the body flying, the blood exploding. In this dream there is a flash and the dreamer is thrown backward by the recoil, the gun flies away. Then the swing is drifting emptily, the open mouths of grownups moaning in dismay and despair, and demanding: Why? Why?

And the dreamer says: I just wanted to see what it was like. And then the horrible, horrible realization of what has been done. The most central fact being: That person doesn't exist anymore. That person was a human being. That person had a life. Now it is gone. Absolutely gone. And you did it.

And after a while there would come other dreams of murder. These varied considerably, but all of them featured an assailant who was armed and the dreamer responding to the threat by shooting first. He always shot first. Legally defensible, it was experienced as murder, nonetheless. In the most vivid of these, the dreamer is squatting, his back braced against a wall in a dark room. There is somebody else there, a woman weeping quietly. The dreamer is waiting and he waits a long time, looking about the darkened room fearfully, though not in terror, just alertly. And suddenly a man appears in a doorway, only very close to the floor, on the floor, in fact. And it isn't a whole man, at first. It is a long, snaky arm that carries a long-barreled pistol that seems like a snake's head, or the fist is the head and the barrel is the tongue, and it slides into the room along the floor, looking about, licking about, and then the fist/head stops and focuses on the squatting dreamer, staring, and the finger begins an agonizing curl. The dreamer registers the threat. And he shoots automatically, without thinking. Several times. The pistol in his own hand jumping and jumping, until the head is dead.

Except that the head isn't really dead. It takes a long time to die, while the dreamer sits by the body and waits, gun in hand, ready to shoot again. But finally it dies and the dream fades.

There were more dreams, many more, all of them quite gruesome and awful, but the dreamer didn't really mind. Or, at least, the dreamer was resigned to this parade of nightmares, aware that this was life, some kind of life anyway, and not death.

It had been clear for some time that Deadman was going to recover. What the doctors couldn't know was just how much and in what way he would recover. But there was considerable brain activity, that was obvious.

He'd had surgery to reconstruct the jaw that had been fractured by the bullet. The bullet, or rather its various fragments, had been removed from behind the ear, magnetically drawn out of portions of the cranium and the jaw. Some of the fragments had been removed from the brain itself, although there didn't appear to be any loss of brain tissue. Dr. Wilder said it was all still there, though a little scrambled. Where there is no great displacement of tissue, the nerve paths seem quite capable of rerouting and reestablishing themselves, but it is always a chancy, iffy thing. The surgeon was sure that Deadman would be unable to move his right arm and leg, and so it appeared, for a while.

A portion of the tongue had been destroyed as well, which added to the difficulties of potential speech, although Deadman was a long ways from speech. What he was looking at was a long period of rehabilitation, with the likelihood that he would never fully recover from this horrendous trauma.

He had several assets, however, in his quest for recovery. One was his remarkable physical condition, now somewhat atrophied from prolonged confinement to bed. Another was Cateyo.

For reasons she could not really articulate, Cateyo was deeply attracted to this patient. Although he obviously wasn't looking in top form at present, she could see that he was—or had been—a fine-looking young man with a remarkable physique. He wasn't much larger than her own five feet four inches, and that seemed to encourage her, or at least not intimidate her. He had been found in disreputable circumstances, true, which argued a kind of rough existence. Still, he may have been, as she was more than willing to assume, a completely innocent victim of a heinous crime. Probably a good samaritan, if she could believe the press reports (derived from Jacky Lee's terse account), who had stopped to pick up a hitchhiker who turned out to be a robber and a would-be killer.

Cateyo was, by contrast, a very sweet, good-tempered young lady who had experienced a kind of religious revival in the last couple of years. Cateyo's father had been deeply religious, a self-taught Montana range preacher. He'd never been ordained nor had he even studied the Bible in a formal way, but he had studied it intensely. Like many another self-taught man, this valley farmer had held idiosyncratic views of the Christian religion. Toward the end he'd been particularly interested in prophecy, poring over Revelation and St. John for some clue to what was going to happen. He was very surprised indeed when the heart attack hit him, while driving a load of hay out to the cows one bitter winter day. He didn't think it was supposed to go like that. There wasn't even time to be annoyed with God before the lights went out. The pickup truck just rambled across the field, dispersing the cows until it buried itself in a snowbank. A couple of hours later, one of his neighbors, or as it was more commonly reported, his neighbor's "Indin," had noticed the truck in the snowbank, hay bales still aboard although now being eaten at by hungry cattle standing around. The Indin called old Yoder's daughter, away at St. James Hospital, in Butte.

Cateyo had not previously been interested in religion, in reaction to her father's cranky obsession with it, but not long after his death (her mother having passed on a few years earlier), she met a young man at a party who seemed interested when she told him about some of her father's beliefs. She was attracted to this man who, like her patient, was smallish but intense. Alas, he proved not to be interested in her, it seemed, or a little leery anyway, and he soon moved on. But his interest in her father's ideas—if they could be called that—in a perverse way seemed to validate them, as ideas. Cateyo began to take them more seriously. Like her father she began to read the Bible very closely and develop her own ideas about Christianity. Intense ideas at that. Whereas her father had been fascinated with questions of the end of things, apocalypses and armageddons, she was particularly struck by the notion of new beginnings, rebirth, of a new life. St. Paul particularly fascinated her. She began to research his life and read books from the local Christian bookstore. She felt that she had a new life, all of a sudden, that she wasn't so aimless and lonely.

Cateyo was a beauty. Pretty, with a full, squarish face and silky fair hair, she had one of those incredible complexions that explain how clichés like "peaches and cream" originate. Her eyes were wide and a clear blue. Her mouth was wide, as well, with full, deep pink lips over perfect white teeth. It's true that she was not very long legged, but she had nice proportions. A tendency toward sturdiness, perhaps, but as she was slim and in excellent shape, "stocky" wasn't likely to be the first word that sprang to the observer's lips . . . "solid," perhaps. This was just a fine-looking young woman. The mystery was why she was so alone.

This was one of those occasional, but well-known conundrums, and none of her friends could solve it. Is it possible to be too pretty, too sweet? Or was she just a little intense and introspective at times? Were most men just scared of her, awed by her vibrant loveliness? Or had they too quickly decided that she must be already taken? A fast-forward video of her life would show men rushing up to her, mouths open, stopping, then hurriedly retreating. She didn't have bad breath or an offensive odor. It was something else. It was a mystery.

At a very early stage, when Deadman was still in a coma, she began to spend more time with him than was normal. Her supervisor, Janice Work, was concerned. Cateyo would come in at odd hours, at night sometimes, and just putter around Deadman's room. Nurse Work found her sitting by his bedside once, holding his hand and talking softly in the dim night. Deadman was totally unconscious. When Janice entered, Cateyo instantly shifted her hand into the position for taking a pulse and lifted her other wrist to check her watch, but Janice was not fooled.

"Doing pretty well," Cateyo said, dropping the patient's wrist. "I was just talking at him. I think it helps. He seems to like it."

"Sort of like talking to the houseplants while you water them, eh?" Nurse Work said, with an amused smile. "Well, he is kind of a vegetable, isn't he? But he'll come around. Listen, honey, you know better than to get too invested in a patient, don't you?"

Cateyo laughed unconvincingly. "Me? Oh goodness, Jan. I guess I know better."

The next day Janice invited Cateyo over for volleyball and pizza with a group of other nurses and their boyfriends, but while she came and participated, it didn't seem to interest her much. An unattached intern was attracted to her, but she seemed distant and he soon shrugged and abandoned the chase.

When Deadman came out of the coma, opened his eyes, responded, Cateyo was thrilled. She began to spend more time in his room, after her normal shift. This was more disquieting to Janice Work, but she didn't make much of it. She was too busy herself, and the other nurses were happy to have Cateyo help out, although they naturally kidded her a great deal about her "boyfriend."

One afternoon when Deadman was awake, Cateyo puttered about the room talking as usual, addressing him almost mindlessly as

"Carmine." "It's getting on toward winter, Carmine," she said. "It gets so cold here in Butte, but I suppose you know that. There will be ice-skating before you know it. The city floods vacant lots, you know. I'd love to take you skating, maybe up on the Hill, around Meaderville. Would you like that? I bet you're a real good skater, Carmine."

She happened to glance at him and was stunned to see him shake his head—carefully, as if it might fly apart—and close his eyes when she called him Carmine.

"Not Carmine?" she asked, instantly receptive.

Slight nod.

"Deadman?" she asked, with a dubious, not quite approving tone.

He shrugged minutely and tilted his head as if it didn't matter.

Some days later, when she was once again pursuing this question of a name, he made a hand gesture, as if writing, and she brought him a pad and pencil. He struggled to make some kind of legible signs, but it was beyond him. Frustrated, he let the pencil drop, and it rolled off the bed onto the floor. But less than an hour later he made another attempt and this time succeeded in inscribing something that looked like a series of waves. Cateyo carried the scribble home and studied it, concluding that it meant "newman," or possibly, "human."

"Newman?" Cateyo asked her patient the next day, holding up the note. The patient stared at her, expectantly or, it may have been, blankly. "New man?"

The more-or-less shrug, the tilt of the head.

It was more than enough for Cateyo. "Yes," she said, emphatically and approvingly, "you are a new man. You have come out of your old life. You are born again. Hunh?"

Newman, as she now thought of him, seemed to smile and nod. Delighted, Cateyo went on with the bath she was giving him. As usual, when she soaped and rinsed his penis, it rose triumphantly, rampantly. As usual, she suppressed it with a pinch at the base.

"I believe I'll call you Paul," she announced, absentmindedly

soaping his penis so that it stiffened again. "As in Newman." She gig-
gled. "But more important, as in St. Paul. He was a new man. When
his eyes were opened to the Lord, he became a new man. You are like
Paul."

Suddenly, the new man groaned and his penis erupted. Semen
flew several feet into the air. Cateyo's mouth fell open and her eyes
grew wide. "Good lord," she whispered.

8
Lady Killer

Humphrey DiEbola wasn't really surprised not to hear from Mario. He'd had no great estimate of the man's abilities. His contacts inside the Detroit Police Department had duly reported the discovery of the man's body on a mountainside in Montana. He was interested to hear that Mulheisen had gone to Montana, presumably to investigate the circumstances of this death, but there was no additional information. Apparently, Mulheisen had looked into it, but thus far nothing seemed to have come of the investigation. Perhaps he thought that it wasn't really related to the death of Carmine.

Humphrey phoned his major contact in the department, a certain precinct commander. He disliked this little creep, but he was generally useful, so he was disappointed when the precinct commander didn't have much information on Mulheisen's activities.

"Somebody's pulling strings again," Commander Buchanan said petulantly. "They're trying to send Mulheisen on some kind of extended vacation out west, detached from the Ninth. It's politics. The bastard has always been in thick with the powers."

"What powers?" Humphrey asked, trying to quietly slurp up a fiery stew of fish, clams, and tiny octopuses. He was enjoying a quiet evening at home, sitting at the kitchen counter on a stool while his chef, Pepe, puttered about.

"The mayor, the commish, the governor . . . Hell, his old man practically ran the Democratic Party, in the old days."

"I didn't know that," Humphrey said. "So, how come Mul is still a sergeant? That don't sound like pull to me."

"He's lazy. He won't take the lieutenant's exam, and they all cover for him downtown. He says he prefers to work in the field instead of behind a desk, but I know better."

"That don't sound lazy," Humphrey said. "So what's he doing these days?"

"They're talking about some big deal," the commander complained. "I didn't even hear about it until he was already out west, on this other thing. Some regional task force that the Feds are funding, or maybe it's the states themselves. That's gotta be political."

"What is this task force?" Humphrey asked, tearing off a chunk of fresh Italian bread and slathering it with butter.

"Northern Tier Crime Task Force, or something like that. It's all the upper Midwest states, extending out to the Rockies. Maybe they think the mob is moving in on the north country, or something."

Humphrey smiled. "There'd have to be more people." Privately, he knew that the mob wasn't moving in on anybody these days. They were too busy trying to hang on to what they once had. He wondered if it didn't have something to do with a rise in activity from the West Coast, from so-called Chinese Mafia activities. From what he'd heard, there was getting to be an awful lot of money coming in from the Far East, a lot of muscle. He'd heard it had something to do with the impending shutdown of Hong Kong, when the mainland Chinese took over. The big operators there were looking for new fields. Seattle was hot, he'd heard. Maybe it extended inland.

"You should be happy," Humphrey said, "you got him out of the precinct."

"Oh sure, but it isn't permanent, even if it comes off. So in the meantime I'm shorthanded and you got people coming in every day, they want to talk to Mulheisen, won't talk to nobody else. You know, a lot of people are really fooled about this guy."

"Sure, sure," Humphrey said, "but basically, he's just gone to Butte, about this so-called hit man. Is that it?"

"So far," the commander agreed, "but what is it? It's just some guy they found in a ditch, so Mulheisen gets a free vacation, paid by the taxpayers, and the Ninth has to carry his load. And then if this Northern Tier bullshit flies, who knows how long he'll be gone?"

No satisfying some people, Humphrey thought, but he hastened to say, "It's a damn shame. No wonder our taxes are so high." DiEbola himself went to some lengths to provide himself with a reasonable-looking income, so he could pay taxes and present a legitimate appearance. He thought he should appear to have an income of about a hundred thousand or so and pay all the appropriate taxes.

The next day he sent Rossamani out for the Yak.

"Any more cards from Helen?" Humphrey asked.

"No, but there was a phone call," the big lump said. "Missus Sid said it was from Nelly."

"Where did she call from?"

"I dunno. Maybe California?"

"Why do you think that, Roman?" Humphrey asked. "Did she mention anything?"

The Yak frowned, concentrating. "I dunno why I thought that. Maybe 'cause she called so late? After Missus Sid went to bed?" His face lit up with understanding. "Liddle Helen should know her ma goes to bed at nine. It was after ten when she called. I answered the phone. I to'd her it was late. And she said she forgot the time difference. That'd be California, wooden it?"

"Maybe," Humphrey said. "You did good. But why didn't you tell me she called? When was this?"

"It was a week ago, I think," the Yak said. "You didden say nothing about phone calls, F—, er, Mr. Diablo."

"Just call me Humphrey, old friend. Well, let me know next time, whenever you hear from Helen, telephone or otherwise. Okay? Anyway, Montana is two time zones away, isn't it?" He turned to Rossamani for confirmation, but Rossamani just shrugged.

"Well," the Yak offered hopefully, "she said it was warm where she was. She to'd Missus Sid that. Missus Sid was afraid she'd be cold in Montana, in November."

"But Helen didn't say where she was, just that it was warm there? Did she say she would be in touch again?"

"Yanh. She said she might be home for Christmas."

"Well, that's good, that's good," Humphrey said. "Children should come home for Christmas. The next time Helen calls I want you to tell her to call me. I understand her, Roman. I've known her since she was a baby. I'm worried about her, old friend. It worried me that she would go off with this guy, with Joe. I liked Joe, you know, I thought I could trust him. But it looks like he was not the man we thought he was. But I don't blame little Helen for this. You tell her that. Tell her to call Uncle Umberto. Remember she used to call me Unca Umby? She was the only one who ever called me that. But don't tell her what I said about Joe. That's between you and me. So, she made a mistake about Joe, we all did. I don't hold it against her. Listen, does Mrs. Sid still do the big dinners on Sunday?"

"She kind of give that up after Big Sid died," the Yak said, "but I think she'll do something for Christmas. She's been feeling a little better. Some of her friends have been coming over. Yanh, I think they'll prob'ly have a big Christmas."

"That's great," Humphrey enthused. "You keep me posted, Roman. Maybe I'll drop by, if it's all right with Mrs. Sid."

The Yak looked a little doubtful, but he said he'd run it by the widow. "Missus Sid don't have nothing against you, Humphrey," he said, "it was just Carmine. But I dunno."

When he had gone, Humphrey asked Rossamani, "Who do we have? What kind of hitters do we have? I don't want no more of Mitch's pricks. This is our business, our job. Do we have any kind of local boy?"

Rossamani pondered. He was an able enough man, a born henchman, shrewd but conservative. Privately he had always been skeptical of Humphrey's way of running things. He had liked it better when Humphrey only advised Carmine, who tended to shoot first and ask questions later. Humphrey was too much of a thinker for him. "Well, we got half a dozen kids over in the house," he motioned with his head toward the refurbished flats that lay within the Krispee Chips well-fenced grounds. These flats were occupied at various times by immigrant lads from the Old Country. Some of them worked in the Krispee Chips factory, some were being groomed for more responsible positions in the mob organization; all of them were here as nominal spouses of young women who worked for Krispee Chips. They were married by proxy, usually, while the young man was still overseas, and surprisingly, many of the marriages held up very well. It was one of their number who had driven Carmine's car on the fatal day.

Humphrey shook his head. "We can't send a kid like them out to Montana," he said. "He'd end up in Canada, or China, maybe."

Rossamani shook his head doubtfully. "I'll look around," he said. "There must be someone."

Humphrey sighed. "We have fallen on bad days, Rossie. It's like the fall of the Roman Empire. The Visigoths are at the gates and where are my centurions? Find me a boy. And find out who we got in Butte. We must know somebody out there. Mulheisen isn't into this Northern Tier thing for no reason."

* * *

A couple of days later, Rossamani ushered a woman into Humphrey's presence, at the Krispee Chips office. She could have been thirty or forty, a tall square-shouldered woman with a hard face, little or no makeup, and her coarse brown hair cut very short. She wasn't really unattractive; if she'd had a twin brother, he'd be quite handsome, but on her it was just a little unsettling. Square shoulders, square jaw, with a strong nose and a wide, thin-lipped mouth on which she wore no cosmetics. Her heavy dark eyebrows frowned over a pair of dim brown eyes. She wore pleated wool slacks and a very tweedy jacket in a color usually called "heather." It was appropriate, because her name was Heather, she said.

Humphrey felt an air of menace, but he licked his red lips and asked, "What's your thing, Heather?"

"My thing?" Her voice was surprisingly soft, but with a bristly edge. "I don't have a thing, Mr. DiEbola. Men have things." She pronounced the word with a kind of withering contempt. Humphrey's thing would certainly have withered if it hadn't already been in a quiescent state.

Humphrey smiled, a sickly, pained smile. "Some of the guys have a preferred method, Heather, that's all I meant. Some guys are shooters. Most of them are shooters, in fact. But I know a couple guys who are partial to blades—used to know 'em," he amended. "Not too many of 'em around these days."

"Do you ask the guys what their method is?" Heather said. "No, I didn't think so. But you ask me. 'Cause I'm a woman."

She held up her square hands. They were large and reddish, with large knuckles. "This is what I usually use," Heather said. "I can shoot, if you want me to shoot, or I can use a blade . . . a hatchet, maybe? A sharp stick is good. A rock can be useful."

Humphrey suppressed a shudder. He found that he couldn't meet her eyes. The eyes were a giveaway, he thought. Lots of people look intelligent; a high, smooth brow, a neat and orderly appearance, an air of self-assurance . . . and sometimes, even the eyes have that look of keenness, of awareness, that bespeaks intelligence. Once in a while he would meet a young fellow, often Italian, who exuded this kind of vibrant healthiness, seemed alert and bright, and even when you looked into those eyes it seemed possible that the kid was on the ball. In time, alas, it rarely worked out that way. Heather was impressive in this way, except for the eyes. You couldn't see into them at all; there was a kind of veil, a film of . . . of what? Nuttiness? Stupidity? He couldn't tell, and he was too astute a manager of personnel to rely on appearances, but it was bothersome.

He swiveled his chair away and gazed at a painting of a winter scene, another of Carmine's arty purchases, or his wife's. It was very dark and lugubrious, a snowy hillside with dark trees and an occasional boulder on the slope, everything dull and brownish and fading into a kind of noncolor in the distance. Snow was falling in the scene and there wasn't a sign of life. Humphrey had come to think of this as Montana.

"A guy already went out to Montana," Humphrey said, talking to the picture, "and the guy came back in a bag. We ain't sure what happened. Maybe he pulled off the hit before he got it, but we don't know. Now we hear there's a guy in a hospital in Butte, we think he might be the guy our boy was supposed to hit, but if he is, he didn't get hit hard enough. A friend of ours in Butte says this unknown fella in the hospital out there was booked in as 'Carmine Deadman.' Now, I never heard of no Carmine Deadman, but that's too much of a coincidence for me, so can you go to Butte and look into it?"

Heather nodded. "I can look into it. That all you want?"

"No. If this Carmine Deadman is the right guy, then you should make sure he's a real dead man."

"How do I know if he's the right guy?" she asked.

"Go look. We're looking for a guy in his late twenties, about five-five, five-six, black hair and blue eyes, kind of a good-looking guy. He goes by the name of Joe Service. You see this Deadman and if he looks right, then you call me and tell me what you found out. Then you can go look for a rock, or whatever," Humphrey said. "That okay? Five bucks to go look, another ten if you need to, um, take action."

"Ten and ten," Heather said. "I can't do anything on five."

Humphrey shook his head. "Get her the fuck outta here," he said to Rossamani, "she gives me the creeps."

"You're the creep," Heather said. "I'm not allowed to ask for more? How much did you pay the guy who went out there before, the one who came back in a bag? Does that sound like it was a cake job? Or is it only because I'm a woman?"

"Quit with this woman shit," Humphrey said. "I'm not some equal opportunity employer. I'm offering you a job. You want it or not?"

"Ten and ten," Heather said.

Humphrey drew a deep breath and let it out slowly, staring at the woman. She didn't back down. He kind of liked that, but he still wasn't sure about the eyes. "Wait outside," he said, finally.

When Rossamani returned, Humphrey said, "Where'd you dig her up? She gives me the willies. Did you hear that shit about a sharp stick?"

Rossamani shrugged. "She did a job for Matty, out on the west side, beat a guy's brains out. I don't know all the details, but that's what Matty told me. Said she just went and did it and no problems."

Humphrey stared at the painting for a long time, then said, "What do you think? Can she be trusted? She's not gonna fuck up?"

"She looks okay," Rossamani said, "and Matty says she's okay."

"Screw Matty. Matty is a weirdo. What do *you* think?" Humphrey fixed his lieutenant with his eyes. Rossamani didn't look away and didn't reveal anything, just stared blandly back.

"She seems okay to me," he said.

"Offer her five and fifteen," Humphrey said. "It ain't worth ten just to find out that this Carmine Deadman ain't Joe. If it is Joe, fifteen is cheap for the job."

"What if she don't go for it?"

"She knows too much. If she don't go for it, your next hitter is a clean-up hitter. You get me? He'll have to clean the bases. Who's our guy in Butte?"

"His name is Smokey Stover," Rossamani said. "He runs a tavern called Smokey's Corner. He's okay, runs a small organization, don't make waves."

"If she signs on, tell her she don't talk to nobody but Smokey. I'll talk to him, let him know she's on her way."

"Matty says she's very good," Rossamani said.

"They're all s'posed to be good," Humphrey said. "Get somebody in the on-deck circle, just in case."

Rossamani beckoned to Heather as he walked through the reception area. She followed him down the hall and into his office. He closed the door behind her and locked it. "We got a problem," he said. "The Fat Man don't like you." He sighed, lounging against his desk while she stood, waiting. "Things are still kind of unsettled around here. Matty says you're good, you do what you're told. The way things are around here, the right person could get ahead. You want to get ahead?"

Heather shrugged. "Sure," she said.

Rossamani stared at her frankly, up and down. "I gotta have somebody I can trust, somebody who can take orders. You don't look so bad. Come over here. Get down on your knees," he said, unzipping his trousers.

Heather dropped to her knees on the carpet. Rossamani held her head with both hands. When it was over, he said, "Did you like that? Was it good?" He was a little out of breath.

Heather didn't smile. She wiped her mouth as she stood up. "It was okay," she said.

"Five and fifteen," Rossie said. "That okay? If it don't work out, if Deadman ain't Joe, I'll make it up to you." He stepped close to her and wiped a glistening fleck of something off her cheek with his forefinger. He placed his finger to her lips and she licked it. Rossamani smiled. "I might have a more important job for you, later. I like you. You're good."

"Okay," she said, still not smiling.

Rossamani opened a drawer in his desk and took out an old cigar box. He counted out five thousand dollars. Then he told her how to contact Stover, in Butte. "When you find out anything, call me. Call me first, never call the Fat Man. Understand?"

Heather had driven at least a block from Krispee Chips before she stopped and got out to spit violently, clearing her throat several times. Then she drove to Matty's bar, out McGraw Avenue. An hour later, she was a little drunk, having knocked back several straight shots of bourbon, before Matty showed up. She went into the back with him and as soon as he had closed the door and turned to face her, she knocked him down with a strong right hand. At some time, without his noticing, she had donned black leather gloves. When he got up she knocked him down again. For the next ten minutes she worked him over carefully. At no time did she hit his face, always his head or his chest. Once she kicked him in the buttocks, carefully but closely missing his balls. When she was done, she said, "Don't ever fuck with me, you piece of shit, or next time I'll kill you. You understand?"

Matty, a slender, slick-looking guy, nodded. He grinned ingratiatingly and apologized for not warning her about Rossamani. Finally she smiled, a thin, grim smile, and unzipped her slacks. She perched on the edge of the desk and said, "Come here."

"You know I don't like that," Matty said.

"I didn't like what I had to do," she said. "Now it's your turn, Doggy."

Matty dropped to his knees.

9
Mul of the West

If we go to the airport, go through all the rigmarole of checking in, board the plane, fly for ten hours—say, to the Gulf of Mexico, crossing over Cuba, and then out to sea, all the way to England and back across the ocean—and then land where we took off from . . . have we actually been anywhere? Mulheisen pondered this from time to time, usually while flying to some distant city. While in the air force he had flown on SAC refueling flights like the one just described, and he found it difficult to assess: whether he had actually been anywhere other than in an airplane, an experience not much different than if the plane had never taken off, particularly if he flew at night or above an overcast for most of the route. This is what ordinary travel has become.

Mulheisen mused on this as he took off from the enormous industrial urban area that is Detroit, climbing immediately through a thick overcast and then leveling off, the power easing back, blandly cruising. The flight attendants immediately commenced their flight-long busyness, pulling carts up and down the aisles while Mulheisen tried to ignore the crying children, the never-ending parade of pissers shuffling back and forth to the toilet. Below him there were forests, towns, lakes, ribbons of highway . . . then a very great lake, an inland sea on which tiny freighters dragged tiny wakes. But Mulheisen didn't see any of it, and the aircraft hissed on. "It's always sunny on top," the pilots used to say, but the window at his side continued to display a cloudscape not more interesting than the television before which you have fallen asleep, the broadcasting day completed.

The only drama in this video show were the landings. The voices telling him to lock his seat belt, then the aircraft tilting dangerously, then gliding, then surging forward powerfully, jolting down with an enormous roaring and vibration as the engines' thrust reversed and the flaps went to full and blue lights flashed by and he strained against the strap anxiously, until the power died and they began to taxi. He sat back, relieved but a little guilty about his fear, and he didn't glance around at his fellow passengers, respecting their terror or trying to mask his own terror, which anyway dissipated entirely by the time the plane arrived at the gate. There were at least four of these thrillers: you don't get to Montana nonstop.

However, there is no such thing as a continental overcast and eventually, somewhere west of the Mississippi River, the clouds dissipated. Now he seemed to be getting somewhere. In America, as you move farther west, the terrain becomes grosser. First enormous plains covered with crops or, in season, snow; few towns, fewer houses, lonely roads; then scars in the earth, vast expanses of erosion and geological litter; and finally forests again and the upthrust of mountains. The landings were hairier now. The aircraft banked like a fighter jet and thundered to shrieking, shuddering halts. On takeoff the aircraft climbed steeply, desperately clawing for altitude. Below him, scrolling through his seat-side screen were immense reaches of piled rocks, and in every valley a tiny silver stream with, usually, a small town at the intersections of valleys.

The Butte landing is one of the most harrowing, Mulheisen found. He felt he was almost a qualified fighter jock by the time he wrenched his way around the mountains and raced to a belt-straining halt. When he reached the front door, the air was cool and fresh. The airports are small out west, in the lesser cities like Bismarck, Bozeman, and Butte. Often they don't have mobile ramps and you have to de-plane onto the windy tarmac. But that in itself is rather nice, at least Mulheisen thought so. He liked to get a good look at the airport activity, the small aircraft, the people driving baggage trucks and handling the fuel. He liked the smell of jet fuel: It reminded him of his youth in the air force.

In these small airports there is a distinct absence of threat. A person from a city like Detroit feels strangely confident and almost at ease. It is never far to the main reception area, and anyway, there was a man to meet him.

"Sergeant Mulheiser?" he said. He wore a gabardine uniform, with a lot of gun belt and holster and a kind of cowboy hat. As tall as he was, he wore high-heeled cowboy boots. His face was huge and dimly pitted. He seemed to be smiling, but perhaps not.

Mulheisen eyed the brass nameplate over the pocket and said, "Zhock?"

The deputy frowned. "Jacky Lee," he said, then extended a hand so large and stiff you could never imagine a glove on it, but at least it wasn't a crusher.

"Just call me Mul."

"Mr. Antoni said he's sorry, but . . ." He pronounced it "An-TONY," just as Mulheisen always did. Antoni was deeply involved in a drug case, it seemed. However, he would pick up Mulheisen from his hotel that evening, for dinner.

"You want a drink?" Jacky said.

"Absolutely," Mulheisen said. He'd had more than a couple in the four-stop route from Detroit, but that last landing had erased all the ease that the previous drinks had provided.

Jacky Lee was not a man to waste money on the airport bar. They drove toward the town, which Mulheisen could see in the distance, perched up the hillside. On one side was an enormous craggy range of mountains, so close you could lean on them. Mulheisen was strangely pleased to hear Jacky refer to these mountains, with a slight gesture of the hand, as "the Continental Divide." What a powerful notion was hidden in that offhand gesture, Mulheisen thought. In front of them, only partially obscured by the ugly panoply of chain-restaurant and auto-dealership signs, was a huge, raw hill—larger than any mountain in Michigan—that was covered with buildings, except for a scattering of scabrous bare patches. On the airliner's approach, Mulheisen had seen the immense crater filled with water that was the remnant of years of pit mining. It was bizarre. An industrial lake on the very edge of a city, scooped out of a mountain. This was Butte.

Jacky stopped at a little bar that had a faux A-frame portico. They sat down to shots of whiskey with beer chasers. Mulheisen was pleased to find that they had Stroh's beer.

"I was the one who found him," Jacky said.

"Uh-huh," Mulheisen said. "He must have been a mess."

"He was. We didn't think he'd live. Hell, I didn't even think he was alive."

Mulheisen instantly perceived they were talking about someone other than the mob killer Gianni Antoni had called him about. But he just sipped his whiskey and looked out the window at the amazing mountains. There was some kind of superhighway issuing from the mountains. He could make out large trucks creeping up and down. Everything seemed about ten miles away. "What's up there?" he asked, indicating an enormous white object on the very ridge of the Divide, overlooking the valley.

"Statue," Jacky said. "Our Lady of the Rockies. It's lit at night. Those trucks are coming down from Homestake Pass. There's another pass to the north . . . Elk Park."

"The pass," Mulheisen echoed, marveling to himself. Just imagine being able to offhandedly say "up on the pass," or "over the pass." It didn't mean much to these people, of course, but to a Detroit boy it had a magical twang.

"Doin' all right now, though," Jacky said.

"Uh-huh," Mulheisen said. "What does he say?"

"Nothing," Jacky said.

Mulheisen liked the way Lee said that. He understood that the man, whoever he was, whomever Lee was talking about, had not said anything, as opposed to having said something that turned out to be inconsequential.

"What about Helen Sedlacek?" Mulheisen said.

"Oh, her. Well, she was living down to Tinstar," Jacky said, "and now she's gone. No sign of her. Her boyfriend, Humann, there's no sign of him."

"No sign, eh?" Mulheisen said. "Well, who are we talking about, then?"

"Deadman," Jacky said.

"A dead man, sure," Mulheisen said. "But I thought you made an identification? Through the FBI?"

"Oh, that guy," Jacky said. He actually lifted his eyebrows and widened his eyes to register that he understood that they had been talking at cross-purposes. "Soper, or whatever. You know him?"

"I know of him," Mulheisen said. He took a long draught of beer. He felt a little better. "Not a loss to the community. Goes by the name of Mario, usually. I picked him up once on a muscle charge. He pulled some time back east. New York," he clarified, realizing that to this lawman, Detroit was also back east. He drank the rest of his shot. It was bourbon. "But you were talking about someone else."

"Yeah, sure. I thought you were here to identify Deadman."

"Dead men?"

"Deadman," Jacky said. "The guy I found on the road."

Mulheisen didn't get it. Jacky explained.

"Carmine Deadman?" Mulheisen said. "Well, it's obvious. Carmine was the mob boss who was hit in Detroit last spring. Your 'deadman' was probably involved. Whoever hit him—Soper?—was just putting out a notice, that this 'deadman' was in repayment for Carmine. His name isn't Carmine Deadman."

"I didn't think it was," Jacky said defensively, "but I had to call him something."

Mulheisen agreed. "It was as good a name to give an unidentified man as any. Rather droll, in fact."

Jacky didn't like that word, "droll." He knew it meant "funny," more or less, but it was too fancy. "I wasn't trying to be droll," he said.

Mulheisen looked at the man carefully, waiting until Jacky turned to face him. "Can we take a step back here, Jacky?" he said. "I'm not some big-city cop out here to make you look like a hick. I'm here because I was told that you had discovered the body of a well-known mob hit man, a fellow named Soper, who was known to associate with the late mob boss Carmine. It's my task, when I'm on my own turf, to find out who killed Carmine. That's all I want. I'm very pleased, however, to learn that in addition to Soper, you've turned up some evidence on a young woman named Helen Sedlacek, whose late father was an associate of Carmine's. We happen to believe that Carmine had Helen's father killed. We also know that Helen disappeared from Detroit the same day that Carmine died. So, we make connections. Now the connections have landed me on your turf. I'm happy to be here, happy to be of assistance, but I assure you that I fully understand that it's your turf. Okay?"

Jacky almost smiled. "Sure," he said. "You want to go see Deadman? Maybe he's part of it."

"Oh, I'd be happy to see him," Mulheisen said, "but I doubt that I'd recognize him. It occurred to me, just now, that it might be a character we know as Joe Service. We don't know much about Service, but apparently he is, or was, some kind of contractor with the mob, for the late Carmine, in fact. He wasn't known to be a hit man, but more of an in-house investigator, a kind of troubleshooter. Helen Sedlacek was seen in the company of Service in the days before she disappeared. The trouble is, I don't have anything on Service. No pictures, no prints. I think I may have seen him, once or twice, but I didn't remark him at the time and . . . well, you get the picture, I'm sure."

Jacky understood. Like Mulheisen, he had simply noted with suspicion that it wasn't often that two strangers end up dead, or near dead, in one sparsely populated county. Not in Montana, anyway. All Mulheisen could say about Service was that he was below average height, about thirty years old or a little less, athletic build, good-looking, with dark hair. That wasn't nearly enough, although it certainly matched with Carmine Deadman, and Joseph Humann.

Back in the car and driving uptown, Jacky said that he had tried to link his "Deadman" with the missing Joseph Humann, Helen Sedlacek's associate in Tinstar. A couple of people from Tinstar had been brought in to see the recovering victim, but his face was so bandaged and contorted that they hadn't been able to say if the man was the one they knew as Humann. They had taken many latent fingerprints from Humann's home, but the word wasn't back on the comparison with the victim, as yet.

"You had lunch?" Jacky asked. "No? Well, I'll take you for a quick tour and we can get a bite, kind of give you a feel for the place. It's gotta be a little strange, just flying in like this."

This was agreeable to Mulheisen. He sat back to absorb what he could, in the hope that he could make some sense of a new town. He had chauffeured visiting cops around Detroit, and he'd always been curious about their impressions. It was normally bewilderment at the sprawling city. Butte, however, was clearly more compact, more digestible.

Mulheisen had occasionally contemplated leaving Detroit. It isn't always easy to love the place. As a student of the history of that strategic straits, he knew that successive Indian nations had considered it important enough to gather there from time to time, but none had ever chosen to stay. Only the European invaders and then the

Americans had stayed and built, but there was a persistent tendency for flight even among them. Indeed, the city was experiencing a dramatic ten-year hegira.

Sometimes it seemed to Mulheisen that everyone he knew had left Detroit. There were Detroit people all over the country. A few years earlier, in fact, he had considered moving to Oregon. But he had always abandoned these notions because the pull of the local milieu was too strong, and anyway, the idea of learning a whole new place seemed too daunting.

Driving uptown with Jacky Lee, he experienced the difficulty intensely. There is almost nothing of Detroit in a place like Butte, Montana. The mountains, the air, the vistas—it was overwhelming. There was, however, a certain resemblance. Like Detroit, Butte is an industrial city in a process of decay and change. In a perverse way, Mulheisen warmed to these empty brick buildings, the littered streets of dilapidated neighborhoods, boarded-up hotels, and weedy lots where a house had been demolished, the rearing silent hoist frames and rusting tin roofs of mines. These mountains were exciting, but they were also alien and unnerving; urban decay and even the brutal, grotesque disfiguration of the hillside by the mines seemed familiar and friendly.

Mulheisen had been to just about all of the major cities in the country, but only on business. Most often it was a quick in and out to pick up an extradited prisoner. The airport, the ride to the city or county police headquarters, the motel, a dinner with an officer or two whom he'd met on similar assignments in Detroit, or at a conference—often with an old friend or acquaintance from Detroit who was now living in San Francisco or Houston or Atlanta. The next morning he'd pick up the prisoner and get back on the plane. San Francisco looked nice; so did Reno. One of his best friends lived near Reno now and was always after Mul to relocate. Mulheisen liked to visit, but the prospect of actually leaving the grungy environs of Detroit, the great steamy, swampy, brutally cold and dank stinking morass of lovely forested and broad-avenued riverside Detroit, for some new and not quite right town where people lacked an edge to their conversation . . . Aw, to hell with it, he would inevitably say.

However, Butte looked okay. It was as awful as he could wish and at the same time pretty grand. He especially liked the people. Jacky Lee's taciturnity notwithstanding, everybody here seemed to be friendly and cheerful. They were walking from the parking lot to the Finlen Hotel, and a passerby looked up and met Mulheisen's eye and said, "Hi ya, pardner." Mulheisen was startled. He looked to Jacky Lee, but Jacky said he didn't know the guy. You don't make eye contact on the streets of Detroit; it invites an unwelcome intimacy, such as a gun alongside the head and ungentle hands tearing at one's clothing. The old guy probably mistook me for someone else, Mulheisen thought. But a few minutes later, as they walked over to the M & M saloon, a young fellow came out of Gamer's Restaurant, stopped to pick his teeth (everybody in Butte picked their teeth, he soon realized), and nodded to Mulheisen. "Howdy," he said. In the great swirling mass of men and women in the M & M saloon, playing keno, drinking beer, eating lunch, several people nodded at him and said hello with a smile. He had no idea what the hell this meant, but it was pleasant, if a little unsettling.

For lunch Jacky Lee had driven him out to the perimeter road, Continental Drive, to a little pasty joint that didn't appear to have a name. It wasn't much of a joint. It reminded Mulheisen of some soul food places in Detroit: not more than a halfhearted attempt at decor, a simple counter with vinyl-covered stools, a couple of Formica-topped tables with mismatched chairs, some kind of ersatz wall covering that was supposed to resemble wood paneling but didn't come close. Clean though. And the pasties were delicious. They were served very simply: a single large pastry stuffed with meat and potatoes lying like a steaming brown island in a lake of brown gravy on a plate. You could get a side order of coleslaw in a Styrofoam container.

The pastry was not delicate. It had to be strong enough to contain the meat and potatoes. Mulheisen liked it very much and asked the young woman in a full apron who had brought the plates out from the kitchen just what the ingredients were.

"Oh, beef, potatoes, onions, sometimes carrots—depends on who is cooking."

"Ground beef?" Mulheisen asked.

Her eyes widened in horror. "Ground beef! Good lord! *Flank* steak." She disappeared back into the kitchen.

Not far from the pasty place, Mulheisen noticed a church with three somewhat Oriental, or Russian-looking domes. Jacky identified it as Holy Trinity, a Serbian Orthodox church. "The priest there is from Detroit," he added.

"From Detroit? You're kidding."

But he wasn't and when they stopped, the young priest was delighted to see them. This was his first parish, he told them, and he'd been amazed to find such a large, flourishing congregation way out west. The church was very beautiful, standing below the towering ridge of the Continental Divide. They chatted about the Tigers for a few minutes, and then Mulheisen asked if a young woman from Detroit, Helen Sedlacek, had been to visit. No one of that name had appeared, the priest said, it didn't even sound like a Serbian name, but when Mulheisen described Helen, he quickly recollected a young, dark-haired woman who had wandered in one afternoon, earlier in the summer. Very attractive, about thirty, with a silver streak in her hair. He knew nothing about her, he said, and he was sure that she hadn't talked to his wife or he would have heard about it, but he would ask around. He hadn't seen her again. He was sure that she hadn't given the name Sedlacek, however. He had assumed she was a tourist—"People drive along the highway there," he said, pointing up at the road coming down from Elk Park, "and they see the church. If they're Orthodox, they recognize what it is, right away, and they stop by. They're always surprised by the size of the community, and sometimes they find familiar names among the congregation, or even distant relations. I did."

Driving back uptown, Lee explained that there had been a lot of ethnic neighborhoods in Butte, once upon a time. "Italians, Irish, Finns, Croats, Serbs, Poles, Cousin Jacks," he waved his hand inclusively at the hills.

"Cousin Jacks?" Mulheisen said.

"Cornish, from Cornwall," Lee explained. "They brought the pasties. They're all miners. Or were. A lot of the neighborhoods were gobbled up by the Pit and now, well you know how it is . . . a couple generations go by and the kids intermarry . . . the neighborhoods just kind of got all mixed up. But you still got a little of it. Hey, I'll take you to a good ol' Cabbage Patch bar—Smokey's Corner."

Bernard Stover was inevitably known as "Smokey," after a comic strip character from the thirties. It may also have had something to do with his involvement in occasional convenient fires later in his career, fires that resulted in insurance payments to acquaintances. He was a Butte lad, born and bred, right out of the Cabbage Patch—a largely Irish conclave on the shoulder of the Hill. In its early days the Patch was a rackety collection of shacks and cribs that harbored immigrant miners and their families, then was renovated with government projects and was now due for another urban renewal process.

Smokey had come a long way from the Cabbage Patch, in a sense, although Smokey's Corner, the tavern that was the flagship of his not-very-far-flung enterprise, was located just a couple of blocks from where he'd been born. He was a good-sized feller, in the local parlance. In his seventies now, he was frankly paunchy, and his long face was jowly, the round blue eyes under that still-unwrinkled dome of a brow as innocently blue as a baby's. He still smoked a pipe, a new corncob every week, loaded with Union Leader tobacco.

He was knowledgeable about the mines and the Company, as one commonly referred to the Anaconda Mining Company, the organization that had operated the great copper mines of The Richest Hill On Earth before closing down and selling out to ARCO in the eighties. There was still some mining in Butte, but not on the grand scale that had made this the biggest, richest town in Montana. Smokey Stover had never spent a single shift in the mines. From childhood he had worked the bars, peddling papers, running for beer, running for sandwiches for gamblers, whatever paid. Later he had run bootleg liquor. Nowadays he was into real estate and development, and he still ran his cranky old tavern, as unreconstructed as possible.

The national mobs had never really had a foothold in Butte. It was hardly worth their trouble. Too few people, even in the heady days of nearly 100,000 population. Nowadays, with only 34,000 in the county, it was even less interesting. The old red-light district was gone and gambling was legalized. But they had always kept in good contact with some locals, primarily Smokey and his predecessors. There was a big Italian population in Butte, and possibly the mob had some contacts there, but it was mainly with Smokey.

Smokey's Corner was as old fashioned as a bar could be in America in the waning years of the twentieth century. The door opened right off the street. The floor was unpolished hardwood and already at ten in the morning it was littered with peanut shells and cigarette butts, mixed with sweeping compound. There were three coin-operated pool tables placed in the center of the narrow room that ran back some sixty feet to the back room, with a row of tables and chairs against the outside wall. The tables and chairs were wooden, seemingly the original furniture—deeply scored from knives and keys, displaying initials, crude representations of genitalia and other more obscure images—but the original furniture had long since been smashed in brawls and whittled into sawdust; these chairs and tables dated from the fifties.

The bar was original equipment, having been hauled by mule

train out to the gold mining camp Alder, down in the Ruby Valley, back in the 1870s and thence to Butte when that camp folded. Along the inner wall the bar ran fully thirty feet with a tall mirrored back bar on which many bottles of whiskey were displayed. The top of the serving bar was deeply scored and gouged, and there were at least two verifiable bullet scars in its wooden surface, one of them not that ancient—a client had absentmindedly pulled out a .357 magnum pistol while searching his pockets for another dollar, and when he slapped it on the bar it went off, blowing away part of the bar and shattering a corner of the back bar. This had happened two years ago; Smokey had banned the perpetrator from the bar for a week.

The old pressed-tin ceiling was still intact and repainted at least once a decade. Half of the brewery signs on the walls were of long-defunct brands. There was no attempt to make the bar look old, or traditional; it was just an old bar that had never been exposed to ephemeral trends of modernization. A very comfortable bar, actually, with a high ceiling that kept it from being too smoky, with fans that rotated infinitely slowly, with high, clear windows (rarely washed) that let in the fine mountain light. It had a kind of spaciousness that was pleasant. It didn't stink, either. While the floor was swept only nightly, the tables and bar and the sinks were kept clean and orderly. It was a regular old corner tavern, of a sort well known to Mulheisen from his youth in Detroit, but long since vanished.

Smokey was in the bar when Mulheisen and Jacky Lee entered. Also in the bar was the woman Heather, sitting at a table in the back, wearing a ski jacket. They didn't notice her. Jacky introduced Mulheisen to Smokey.

"From Detroit, hunh?" Smokey said with interest. He quit counting the take and wiped his hands before shaking Mulheisen's hand. "I know some guys from Detroit, they used to come over here once in a while."

"That so?" Mulheisen said. He looked around the bar, liking what he saw. "Did you know a guy named Mario Soper?"

"Is that the guy you was asking me about, Jacky? Nah, I never seen him. If he came in here I didn't notice. See that guy over there?" Stover pointed to a gaunt, grizzled man who looked to be seventy or more, sitting by himself in one of the wooden chairs along the outer wall. He had a shock of stiff, silvery wire hair and black eyebrows. He peered through thick glasses at a newspaper. At his wrist was a glass of amber whiskey next to a beer chaser. "You should ask him. That's Dick Tracy. He was a reporter for the *Standard* for about a hundred years. If anybody seen him, it would be Dick."

The woman in the ski jacket passed Mulheisen and Lee as they sat down to talk to Tracy. Lee watched her leave but didn't comment. Tracy was a pleasant, soft-spoken man. He seemed pleased to talk to them. He thought he recognized Lee's photo of Mario Soper, but couldn't remember when or where he had seen the man. He didn't know anyone named Joe Service or Joe Humann, or Helen Sedlacek.

"You're from Detroit, eh?" Tracy said. "You see much jazz back there?"

Mulheisen was pleased to talk jazz with the old reporter. They shared an interest in Cozy Cole—Tracy had played drums in his youth, for dance bands, swing bands at the old Columbia Gardens, a long-defunct amusement park that occasionally had brought in groups like Tommy Dorsey and Glenn Miller.

"I sat in once with Ray Anthony's band," Tracy said. "His drummer got drunk and lost some money in cards uptown and then he got noisy and finally his arm broke. So I sat in for him. It was unbelievable! What a band."

He went on to tell them what a villain old Smokey was. "Looks quiet now," Tracy pointed out, "but later the bikers come and others. You can get killed just walking by. A guy was stabbed about six months ago, just walking his dog. He should have known better than to walk a dog by Smokey's Corner."

"Yeah, it can be bad," Jacky affirmed.

Mulheisen found it hard to believe. Compared to Detroit,

Butte looked like a rest home. He asked again if Tracy hadn't seen Mario Soper, perhaps in conversation with Smokey. But Tracy didn't spend any time in Smokey's after about two P.M.

"That's about as early as the bikers and thugs get up around here," he said. "They stagger in here around three or so and knock back a few shots to get well. By then I'm up at the Helsinki—a much quieter bar, at that hour anyway. And then I'm home by eight. Your guy—what is he, a dope dealer?—probably would have been in later. But if he was a dope dealer, he was definitely in here, talking to Smokey. 'Cause nothing like that goes down in Butte without Smokey."

He glanced up at the bar and hoisted his empty glass with a faint smile at Smokey, who brought the bottle of Old Forester and poured out a huge couple of shots. Mulheisen quickly threw down a fiver and was surprised to get a couple of dollars back.

"He's a grand feller," Tracy said, with a mock Irish accent. "We both took catechism at the same time from Father Keneally." He leaned closer and lowered his voice. "Did you see that great strapping butch who just strolled out? She's from Detroit. I was talking to her. She said she was looking for an apartment. Not a pleasant lassie, I can tell you. Hard, very hard. She's got hands like a navvy, as the old-timers would say. She and Smokey have their heads together every day. I saw him passing money to her. Maybe she won a bet, or something."

"She move out here?" Lee asked.

Tracy said she had told him that she had taken a job in town. "Some kind of computer consultant, she says, but she doesn't impress me as a clerical worker. She's in and out of here all day. Someone said she was working at the hospital, saw her over there. Maybe she is a consultant, working on their computers. I guess she found an apartment, but I don't know where."

The old newsman rambled on about one character or another

but nothing, including his dark suspicions of the dykey computer woman, caught the imagination of the two cops. They soon left.

On the street, Mulheisen said, "Dick Tracy? Smokey Stover?"

"Tom Tracy, I think," Lee said, "and Clarence. But you know how these things are." He shrugged. "I can drop you anywhere you want, Mul, but I've got to get back to work. We've been having a lot of arson fires lately, and everybody's got to concentrate on that. But give me a call, anytime, and I'll do what I can to get away if you need help."

Mulheisen had obtained a street map. He said he thought he'd just walk around, try to get a sense of the town.

From his fourth-floor room in the Finlen Hotel, he could see a good deal of Butte. It wasn't a bad hotel, just a little old and dark with creaky floors. He went out for a stroll before dark. He walked all the way up the main drag, Park Street, to a kind of shoulder of the Hill where lay the campus of the School of Mines, or Montana Tech, as it was now called. He stood next to a bronze statue of Marcus Daly, one of the original Copper Kings who had built this western metropolis, and gazed out with Marcus at the city below. It was rather grand. He could see an awful lot of country from here: mountains to the south, mountains to the west, and of course the great wall of the Continental Divide to the east. He took a deep breath and exhaled. It was fine air, cold in the fall afternoon. It was the kind of country that made you want to take a deep breath.

10
Heather

The minute she laid eyes on Cate Yoder, Heather was smitten. The lovely little blonde was wheeling a muffled patient along the sidewalk around the hospital to a place overlooking the large park that spread down the hillside. The patient seemed to be a young man, his face partially bandaged and hidden by dark glasses. His head was covered with a woolly cap, and he wore a warm coat over which was draped a thick plaid wool blanket. He didn't speak or even move.

Heather approached them. "Nice day," she said.

Cateyo looked up, a little wary and defensive for some reason, but smiling. She too wore a woolly cap, and her lustrous gold hair escaped to cascade onto the shoulders of her own warm jacket, a colorful down-filled affair.

It was, in fact, a brilliant, sunny day in October, the temperature barely 40 degrees Fahrenheit. There had been frost but by now, ten-thirty, it had gone.

"Yes, it's lovely, isn't it?" Cateyo said. "I hope it isn't too cold for Paul." She fussed with his blanket for a moment.

Heather noticed the nurse uniform under the jacket and said, "Is this your patient?"

"Oh yes, he is," Cateyo replied, rather possessively, Heather thought. "This is his first time out."

Heather stooped and looked at the patient more carefully. "Hello," she said. Her voice was low and soft, and in her warm ski hat she didn't look unpleasant. Cateyo was disarmed. The patient did not respond.

"Paul doesn't speak," Cateyo said. "Actually, his name isn't Paul. We don't know what it is, really. He's not been able to tell us."

"My goodness," Heather said, straightening up. "Auto accident?"

"No, no," Cateyo said, carefully. "He was . . . a head injury. But he's getting better. Aren't you, Paul?" She laid her mittened hand gently on his shoulder. "He's just recovering from surgery." She gestured at her jaw and ear, as if to indicate the surgical site. "He'll be up and about, one of these days."

"Poor man, what sort of head injury?" Heather smiled at the young woman. She really was delicious, Heather thought, taking in the rosy cheeks and bright blue eyes, the soft pink lips. The bulky jacket didn't offer a very good notion of the woman's body, but Heather was sure it was strong and supple.

"It was a gunshot wound—not self-inflicted," Cateyo hastened to assure the woman. "He was just left for dead, on the highway. Can you believe that people could be so cruel?"

"Oh, I can believe it. Men are very cruel. That's why I had to get away from Detroit."

Below them, some mothers were watching and playing with several young children who were tumbling about the brown grassy hillside. Their voices rang in the clear air. Beyond the hillside and houses one could see in the distance huge white-capped mountains. A large black bird, much too large for a crow, sailed down across the broad hillside toward the Dumpster behind the IGA supermarket below them. Heather thought it must be a raven.

"It's very pretty here," Heather said, "and peaceful."

"Yes. You're from Detroit?" Cateyo asked.

"It's awful back there," Heather said. "I've just moved out to take a job here. I'm looking for an apartment. You wouldn't know of anything?"

"There's usually lots of rentals available. Have you looked in the *Standard?*"

"I looked, but I didn't really know what I was looking for," Heather said. "I was kind of hoping for a roommate . . ."

"Gee, I don't know," Cateyo said, "I'm sure there are people looking for a roommate, but . . ."

Their conversation faded in and out of Joe's consciousness. The word "Detroit" caught his attention, bringing with it an odor of alarm, but it faded away when the word wasn't repeated. His hands were cold. This new woman made him uneasy. Poking her huge face down into his. Why didn't she go away? He wanted Cateyo to talk to him, to stroke his hands, to sit and look at him as she generally did. He didn't even mind if she babbled on about Jesus. It was nice to be outside—the sun was warm on his face—but the breeze was chilling. He was worried. What if he got chilled? Cateyo looked after him very well, but she wouldn't know he was cold, especially if this awful woman kept talking and talking, as she seemed to want to do. His sunglasses were slipping and Cateyo hadn't noticed.

He lifted his head slightly. Not much, only a millimeter or two, but even so, he did it carefully so as not to reveal that he could move at all. Through the dark glasses—somewhat blurry, unfortunately (was it his vision or were they dirty?)—he could see the new woman. She was, as his first view had indicated, quite awful. He hated her now. He wanted her to leave. He concentrated furiously, willing her to leave.

Instead, she took hold of the near handle of the wheelchair, saying to Cateyo, "Here, let me help you with that." There was a low curb over which Cateyo wished to move the chair so that it could be rolled onto the grass.

"No," said Cateyo sharply and struck the woman's hand away.

It was done without thought, but forcefully. Cateyo was appalled. She hadn't meant to react so violently and she was immediately apologetic.

"I'm sorry," Heather said sweetly. "Of course, he is a patient and you are his nurse. You are responsible. I didn't mean to interfere. You take very good care of the poor dear."

The chair had lurched insignificantly, but Joe took the opportunity to groan as loudly as possible.

"Paul! Are you all right?" Cateyo fell to her knees before him, clutching his hands and gazing up into his dark glasses. She pushed them up onto his nose properly.

"Nnnnghhh," Joe muttered.

Cateyo stripped off her mittens and clutched at Joe's hands. "Oh lord, his hands are freezing! I'm sorry, Paul." She tucked his hands under the blanket. "There, that's better. Let's just take a little stroll down along the path."

A narrow footpath descended on a long slant across the shoulder of the hill. There had been a hard frost in the night and the ground was quite hard underfoot. Cateyo began to push the wheelchair slowly but carefully along the path with Heather walking alongside, still chatting about apartments and the clear weather. Joe resisted the tendency to lean sideways, downhill, but then he gave the effort up and toppled. Instantly, the chair capsized and Joe, to his horror, was tumbled out. The brutal, hard earth flew up at him and he only just managed to twist so that he didn't strike his face on the injured side, taking the blow first on his right shoulder and then his right temple. The pain was fabulous and he blacked out.

"Oh my god!" Cateyo screamed and she leaped to save him, but too late. Furiously, she snapped at Heather, "Now look what you've made me do! My god, he might be hurt!" She knelt over him, examining his bandaged face with obvious concern. "Are you all right, Paul? Are you all right?" She struggled to lift him then looked in panic for the chair, which lay on its side.

"Help me," Cateyo said to the woman. "The chair."

"Here, let me lift him," Heather said. "You get the chair." She spoke briskly and Cateyo leaped to do as she suggested.

"He seems all right," Heather said, "but maybe you better run back for some help. I'll watch him. Hurry."

Cateyo dropped the chair and knelt over Paul/Joe. His eyes were open and he blinked encouragingly. "No, I think he's all right," she said. "Let's get him back to the parking lot."

Heather picked up Joe's fallen sunglasses, then scooped him up in her arms. "He's not heavy," she said. "I'll carry him back to the walk. You bring the chair."

She set off up the path and Cateyo, alarmed but uncertain, followed hastily, dragging the chair over the bumpy earth, trying to keep up to Heather's rapid strides and calling after her, "Is he all right? Wait. Wait." But Heather strode on.

Heather stared down into Joe's face intently. His eyes were blue and clear and they stared directly into hers. His mouth was slightly open and a thread of spittle drooled from one corner. "He's okay," Heather called back over her shoulder. The woman carried him briskly and easily. It occurred to her as she reached the paved sidewalk that she could "accidentally" stumble and drop him directly onto his head. There was a good chance that it would do for him. Or, she thought, glancing across the blacktopped surface of the parking area, she could carry him to the side of the hospital and bash his head against the rough brick wall until she was sure he was dead. The girl wouldn't be able to stop her. She set off across the parking lot.

Behind her, Cateyo had stopped to set up the chair and rearrange the fallen plaid blanket, so that Joe/Paul could be resettled in it and wheeled back into the hospital as if nothing had happened. She glanced up when she realized that the woman was walking on.

"Stop!" Cateyo cried out. Her voice was strikingly clear and commanding. "You! Stop!"

The woman stopped and turned toward Cateyo, cradling Joe in her powerful arms. She smiled. "My name is Heather," she said.

"Bring him here," Cateyo commanded.

Heather stared at her for a long moment, then looked down at Joe. He showed no emotion, just stared at her.

"Oh. Sorry," Heather said, and carried her burden tenderly back to the chair, where she carefully lowered him and stood by while Cateyo fussed over him, rearranging the blanket, examining him to be sure that he wasn't hurt.

Finally, Cateyo stood and said, "I think he's all right. No harm done, I guess. But it must have scared him. Poor dear. Well, I better get him inside. I'm sorry I yelled at you . . . Heather. It wasn't your fault. It was my fault. I didn't realize how steep that path was. I should have paid more attention. Please forgive me. I can't thank you enough for helping out."

"Oh, don't think of it," Heather said. "I shouldn't have distracted you. Not when you have such an important responsibility. I'm glad I could be of help. Are you sure he's all right? Good. Well, no harm done, I guess. Listen, what's your name? Could I call you later and we could talk? I really don't know anyone here in Butte, and it's kind of . . . well, lonely. Maybe you could give me some advice on an apartment." She stood casually but firmly in the way of the wheelchair, smiling but not yielding.

"Yes, yes, of course," Cateyo said. "I'm Cate Yoder. I'm in the book. Bye!" And she wheeled the chair around the larger woman and whizzed back toward the warmth and safety of the hospital.

Joe was intensely relieved. He had no idea who the woman was, but she had given him a terrible scare, the way she looked at him, the way she held him. He remembered her hands particularly, large and red, and she flexed them constantly, squeezing him. He had seen something odd in her face, as if she hated him, but he could not imagine why a perfect stranger would hate him. Even before the accident, which he had in a sense willfully precipitated, those spasmodically clenching hands had alarmed him. Perhaps it was why he had allowed himself to tumble.

Once back in his room, however, he forced himself to forget about Heather. He leaned quietly against the bed while Cateyo undressed him, moving his arms one way, then another. He wore flannel pajamas that she had brought him. They were warm and comfortable and they had hockey players on them. He liked that. He liked it too when Cateyo sat him in bed and laid him back, then covered him.

"Oh, you poor thing," she said, talking more or less constantly under her breath, "what a ninny I am. How could I have not noticed how steep that path was? And then to just stand there talking to that woman while you're freezing to death. I'm sorry. I should be more careful. I will be more careful. Are your hands still cold? They are." She began to chafe them, then tucked them under the covers.

"Are you comfy? Is my guy comfy? My handsome Newman. Yes you are, a New Man, the New Man, the newest man there is." She adjusted the covers, checked his pulse, felt his brow, looked into his clear blue eyes. Then she glanced around and knelt to give him a swift kiss on the lips. Joe liked this part best.

Now she would sit, he knew, and talk to him for a while, at least until another nurse came along. All about Jesus, of course. About her theory of the New Man, the one who was coming to save the world from sin. She pointed out the similarities between his life and that of Christ. An unknown person, she said, who came out of nowhere, was killed and then rose from the dead. Of course, she had no idea who Joe was or what his life had been about, but then he wasn't too sure about it himself. Perhaps she was right. Maybe he was some kind of New Man. He wanted to be a New Man. He wasn't sure what he had done to fetch up here, in this bed with this lovely woman babbling at him, but he had a feeling it didn't bear too close examination.

On the other hand, he felt unaccountably anxious. He was

afraid of something, he knew, but what? Perhaps it was that awful woman, Heather, and her mention of Detroit? But he couldn't imagine what she could have to do with him. And more than that he felt he had something important to do, but he had no idea what it was. It had something to do with money, he thought. Yes, whenever he thought of money he got a strange, satisfying feeling. It was good to think about money. He wasn't exactly sure what money was, but he kind of knew, and he had a feeling that very soon it would all be perfectly clear.

Already his face felt more whole, more solid, and his tongue could move, he had discovered. But to move everything at once, the jaw, the tongue, that was too much. But soon. Perhaps in the night, when no one was around, he could practice.

Heather went directly to Smokey's Corner. Smokey was standing at the end of the bar. A skinny woman with hair dyed too red was pouring drinks. Heather nodded to Smokey, and he followed her back to a table in the rear.

"You see your man?" he said.

"I saw him," Heather said.

Smokey nodded. "You're s'posed to call Mr. Rossamani," he said. He gestured to a phone hanging on the wall near the end of the bar. "You can use that. No charge."

When she got through to Rossamani she said, "It was Service, all right. The nurse was taking him for a ride around the hospital, in a chair. The face is still bandaged and he wore dark glasses, but I got a good close look. It couldn't be anybody else. He's not talking, not even moving. He makes little noises, though. He'll talk, eventually . . . if he lives."

Rossamani was pleased. "I'll pass it on to the Fat Man," he said. "I'm sure he'll want you to go ahead. How long will it be?"

"I don't know. I damn near did it today, but then I thought I'd better check it out with you. How much does this old creep here know?"

"Smokey? He don't know nothing, just you're there to check it out, keep an eye on Service. What's your plan?"

"I'll be needing more money. I have to get close to the nurse. She seems to be the key. She watches Service like a hawk."

Rossamani said he'd call back in a few minutes. Heather told Smokey and picked up a copy of the morning *Standard* and went back to the table. A few minutes later the phone rang and Smokey answered it. He talked for a couple of minutes then hung up and came over to sit down near her.

"You gonna be sticking around?" Smokey reached in his back pocket and hauled out a large trucker's wallet, which was attached to his belt with a thin gold chain. He opened it and counted out three thousand dollars in hundred-dollar bills into Heather's large hand.

"Why?"

"I thought maybe we could have dinner," Smokey said. "You're new in town, probably a little lonely. I'm not a married man, myself."

Heather almost smiled at him. "You want a date?"

"Why not?" Smokey said. "You got something against older men?"

"Not particularly," she said. "But I've got a lot of work to do. I need to find out about a nurse."

"What nurse?"

"Cate Yoder, she works at the hospital."

"Cateyo?" Smokey grinned, then he looked at Heather for a long moment and something clicked. "So, you'd like to get close to Cateyo?"

"What does that mean?" Heather demanded. She crammed the money into her coat pocket.

"Nothin'. Good lookin' woman, though, eh?"

"How do you know her? She wouldn't be seen dead in a joint like this."

"She was one a my nurses when I had a triple bypass a coupla years ago," Smokey said. "Kinda made you sorry to get well, knowin' you wouldn't see her anymore."

"So? What do you know about her?"

"Nothin'," Smokey said. "Kind of a religious gal. Real sweet. Like a flower in the field." Smokey snorted, surprised by his own lyricism.

"A flower, hunh?" Heather smiled herself, remembering the woman's fresh loveliness. "Is she married?"

"Married? No, I don't think so." Smokey shook his head. "I never even heard about her going out much. She never talked about any boyfriend or even flirted with the doctors, like most of them do. She's quiet, religious."

"That's interesting. She live alone?"

Smokey caught the hopeful tone and said, with a wry look, "I don't know if she lives alone, or what, but I know she ain't like . . . uh, you know."

"Like what? Like me? You don't know anything about me." She fixed him with her flat brown eyes.

Smokey didn't back down. "Okay," he said, "I don't know shit about you. You want a drink?" He stood up.

"Bring me a shot of something," she said. "Rye, and a beer chaser." She opened the *Standard* to the classifieds and began to look at rentals. When she saw the cop come in, she felt a sudden thrill, especially when she saw the other man, the plainclothes cop. She continued to peruse the ads, however, and when she felt composed, she stood up and walked out. As she passed the men, she was very conscious of Jacky Lee's eyes. Oh, let him make a move, she thought, just one move. But he didn't and she was outside. She hung around for a while, keeping the sheriff's Blazer in view, and when the two men finally left, she returned. Smokey was still standing at the end of the bar, looking at what appeared to be a lingerie catalog.

"Who were those guys?" she asked Smokey, leaning over the bar.

"The deputy is Jacky Lee," Smokey said quietly. "The other one was some kind of dick from Detroit."

"I thought so," Heather said. "Mulheisen. I've seen him."

"That's the name," Smokey said. "He was asking about Soper. I already told Jacky I never seen the bum, but you know how cops are: Everything's gotta be told again, and again. I sicced him onto Tracy." He indicated with his head the gaunt man still sitting against the wall, now reading a book and occasionally sipping whiskey from a glass. "Don't worry," he assured her, "Tracy don't know nothing. He's just an old reporter, trying to drink his way into heaven. They yammered for a while and left."

"Bring me a shot of what Tracy is drinking," she said, "and a beer chaser. And when you talk to Rossamani again, tell him about Mulheisen. Also"—she leaned closer, across the angle of the bar—"you talk to Rossie, not the Fat Man."

Stover gazed at her calmly. "Rossie. Not the Fat Man."

"Good," she said. She sipped the whiskey and looked down at the catalog. There were pictures of beautiful women lounging about in see-through garments and a plethora of straps and lace. She put her finger on one of the pictures, a woman in a bustier, garter belt, and hose, but nothing else. "I've got an outfit just like that, only in red," she said.

"You?" Smokey narrowed his eyes. "I'd love to see it."

"I bet you would," she said. "Maybe I'll show it to you sometime, after dinner."

Smokey was pleased. She was an interesting woman, he thought, full of surprises. "I wouldn't of thought you'd be into this stuff," he said, cautiously.

"Oh yes," Heather said. She tossed down the rest of the whiskey. "I've always been the fem."

That evening, having showered and groomed herself very carefully, Heather rang the doorbell of Cateyo's house. It was a solid brick house with a tiny front yard surrounded with a wrought-iron fence. It was one of several similar houses on a street just a few blocks from the hospital. The houses were just a few feet apart. They had small porches and steep roofs. They looked to have been built in the thirties, or even earlier, but they were all in good repair. The street was on a hillside, but not steep.

Cateyo was surprised to see her.

"Hi," Heather said, smiling pleasantly. She gestured at a brick apartment house across the way and up the hill a few houses, saying, "I was just looking at a place over there, but it was already taken. The phone book said you lived close by, so I thought I'd stop. You were so kind to invite me. Was your patient all right? I hope he wasn't too upset."

"Oh, Paul's okay. I think he might have been a little alarmed, is all. Well, come in. It's cold out there."

The house was quite nice, pleasantly furnished but with too many religious pictures for Heather's taste. But evidently the kitchen had been recently remodeled; it was quite modern. In the way of such houses there was a front parlor, or living room, which opened through an arch into a dining room, then a swinging door into the kitchen, as one moved from the street side toward the alley. There were two bedrooms, separated by a bathroom. There was also a basement, half of which was given over to a narrow garage with space for a single, preferably small car and which one entered from the alley.

All of this Heather learned in the first half hour, as Cateyo took her on a little tour. Most important, it was soon clear that Cateyo lived alone, no sign of a man at all and no roommate. She was obviously quite proud of this house, which she had only recently purchased, although she had rented it for some time. She was full of plans to renovate further.

"It's lovely," Heather enthused. "I love these drapes, and the furniture is just right. You were so right to start your renovation with the kitchen. What's next, the bathroom?"

"I think so," Cateyo said, "but it's so expensive. The kitchen cost me about a thousand dollars more than I expected."

Heather stood in the doorway between the bath, with its plastic shower curtain hanging into the old-fashioned tub, and the empty spare bedroom. The sink was a freestanding pedestal model, dating from the thirties. Heather pointed out that it was still quite attractive, with the original ceramic handles. "You ought to keep that," she said. "You could save quite a bit by doing some of the work yourself. If you get some dumb carpenter in here, he'll want to yank that out first thing. These guys, a lot of the time they aren't really very creative."

"The guy who did the kitchen was really pretty good," Cateyo said, defensively.

"Oh, he did a swell job, as far as I can see," Heather assured her, "but I bet it was you who decided how it should look, who made, you know, the real creative decisions. You can get very nice bathroom cabinets that are pre-built and hang them yourself. It isn't hard, with a little help. I've done it before. I can help you, once I find a place to sleep." She turned and looked frankly into the empty back bedroom. Cateyo was using it as a temporary storage space. Skis, a tennis racket, an old dresser, and a couple piles of old magazines were all that occupied the little room.

Cateyo watched her and felt a tiny pang of guilt. She had plenty of room, and she had sometimes thought of advertising for a roommate, but then she'd thought she would just wait until another single nurse came in to St. James and, if she liked her, offer the room. And then, lately, she had harbored a little fantasy about Paul. Maybe, when he got better and was discharged, she could bring him here. This was so remote and the means of effecting it so unclear that she hadn't dared to really think about it.

There was something about Heather, though. She seemed at once big and strong, exuding power . . . but then there was an odd vulnerability, a faint breath of tenderness. Cateyo liked to stand next to her, sensing the older woman's power. It was a curious combination, perhaps only displayed by physically imposing women. Or certain beasts, such as gorillas.

Heather turned back and thrust her ugly hands into her pockets. She had learned early that for some reason people felt easier around her when her hands were in her pockets. She observed the irresolute expression on Cateyo's face: guilt contending with something unknown. Fear? A desire to be left alone?

"Part of the problem with finding a place," Heather said, "is that I can't stay long. This job with the power company is only for a couple of months, and then I'll be off to the next one. Probably Seattle."

"You could stay here," Cateyo said, relieved.

"Are you sure? You don't even have a bed . . ." she gestured at the spare room.

"That's no problem, I'm sure. And the rent would be reasonable. Really, I'm sure you'd be a great help."

Heather took a man's wallet out of her coat pocket and fingered the thick sheaf of hundred-dollar bills. "How much?" she said.

The two women laughed, beaming at each other. They both envisioned long winter evenings of companionship, girl talk, woman talk. But with significant differences. For Cateyo, here at last was someone sympathetic, to whom she could talk about Paul. For Heather—she glanced at the old-fashioned clawfoot bathtub, envisioning the rosy, golden girl who would step out of that tub, reaching for a towel—it was an almost impossible dream of access, not only to the girl, but to the target.

11

Antoni

Gianni Antoni had become Johnny. " 'Gianni' doesn't look so good on a campaign sign anymore," Johnny explained to Mulheisen as they drove from the Finlen Hotel down the hill to Antoni's home. "Used to be there were so many Italians here in Butte that 'Gianni' was a plus—it made you seem more Italian than 'Bud' Cocciarella. But now . . . even the Italians aren't very Italian."

Antoni was looking good. Precisely Mulheisen's age, he looked at least five years younger. Lean, fit, his thick hair steel-gray and stylishly trimmed, his complexion a ruddy tan—he looked like a combination of cowboy and stockbroker. He had now been elected county attorney three straight terms, and many thought he should run for state attorney general, the traditional threshold to political ambition.

By contrast, Mulheisen looked sallow and puffy. "Had a rough night, Mul?" Antoni asked. "Gee, I don't know how you do it. I gave that stuff up long ago. Remember that time we got off the base at Rantoul for the weekend and bought a case of beer that we lost?" He shook his head ruefully. "Boy, were we stupid! Drive out in the Illinois countryside with a couple of babes, lug the beer to the side of a stream, then you get the bright idea to drive back to town for more beer before the case runs out."

Mulheisen had completely forgotten this incident. It amused him enough to ignore Antoni's gibe about a rough night; Mulheisen had in fact gone to bed early, exhausted by flying and driving around with the indefatigable Jacky Lee. He had read two pages of Bernard DeVoto's introduction to the Lewis and Clark journals before falling deeply asleep. As he recalled the earlier incident, it was Antoni who had insisted that they drive back to Kankakee—which was where they had picked up the girls and the beer in the first place—leaving the girls streamside to "guard" the beer. The real reason behind this goofy plan was that Antoni feared that the girls were prostitutes, would infect them with gonorrhea, and he had no condoms. All the way into town, Mulheisen had argued that they weren't prostitutes, merely shopgirls still in their teens. And the tragic ending: They never found the stream, or the girls, or the beer again. It was worth a laugh now, but Mulheisen had felt very bad about stranding those girls. But it was Antoni's car, and they had to be back on base before nine o'clock.

"I thought you were going into law," Antoni said. They drove out along Continental Drive, past the Serbian church and on toward a newer part of the city, lying in the shadow of the Divide. These were newer houses, expensive homes of redwood and glass, plenty of heavy timbers and rough-faced stone fireplaces. The country club was here as well. The old mansions on the hill were no longer the desired homes of the executives and wheeler-dealers of the new post-Company Butte. "Didn't you go to Michigan for a while? We kind of lost track there."

"Oh, I thought about it," Mulheisen said with a mild sigh. "I was going with this gal, she was a prosecutor. We were going to get married, I'd go to law school while she supported me, and I guess the idea was we'd end up in Portland, or Seattle, or someplace. It didn't work out."

The flat way he uttered the final statement warned Antoni not to pursue the subject. He just nodded and grunted. "But you like the cop biz?" he said. "They sure talk you up back there. What's-his-name, McClain, says you're the best they've got. So how come you're still a sergeant? You bust some captain in the nose?"

"I've thought about it," Mulheisen said, with a humorous lilt to his voice, "but . . . I don't know, I didn't need the rank, and staying a sergeant is the only way you can avoid becoming a paper pusher. I like the beat. Is this your place? Nice crib."

"Crib!" Antoni snorted. He wheeled the new Lincoln into a driveway already crowded with an enormous four-wheel-drive Dodge pickup with an extended cab and huge, knobby tires, plus a sleek little red Miata and a four-wheel-drive Toyota pickup. There was an attached garage, but it too was filled with a boat on a trailer and another large, but slightly older model sedan. "That's Pat's car," Antoni said, indicating the Miata, "and the Dodge is my fishing wagon. Suzy and Jeff belong to these other rigs." Mulheisen correctly deduced that the latter two were Antoni's children.

The house was large and sprawling, on two or three levels. Like its neighbors it was glass and stained cedar with tons of stone and had a low-pitched roof covered with rough, hand-hewn cedar shakes. It was the kind of modern, overequipped house that Mulheisen only ever saw in Hollywood films. Nobody he knew actually lived like this.

A pretty blond woman dashed into the sunken living room to greet them, toting on her hip a hefty two- or three-year-old boy with curly blond locks. Mulheisen thought she might be in her late thirties, but the kid gave him pause. She could easily be a sun-dried twenty-eight. But, no, she was Johnny's one and only wife, Pat, the one he'd babbled incessantly about in the air force (and perhaps the hidden reason they'd driven off and left the two girls by the stream with the beer).

"Hi, Mul!" Pat yelled. She jammed the kid into his daddy's arms and surprised Mulheisen with a big hug. "I've talked to you on the phone and I've heard all about you for years. It's 'as Mul used to say' and 'Mul always says,' around here, you know."

Mulheisen didn't know how to respond to this. She was a real armful and he held her awkwardly. He almost blushed. A very tall, very robust young man entered, looking a lot like a giant version of his father, complete with a five o'clock shadow and the stiff but black hair. He was in some kind of hunting outfit, all boots and canvas with cartridge loops and many, many pockets. "Hey, Mul," he roared, "good to finally meet ya. You gonna be around for a while?" He grabbed Mulheisen's hand in his powerful paw and wrung it for a second, then threw it back. "I'd like to stay and talk, or rather, hear all yours and Dad's stories, but I'm driving over to Ekalaka for the antelope. I'll be back in a couple days. Hey, Dad, I'm taking the Winchester and the H & H, okay?"

Johnny grinned and proudly slammed his huge son's back. "Jeff!" he bellowed, as if introducing a prize bull to an arena. "He's a lotta kid, eh, Mul? Get outta here. Drive safely and no drinking and driving! Hey! Is your fishing gear in your rig? Get it out! Me and Mul are gonna float the Big Hole tomorrow! Mul can use your stuff, okay?"

"Great!" the kid hollered back over his disappearing shoulder. "I'll throw my stuff in your wagon!" And he was gone.

Mulheisen stood foolishly, trying not to nurse his damaged hand. "Quite a kid," he managed to say.

"You said it," Johnny agreed. "Hey, everybody, let's have a drink and celebrate the arrival in Butte-America of the great Mulheisen!"

Pat seemed enthusiastic, and shortly they were all equipped with glasses full of gin or bourbon. Soon they were joined by a pretty, long-legged sixteen-year-old: Suzy, long black hair and blazing blue eyes, at least six feet tall and clearly not through growing. She was bedecked in an array of sports clothing—spandex, knee socks, running shoes, sweater, jacket, shorts—the exuberant profusion of it all leading Mulheisen to think that she had just come from a combined field hockey/soccer/basketball/track meet. Like the rest of the family (except the shy little Cal, who hid his thumb in his mouth and looked at Mulheisen only over a furtive shoulder), Suzy was a yeller and a grinner, a slapper of backs and a kisser of moms, dads, and even Mul.

Mulheisen shrank from her approach, but there was no escape. She hugged him furiously and kissed his cheek. Her face was red from the wind and the sun but fresh and cold, and her tangled hair smelled of windblown sage. She'd been out running. Just running. Felt like running, that's all. She ran to the kitchen and came back with a cold diet Coke and guzzled it down in two long, gasping guzzles.

Contact with these people could be exhausting, Mulheisen thought. He tried to remember Johnny (Gianni) as a pell-mell airman, but couldn't. Not an eager beaver in those days. Something had happened to him. Pat, he supposed. Yes, that must be it. She flashed back and forth to the kitchen, the dining room, upstairs, back to the living room to gulp at her gin and tonic, pick up the kid, hug him, put him down, flash away to the kitchen.

Mulheisen and Johnny took the obligatory stroll around the grounds. There was, as even the poorest Butteant enjoyed, a magnificent view to just about all quadrants, though the view of the Hill might not appeal to some, with its bald patches and lonely looking mine hoists—gallows frames, Mul had heard someone in an uptown tavern call them. But it all looked grand to Mulheisen. They looked over at the country club, and Mulheisen assured Johnny that he wasn't interested in a quick nine. They wandered out to Johnny's wagon, the beefy Dodge pickup that was loaded with fishing gear. Johnny assured him that they would float the Big Hole River tomorrow.

"Is it . . . ah, white water?" Mulheisen asked.

"Nah. Well, not really. A few rocks, here and there. Water's low this time of year. If it's like this, and it should be"—Johnny gestured at the sun setting in a blaze of red and gold beyond the western peaks—"it'll be great. Something'll be hatching. You do much fly-fishing back in Michigan?"

"Not really," Mulheisen said.

"No? Too bad. There's some great trout streams, famous ones, back there—the Au Sable, the Manistee, the Boardman . . ."

"I've heard of them," Mulheisen lied. Well, he had sort of heard of the Manistee, but he wasn't sure in what context. Hadn't some guy killed half a dozen of his neighbors up there and stashed them in his freezer? Something like that. Or it could have been the town of Manistee, or was it Manistique, in the Upper Peninsula? He couldn't remember. "I live on the St. Clair," he offered hopefully. "Some of the guys go out for sturgeon, I think, and there's some kind of carp that spawn there. But I haven't really done much fly-fishing."

Johnny seemed shocked. He hauled out an aluminum tube and shook out two wispy sections that fit together to make a nine-foot whip, or so it looked to Mulheisen. It had a cork handle and tapered to a mere twig point. It was extremely flexible. It seemed to float in the hand, so light he could hardly hang on to it. Johnny quickly attached a reel and strung a tawny plastic line through the metal loops on the rod. They stepped away from the garage onto about three acres of well-mown grass, still as green as June, despite October frosts. With a few quick gestures Johnny had fifty feet or more of the line looping gracefully through the evening air; then he stopped his forward gesture, and another fifty feet or so went shooting out, and the line flew straight as a bluejay, then settled gently to the grass.

"Here, you try it," Johnny said, reeling up most of the line and handing the rod to Mulheisen. "Remember, you're not casting a lure on the end of a spinning line, but casting the fly line itself, letting it release . . . yes, that's it, don't let it drop behind you, give it more power as you move it forward, just like a whip, sort of, that's it, that's it, now let it go for—well, we'll practice more tomorrow. Sounds like dinner's ready."

This last was delivered as the line coiled around Mulheisen's head and then flopped and folded about him. It didn't tangle much and was fairly easily reeled up. They went in to dinner, a terrific roast loin of pork with lovely browned onions and carrots and turnips, with smooth, hot whipped potatoes and incredible gravy. The dinner rolls were freshly baked, and the green beans were fresh and very green and very tender, steamed with lemon butter. It was delicious.

Then everything was hurled into the dishwasher and forgotten. Suzy sprinted off to do homework; she had an A average and was planning to graduate early from Immaculate Conception and take a scholarship to Brown or Stanford, she couldn't decide which. Track scholarship on top of an academic one. Hurdles. Pole vault. High jump. Soccer, too. Probably ecology, maybe the law (later).

"Environmental law," her dad said firmly. "It's big and getting bigger. It'll probably be the biggest thing ever, down the road."

They drank coffee and sipped cognac—very old cognac, specially imported, not available in the Montana state liquor stores. Pat took the kid up for a bath, and Mulheisen and Johnny trotted off to the den, an incredibly expensive-looking room in the lookout basement, with its own view of the mountains and the masses of stars through a sliding glass door. The walls were clad in some kind of oiled teak, or zebrawood . . . it didn't look to Mulheisen like something that occurred naturally in large enough quantities to be milled and screwed with brass screws to the walls of a basement—knife handles, sure, or gunstocks, maybe, but not planks.

There was also about $10,000 worth of electronics stuck into the walls, but Johnny didn't seem interested in music or movies or whatever it provided. He wanted to talk about the Northern Tier Crime Task Force.

"Could be the biggest thing ever, out here, Mul," he said. He actually lowered his voice, perhaps due to the hour and the impending bedtime of little Cal, who was brought down in footed jammies to be kissed by all, even Mul, who brought a tremble but not a yelp to the brave lad's lip. "And you could be big in it," Johnny concluded, as if there had been no interruption.

"Me? I live in Detroit," Mulheisen said. "I'm seventeen hundred miles from here, Johnny."

"Not-nee-more, Mul. Not with computers. An nennyway"—
the brandy seemed to be having an eliding effect, Mulheisen noticed—"why are you'n Detroit? Be here! Be the chief investigator!
The big cheese. Chief Inspector Mulheisen! Captain! Hell, Admiral
. . . Field Marshal Mulheisen!" He laughed. They both laughed. And
Johnny poured them some special calvados from a collection of cal-
vadoses he had gathered in France a couple of years ago.

"Investigate what?" Mulheisen said.

Johnny squinted and smiled as broadly as he could, his teeth protruding comically, and said, "The New East Asia Co-Prosperity . . ."
He held the "eee" sound until Mulheisen began to sibilate a conclusive "Sssphee—," then interrupted him to end with a violently
ejected "FEAR!" He laughed. "Not to be racist, Mul, but it's the Chinese Mafia. That's the big number these days. Everybody's afraid that
when the Reds take over Hong Kong, the big Asian crime money is
coming here."

"To Montana?" Mulheisen arched a brow.

"Eventually. First to Seattle, Vancouver, Portland, Spokane
. . . and slowly, on across the Northern Plains into Lethbridge, Cal-
gary, Edmonton, Winnipeg, Minneapolis . . . Along the way they gob-
ble up Missoula, Butte, Billings . . . We're small taters for these guys,
but they don't overlook even the tater tots, Mul. That's the story,
anyway. Heavy-duty dudes, Mul."

Mulheisen waved an H. Upmann Petit Corona. "Mind if I
smoke?"

"Oh god," Johnny said, eyeing the cigar. "Oh sure, why not?
Here, I'll open the door." He jumped up and slid the glass door open.
A cold breeze crept in. The temperature must have dropped 20 de-
grees from the afternoon 50s.

"That's all right," Mulheisen said, "I'll have it later."

"No, go ahead. Light up. I insist. Hey, I'll have one, too. I've
got some around here." He waved away Mulheisen's offer of one of
his, and delved into a splendid cherrywood humidor on one of the

bookshelves lining an inner wall. He came up with a very large Havana, a Romeo y Julieta. "I have these, but I never smoke them. Joe Spalding gave me 'em, he's the chairman of the board at the power company. Here, have some." He grabbed a handful and stuffed them into the breast pocket of Mulheisen's sport coat, about seventy-five dollars' worth of cigars.

When the cigars were lit and drawing well and the initial smoke had cleared, whisked out by the door and/or some kind of faintly humming air-exchange system that Johnny had turned on, Mulheisen said, "So there is a big job. Is it in your power to give?"

Johnny nodded. "Effectively. I don't have ukase muscle: 'Listen up, guys! Mulheisen's our new head cop.' But if I suggest you, I will certainly have already made sure that no one will seriously oppose the nomination. No prob, Mul."

"But it'll just be a desk job," Mulheisen said. "Organizing squads of investigators, having meetings with mayors, police chiefs, Feds of all kinds, looking at miles of organizational posters, video proposals, funding strategies . . ."

"Nah, nah," Johnny said, waving his cigar. He set it aside and never picked it up again, only an inch or two of it tasted. "Youkin nav monkeys'll do that. Secretaries. Beautiful secretaries, maybe." He looked hopeful, then sighed and shook his head regretfully. He raised his hand to hide his whispered comment, "Notso weasy to get beautiful seckataries anymore. Turns out everybody's beautiful is also smart." He sat back, dropping the pretense of some confidential information. "Dunno why that is. D'you? Usetabe, beautiful was dumb. Not-nee-more. Speshly wimmen. Well, you think about it. We'll go fishin' tomorrow. I'll pick you up at . . . oh, nine? Ten? No point in goin' early, this time of year. Too cold in the mornin', fish don't bite till noon. Let's have a sauna." He pronounced it "sow-na," in the approved manner, and sprang to his feet a little unsteadily.

They walked out along a little path in the cold night air. There were many more stars than Mulheisen could remember seeing, at least for a long time. Perhaps there had been this many stars when he was younger, in the service and stationed in some remote corner. Yes, he thought he could vaguely remember that. But there were plenty here.

The path ran along the shoulder of a gentle declivity that ran down, as Mulheisen recalled, toward the country club. To match the stars overhead there were many thousands of lights out across the valley, but now somewhat obscured by ground fog. They came to a copse of evergreens and stepped into their aromatic embrace, and Johnny opened the door to a small wooden outbuilding that smelled even more aromatically of cedar. There was a tiny dressing anteroom, with a portentous shower stall in one corner, waiting to chill their en-flamed bodies. Johnny flicked some switches and sat down to take off his shoes.

"It's heating up," he said. "It'll be a coupla minutes. I should have brought my cigar."

Mulheisen shed his shoes and pants. "This Northern Tier thing seems a long way off," he said.

"No, no, no," Johnny said. "It's starting. It's started. They're already seeing infiltration of the drug business, the gambling especially, in Washington and Oregon and Bri-ish—British Columbia. Gambling could be big here. The Indians are into gambling and they want to get in bigger—casinos. Montana has always been pretty good at keeping Mafia—traditional Mafia—out of the gambling. That's why we've kept out casino gambling . . . but it could happen. I expect the Asians will hit gambling hardest in Montana. A cop in Missoula called me a couple weeks ago. He said a major Mafia figure met with the Asians in Missoula in September. That's the word. You should talk to this guy. Fact you will, Monday mornin'. We're havin' a little meeting. Some a the guys from Missoula are comin' over."

By this time they were both nude, and they gratefully eased into the hot air of the sauna. It was not a large space, two tiers of seats in a fully cedar-paneled chamber, with a powerful rock-filled heater on the floor. They had just settled and begun to relish the head-clearing heat, when Mulheisen noticed that the heavy door trembled slightly. He didn't say anything, but a few minutes later he yelped when the door swung open and Mrs. Antoni zipped inside. Completely naked.

Mulheisen stared as she clambered onto the upper shelf across from him. She was indeed a comely woman. She took a great deep breath.

Johnny looked up. "Hi, Hon. Cal go down okay?"

"Like a light," she said. "He's tired after a day of digging and running. Almost crashed in the tub."

"Good, good," Johnny murmured. He lowered his head, gratefully absorbing the heat in his lean, muscular body. Mulheisen clenched his own thighs tightly together and looked down also.

Again the door flew open and this time the stunning torso of Miss Antoni bounced in. She plunked down only a foot away from Mulheisen. He shifted away from her uneasily, trying not to look beyond those long arms framing the youthful pink-tipped breasts.

"I heard you sneaking out here," she accused her father. "I thought you said we were using too much electricity and you wanted to cut down."

Johnny looked at her blankly. He was feeling the heat, you could see. The moisture was pouring off him. He shook his head gently at her and lifted his gaze languorously to meet Mulheisen's panicked stare. "Finns," he breathed thickly.

"What?" Mulheisen croaked.

"I'm surrounded by Finns," Johnny said, tossing a dipperful of cold water onto the hot rocks. The searing steam rose into Mulheisen's nose and lungs. Johnny nodded at his wife. "Pat Juntonen. Born in Finntown." His head swiveled slowly to his spectacular daughter. "Soo-zoolalah Antononen, that's what we should call her. They'd live in the sauna if I didn't lock it once in a while. You gettin' hot?" he asked Mulheisen.

Mulheisen nodded. He watched in awe as the man stood up,

his penis hanging long and thick as he lumbered out. Mulheisen closed his eyes, took a deep breath and then, as nonchalantly as he had ever done, he dove for the door and whisked out.

The cold shower was running full blast. Johnny stepped out from under and grabbed for an enormous, fluffy towel hanging among others on pegs against the opposite wall. He gestured to the shower and Mulheisen gratefully plunged under. It felt magnificent. He felt magnificent. But he didn't linger. The minute he began to cool he raced for a towel and hastily dried himself, expecting the women to emerge any second. It was an agonizing process, however, as he was dead tired, and the effects of the cold shower soon gave way to the lassitudinous languor of the post-sauna syndrome: He felt good, he felt light, but he couldn't move very fast.

"Take your time, take your time," Johnny said, his voice as soft and easy as it would ever likely be, "they'll squat in there until they turn into beets. They always do. Sometimes I have to drag them out."

But Mulheisen didn't feel at ease until he was back out in the cold night, feeling his still-wet hair congeal frostily. A few minutes later they were in the Lincoln and cruising back uptown. Mulheisen almost fell asleep en route, and he barely made it up the elevator to his room.

Mulheisen's affection for Montana was at low ebb at about noon on the following day, when he found himself totally immersed in the Big Hole River, bouncing off jagged boulders, gasping for breath as he periodically surfaced, still clinging desperately to a fly rod from which many yards of line continued to reel out. He looked up through white froth at one point and saw Johnny's large gray rubber raft bearing down on him. Gratefully, he raised his free arm so that Johnny could save him. The water roared about him furiously and it was cold.

To his stunned surprise, Johnny merely grinned and waved

him to one side, crying "Grab the boat!" while in the front seat Judge Leahy calmly made a cast into a pocket off the main current. Almost immediately, the judge exclaimed "Yeah!" and lifted his rod, which bent deeply, indicating that he had a large fish on. At this point Johnny shipped his oars and stepped nimbly from his position in the center of the raft to stand at waist level in the raging stream. Johnny held the raft for the judge while he played the fish, and Mulheisen realized with a start that the water was only waist deep, and he staggered to his feet. They were in the slack water behind some rocks, the water clear and placid, the gravelly bottom secure and stable here. He was surprised to find that he still held the fly rod.

"Reel up and get in," Johnny called out, grinning.

Mulheisen began to reel up the yards of line that now ran straight down the current. The judge continued to play the trout, and within a minute or two had brought it leaping and lunging to the side of the rubber boat, where Johnny deftly scooped it up with a wooden-handled net that hung from his vest. It was a huge trout, silvery with splendid reds and blues and greens shimmering along its sides like the aurora borealis.

Mulheisen had the fly line completely reeled up at last, just as the judge lifted the nearly two-foot-long trout from the net and carefully extracted the fly from its jaw, then reverently lowered the now placid trout back into the water where it flexed and instantly disappeared. He turned triumphantly to Johnny and declared, "Five pounds if it was an ounce," his face wreathed in delight.

Mulheisen clambered glumly into the high rear seat of the boat again. His shirt was soaked but otherwise he was dry in the marvelously form-fitting blue neoprene bibbed waders. His hat had gone, but it wasn't his hat anyway, it was one of Johnny's. And now Johnny reached into the bottom of the boat, where water sloshed about, and lifted the dripping hat. He handed it to Mulheisen. It was a baseball-type hat with an emblem on it of an angler tangled in his own line and the words, "Frustrated Fishermen." Mulheisen flapped the moisture out of it and tugged it onto his wet hair. He felt like his teeth ought to chatter, but in the bright sunlight they just wouldn't.

"Fun, eh?" Johnny laughed and pushed the boat out from the rocks and leapt into his driver's seat as they shot down the current. A few minutes later they entered a wide and placid stretch of the river and floated calmly and gently. The judge was casting repeatedly and Mulheisen had regained his breath and composure. He gratefully accepted steaming coffee in the thermos top. Johnny handed him a pint of whiskey, saying, "Stiffen that up a bit." Mulheisen did, with a generous dollop of Jim Beam, and he soon felt considerably better. Within ten minutes he was even casting again, though not with any distance or precision.

He was still trying to convince himself that he had almost drowned, but it was getting harder and harder to do as the intensity of the event faded in the calm sunlight. Not very many minutes earlier, he thought, leaning back comfortably in the seat, he had been innocently trying to recreate the image of Johnny's daughter Suzy, as she stepped into the sauna last night. He wasn't having much luck in this. He'd been so astounded that he'd not had time to really notice, to observe, what this teenager had looked like in the nude. He had never seen a sixteen-year-old girl naked, and so he had no stock footage, as it were, to fall back on. But he had a shadowy impression of long black hair, of youthful limbs and a dark triangle. It wasn't sexy, it was too artless to be sexy, but it was a compelling image. And then Johnny had turned the boat sideways, apparently to give the judge a good shot at a holding position behind a rock, and in doing so the stern of the rubber raft had bumped against another rock. It was just a momentary bump, but Mulheisen was not prepared for it and he was off balance, turning to look at something, a heron, and the bump had caused him to slide off the seat and into the main current. He had been swept along for perhaps a hundred feet before he willy-nilly kicked his way into the field of rocks that lay on the far edge of the current. Now, reconstructing events, he realized that Johnny had very calmly assessed the situation, had refused to abandon the judge's position, but had adjusted so that the boat would shortly overtake Mulheisen and box him into the calm water where he could get back on his feet. It had been very masterful, almost offhandedly accomplished.

Mulheisen was grateful, but he was beginning to wonder how long this float trip would take. They had put the boat in the river at a fishing resort or camp about an hour earlier. He had been shown how to get into Jeff's waders and boots, and there had been another brief lesson in casting, which had gone a little better this time. Jeff's fishing vest, festooned with hanging implements and trout flies, was also inflatable as a life preserver. The whole outfit—inflated vest, form-fitting insulated waders, the felt-soled wading boots, wool shirt, hat—had given Mulheisen a clumsy feeling, as of a knight in plastic armor, complete with a lancelike rod of highly flexible graphite.

Their companion this morning was a district judge from Butte, Ed Leahy. He looked more like a judge than one should look: pushing seventy but hale and hearty, a well-trimmed white moustache, portly. He was in brown waders and a venerable fishing vest and canvas hat. "Glad to meet you, Mul. Heard a lot about you. I guess you'll be at the Task Force meeting on Monday?" Then he abruptly dropped any mention of business and explained to Mulheisen that the dark glasses on a flexible strap around his neck were polarized, so he could see the fish through the surface glare. They had magnifying lenses below the regular prescription lenses, so he could see to tie on the tiny flies— "The eyes gave out a long time ago," he said.

The boat had giant inflated tubes, with a light aluminum frame strapped tightly to D rings mounted on the tubes. It featured comfortable padded seats for fishermen fore and aft, and it floated on the surface with stunning buoyancy, hardly settling in the water, despite the three men, the cooler full of beer and lunch, the extra gear. It was a marvelous contraption, and it slipped blithely through surging water with Johnny perched in a central seat wielding the oars. He deftly avoided most of the threatening rocks and was able to position the raft, holding it on the edge of the current so that the anglers could cast to likely holding spots. Now, in this smoother section, it drifted as blissfully as Huck's raft on the broad back of the Mississippi. But ahead were canyons and more white water, an ominous roaring noise.

Four exhilarating hours later Mulheisen felt like a veteran. He had caught a fish—only twelve inches, but a genuine wild rainbow— he had run more rapids, he had even been allowed to row for a stretch of calmer water. He had long forgotten the cool, brisk morning with the odor of pines and the slickness of mossy rocks where they had gotten into the river. They pulled the raft out in warm afternoon sunlight and loaded it on the Dodge pickup, which had been shuttled downstream for them by a gawky teenager. But the whole experience wafted back into his memory that evening when he laid his tired bones into the cool sheets at the Finlen Hotel. He imagined himself making a difficult cast toward the shore and just before he swept into dreamless bliss, he glimpsed a long-legged girl standing naked on the bank.

12
Tinstar

Mulheisen went to St. James Hospital to look in on "Carmine Deadman." The patient was in a private room, his head swathed in bandages. He was asleep. He was still on an IV, but Mulheisen was told that he was now taking food orally, broths and so forth. The bandages didn't hide all of the face, but what was visible was still puffy and swollen, distorted. The man had blue eyes, they said. Mulheisen didn't recognize him.

The nurse was very protective of him. "Oh, he's just the best patient," Nurse Yoder said. "What a good boy!" She patted a foot gently but fondly.

Mulheisen went away but as he walked down the hall with Jacky he said, out of the corner of his mouth, "A nurse like that would have me up in no time."

"I know what you mean," Jacky said.

Out in the parking lot Mulheisen paused to look out over the valley floor below them, the blue snowcapped mountains beyond. There was a high thin wisp of cirrus, and the wind was brisk and cold in November. "Let's go see where you found Mario," he said.

They took the highway east, sweeping up the mountainside toward the Divide. The great white statue of Our Lady shimmered in weak sunlight, gazing benignly over the valley. Then they wound around and lost her, zooming up to the pass, effortlessly overtaking huge, lumbering semis and the occasional late tourist in a motor home. In the mountains there were acres and acres of bizarre cones and pillars of extruded rock—pipestone, Jacky called it.

On the other side was an immense valley, and you could see the road for twenty or thirty miles ahead, but they soon turned off and drove south, down into another valley. Here the mountains were not so large and there were farms and ranches. Eventually they came to a small place that proclaimed itself the town of Tinstar. It was just a crossroads. A gas station, a saloon called The Tinstar, a laundromat (closed), a little convenience store, and a few houses and trailers. Jacky gestured at it without comment and drove on through, as if to say, That's all there is to that. A few miles farther on, they turned off the highway onto a dirt road that crossed over a railroad track and then entered a private road that had a tall arch of huge ponderosa logs over a cattle guard. Miles of wooden fence ran off on either side. From the log crosspiece of the arch hung a wooden sign that had been carved or routed out to say XOX—GARLAND RANCH.

They drove up this long private drive across a big meadow filled with grazing cattle. In the distance was a barn and a corral and a collection of smaller buildings including a low ranch house, but long before they reached it another road ran off to the left and Jacky took that. The road curved around the side of Garland Butte, the small mountain that lay back of the Garland Ranch. They soon came to another gate, with a cattle guard, and a sign that said, simply: PRIVATE PROPERTY. KEEP OUT! Just beyond it was a sign neatly lettered, black on white: IF YOU HAVE NOT CALLED AND RECEIVED PERMISSION TO ENTER, GO BACK NOW. It did not give a phone number to call. Presumably, anyone who would be given permission to enter would know the number and the owner. On either side of the gate and at regular intervals along the barbed wire fence hung metal signs that displayed a bolt of lightning and the word DANGER!

"Mr. Humann is security conscious," Mulheisen said.

"You don't know the half of it," Jacky said. He got out and unlocked the gate, which had a police warning on it: DO NOT ENTER/CRIME SCENE. The road continued around the mountainside, climbing higher and maneuvering through two switchbacks before it crossed another cattle guard and an even sturdier gate, steel and mounted on huge timbers that guarded the road. From the timbers extended a tall steel fence with a running coil of razor wire along the top, extending away around the hillsides, sporting the electrical warning signs. As before, the gate was closed and locked, with a police notice. Jacky got out and opened it, and they drove through. There were trees up here, but none in a wedge-shaped swath that led to the house. The phrase "field of fire" came to Mulheisen's mind.

The house was a very Western house, to Mulheisen's eyes. It was built of large, horizontal logs, and it was on a single floor. The roof was moderately steep, sheathed in dark green steel, and it extended out to cover a porch or deck that ran the length of the front of the house, with a wooden railing. Beyond the house, perhaps fifty yards, the pine forest reared up and clothed the top of the mountain, some four or five hundred feet higher and a quarter-mile away.

Jacky parked and they got out into the pale sunlight. There was a wonderful odor of pines, three or four large ponderosas having been spared to provide shade and a windbreak around the house. The lawn was not a lawn as such, just sparse grass and a lot of pine needles, otherwise bare earth and a few large, lichened rocks.

"Have you been inside?" Mulheisen gestured at the house.

Lee nodded. "Reasonable extension of a crime scene, especially since the ditch rider found a gun in the hot springs. We found more guns inside."

"A lot more?"

"A couple of revolvers and a couple of sawed-off shotguns. I've got 'em all down to the shop, if you want to see 'em."

"A sawed-off shotgun was used in the Carmine killing," Mulheisen said. "Maybe we should look at them."

"What can you tell from a shotgun?" Lee asked. "No ballistic evidence."

"No, but in this case . . ." Mulheisen hesitated, recollecting the bloody scene inside Carmine's limousine. "There could be splashes of blood, fragments of tissue or bone, maybe fibers from clothing or upholstery. These things could possibly have adhered to the weapon, even if it was wiped off or cleaned later."

Lee looked around the silent yard. "I don't think our forensic facilities are up to that kind of thing, Mul."

"I could take it to our man in Detroit," Mulheisen suggested. "But for it to mean anything we'd probably have to have the forensic crew sweep the house, Humann's clothes and Helen's." He sighed. "What else did you find?"

"Quite a bit of money. Pert near fifty thousand dollars, in old bills, mostly fives and tens and twenties." He detached a "Police Crime Scene" ribbon from across the door and unlocked it. They stepped inside.

It was an interesting house, Mulheisen thought. He liked it a lot. It was basically one large room with four small rooms arranged against the back: two tiny bedrooms, only one of them equipped with an ample brass bed but both with built-in closets; an equally tiny "spare" room where Jacky had found the guns (a kind of office, or study, it also had a personal computer, a desk, and a filing cabinet and its closet was filled with women's clothing, evidently a spillover from the other bedrooms); and a bathroom with a tiled shower stall and a large, sunken tub. The large main room had a kitchen on one end and a fireplace with a sofa and chairs at the other end. There were a couple of practical-looking tables, one of which, by the entry, had a telephone/answering machine on it. There were a few pictures on the walls, mostly nicely framed prints of Winslow Homer and Thomas

Eakins (a little odd, Mulheisen thought: no Western scenes, but Eastern scenes). It seemed a very livable, practical space.

Mulheisen pointed at the answering machine. A red light indicated it was on, and a zero appeared in the message slot. "No messages?" he asked.

"Just what's-his-name's voice, the greeting," Lee said. "I left it
on, just in case."

Mulheisen nodded approvingly. "What did you do with the
money?" he asked.

"It was in a desk drawer, loose. I put it in a box," Lee said, "and
I took it to the First Metals Bank in Butte and put it in their vault. I
had one of the bank officers count the money and give me a receipt.
Then I put the receipt in the Butte–Silver Bow evidence locker."

Mulheisen raised an eyebrow. "That what the sheriff told you
to do?"

"I didn't ask him," Jacky said. "I just did it. I didn't want anyone saying I stole any of it, and I couldn't see letting it sit around
the station house. I got Kenny Dukes, the other deputy, to witness
what I did with it when I found it, and also Sally McIntyre, the
ditch rider."

"She came up here with you?"

"She showed me where she found the gun in the hot springs
and then she came on up here."

"Can I talk to this ditch rider?" Mulheisen asked.

"Sure. You want to see anything else in here?"

"I'd like to look at that computer some time," Mulheisen said,
"and the files. I'd like to know the legal considerations, seeing that
Humann isn't under arrest or anything. Of course, possession of a
sawed-off shotgun is some kind of criminal offense, isn't it?"

"I'm not so sure about that," Lee said. "Is that a federal statute?
I'd have to look up the Montana law. But, hey, you'll be interested in
this." He opened the door of what appeared to be a utility closet off
the kitchen. He pushed aside the usual array of mops and brooms and

slid back a concealed panel revealing an assemblage of electronic gear: three small television screens, a reel-to-reel tape deck, various switches.

"I didn't check it out fully," Jacky said, "but from this panel he can activate electric fences, lights, security TV cameras, tape conversations . . . who knows what all? The interesting thing is, there's no sticker from any electrician or electronics outfit. I checked around Butte, nobody there worked on this. It looks like Humann did it all himself. Far as I can tell, it all works. There's no labels on anything, so I wasn't able to figure out what it can actually do, but at least one of the screens shows the yard. The whole thing was turned off when I found it."

Mulheisen glanced around. "Where are the cameras?"

"There's two of them down by the gates," Jacky said. "There might be others. I haven't seen them."

"I didn't see any cameras."

"No, but you probably noticed a couple of bluebird houses on the fence posts," Jacky said.

"Bluebird houses. I didn't pay any attention." Mulheisen smiled. "My mother would be outraged. This guy isn't just security conscious, he's a nut."

Jacky locked the front door and reattached the crime scene ribbon. Then he went to the Blazer and got on the radio, while Mulheisen strolled around the yard. It was extremely pleasant up on this mountain, Mulheisen thought. The wind soughing in the tall pines, the dry scuff of needles underfoot. He wandered up behind the house, along the narrow path that led over the ridge. A blue jay yelled at him and flitted away. It was too dark for a blue jay, he thought. Must be some Western counterpart of the Eastern blue jay. His mother would know.

Jacky caught up to him. "Sally's at home, in Tinstar," he said. "It'd take her a half hour to get up here. You want me to ask her to come?"

"Why not?" Mulheisen said. "Or we could stop and see her on the way back to town. The hot springs is down this trail?"

Lee nodded. "Go on down. It ain't far. I'll see if Sally'd rather we came down to her place."

Before Mulheisen reached the pool, Lee caught up to him, saying, "I couldn't raise her, she must have took off. We can stop by her place on the way down."

They stood on the rocks overlooking the pool and looked down into the greenish blue water. It was very clear and the bottom was lined with old needles with patches of fine, gravelly sand showing here and there. You could feel the heat rising off, and in the cool autumn air there were periodic blossoms of steam off the rocks and the surface of the pond, quickly swept away by the breeze.

"Beautiful," Mulheisen said.

Lee nodded. "Sally said she found the gun right out in the middle." He stared out at the water, then sat down on a large flat rock that appeared to have been placed there for the purpose and shucked off his boots. Next came the complicated belt and holster and then his starched gabardine trousers, which he folded carefully. Mulheisen looked on with amusement. Jacky Lee's relatively short, skinny legs sticking out of khaki shorts seemed like mere props for his oversized trunk, still clad in shirt and jacket. He looked at Mulheisen. "Want to?"

"Well . . ." Mulheisen said, glancing around. It was as remote and lonely a place as one could wish. A few minutes later the two men were wading back and forth in the warm water, staring downward with arms clasped behind their backs, ostensibly searching for discarded weapons, but clearly enjoying the experience. No doubt they looked ridiculous, a couple of grown men in their baggy underwear with shirts and, in Mulheisen's case, a necktie.

"Wheww." Mulheisen breathed out gratefully. "This is pretty fine." He relished the soft flutter of sand between his toes and soon he stopped to stare up at the circle of sky above them. The strands of gossamer still drifted high up. A raven flew into the top of one of the ponderosas and sat there, pointedly not looking at the ridiculous spectacle of the waders. It made a strange noise, almost like a wooden musical instrument—a Balinese xylophone, perhaps, Mulheisen thought—a rising "tick," followed by three descending hollow "tocks."

"Ah hah," Jacky Lee said. He rolled up a shirt sleeve and stooped. He held up a shiny pistol, dangling it from the trigger guard with his forefinger. Encouraged, the two resumed their watery shuffle, but another half hour of feeling about with their feet, occasionally picking up pieces of quartz or old waterlogged sticks, convinced them that they had found what could be found. They were about to get out and dress when a laugh froze them in their tracks.

Sally McIntyre stood on the path. "I don't believe I have ever seen such a thing," she said. "Mister Dee-troit Cop, I have to apologize for our local constabulary. It appears he has not told you the proper Montana way to use a hot springs." So saying, she flung her sweat-stained Western hat aside and sat down to tug off her battered cowboy boots.

"Now, Sally . . ." Jacky Lee said, warningly.

The woman's eyes flashed as she stood up and unbuttoned her jeans. "Don't tell me an Indin deputy, who once told me that Indins have no false modesty, that they're simple, direct people who don't let the white man's foolish ways shame them . . ." she said, now unbuttoning her shirt.

"Sally, goddamn it . . ." Lee said.

The brassiere and the panties were daintily deposited on the jeans and shirt. Mulheisen was stunned. What was it with these Montana women?

Sally waded into the pool, directly to Mulheisen, who steadfastly kept his eyes fastened on her smiling face. She stuck out her hand and, although he recoiled at first, he took it and allowed her to pump his in a friendly way, saying, "I'm Sally McIntyre, the ditch rider. And you are . . . ?"

"Mulheisen," he said.

"Well, Mul," she replied, "this is how we do it." She spread her muscular arms and he noticed that she did not shave under them. The same red hair as on her head and between her thighs. And then she fell slowly backward, splashing into the hot pool. She came up gasping but laughing and kicked backward toward the ledge. "It's grand, boys," she cried. "Try it."

Jacky Lee shrugged and waded out. He dropped his drawers with his back to them, then added his shirt to his pile. He avoided Mulheisen's eyes as he waded back in and dove headfirst into the warm water.

There was nothing for it. Mulheisen followed suit. Lying in the water, fully submerged, it soon seemed absurd to be embarrassed. But what, he wondered, was the protocol for conversation?

"That's gossamer," Sally said, gesturing with her chin toward their lofty canopy. "Tiny, tiny spiders make it. Happens every year, 'bout this time."

"Ah," said Mulheisen, glancing surreptitiously at her floating breasts, the areolas large and suffused with the hot water. "Gossamer?"

"I looked it up in the dictionary," she confessed, casually eyeing the head of Mulheisen's cock, poking out of the surface; he sunk down. "It's from Middle English, it says, *gosesomer*, or 'goose summer.' Probably like Indin Summer."

"I see," Mulheisen said. Jacky Lee said nothing. He lay on his back, his eyes closed. A very large hawk, quite high up, sailed into the gossamer-curtained window. Nobody said anything for a good long time.

"I could sure use a cigarette," Sally said, "sacrilegious as it sounds." She stood up and waded dreamily to the edge to rummage in her pockets. She sat on the big rock, next to Jacky's clothes, and lit her cigarette. She smoked gratefully, elbows on knees. Mulheisen thought she looked pretty, also humorous and refreshingly direct. He got out and joined her, lighting up a La Regenta.

"That smells good," she said, "strong and clean. Can I try it?"

He handed her the cigar. She drew on it. "Mmm, milder than I'da thought." She handed it back. Mulheisen could not recall another woman in his experience who had done or said such a thing.

Out in the pool Jacky had moved to the shallows and sat on his butt, splashing water and rubbing it into his black hair and scrubbing his face. He lay back full-length and rotated violently, then stood up. "I'm done," he said. He waded out and squatted next to them.

Sally looked down at the chromed pistol lying on Jacky's clothes. "Is that another one?" she said. Jacky said it was. "Be a shame to have to drain this pool," she said. She began to dress. Mulheisen was very taken with the unself-conscious way she bent forward to lever and adjust her breasts into the cups of her bra.

"I hope we won't have to do that," Jacky said.

Mulheisen agreed. By now they were all dry and dressing.

"Now I feel like a detective again," Mulheisen said, knotting his tie.

Lee grunted. It could have been a laugh or maybe it was just the effort of pulling his boots on his damp feet. "You do much of this back in Detroit?"

Mulheisen and Sally laughed.

The three of them strolled down to the meadow and the creek where Sally had found the body. Jacky pointed out that he had very early concluded that Soper was not killed at the site: There was no bloody ground, no cartridge cases, no sign of a struggle. A search of the house gave no indication that it had happened there, and so with the grounds. But he had found several .32-caliber cartridge casings about the path near the hot springs. He had also found the wheelbarrow in the shed. The forensic evidence wasn't back yet, but he felt there was a good chance that the victim, who had been shot at least nine times with two different caliber guns, had been shot somewhere around the pool. His assailant probably used the wheelbarrow to carry the body down to the creek. There was dried blood in the wheelbarrow, not a lot, but some. He also had a feeling that the same .32-caliber automatic, the one Sally had found in the pool, had been used on Carmine Deadman, aka Joseph Humann, aka Joe Service.

He recounted all this leisurely as they climbed back up the path, past the pool, stopping to indicate where he had found the cartridges, and ending neatly as they stood in the yard by the cabin. It all seemed plausible to Mulheisen. He was impressed with the thoroughness of Jacky's work and the imagination it required to lead him in the proper direction. He told Jacky so and Jacky shrugged noncommittally.

"What it don't tell us," Jacky said, "is who did it. There's some smeared fingerprints on the thirty-two, probably more on this thirty-eight we just found, and maybe that'll do it, but I never found fingerprints to work out the way you want them to."

Mulheisen knew what he meant. Fingerprints were helpful, but not definitive. What they had was a man left for dead on a highway, another killed in the mountains, a missing associate of the first man, and possibly a missing associate of the second man. Presumably whoever almost killed Joe Service and then did kill Soper was one of the two missing persons—Helen, or the nameless associate that had been mentioned as a hitchhiker. Mulheisen sighed and let all this speculation drift to the back of his mind for further consideration.

Sally showed them pretty much what she had observed when she first came up to the cabin, and she confirmed what Jacky had said about the interior. She recounted what she had heard from Mrs. Garland about Joseph Humann and his girlfriend, Helen, about the daily shooting practice, their frequent if relatively brief absences, Humann's general friendliness—everybody around here liked him, though no one knew him very well. Not many people had found Helen very friendly, however.

Mulheisen thanked her for her help and asked if she'd keep an eye on the place—nothing special, just be attentive to rumors or, if she was passing, kind of look in. If anything came up, she should contact Jacky, or if that wasn't possible, she could call him collect in Detroit. He gave her a card.

"In goose summer you kill the goose," Sally said, as they stood in the sunny yard by their cars. "Unfortunately, I didn't raise no goose this year. But I did have a half-interest in a hog. Do you boys like side meat?"

Mulheisen had no idea what side meat was, but he was desperately hungry after his hike and the bath in the hot springs. He looked inquisitively to Jacky.

"Not me," Jacky said firmly. "I got to be getting back. Mul, you can stay if you want to. I can probably come back for you, or maybe you could get a ride."

This wasn't satisfactory. It seemed clear to Mulheisen that Sally was interested in him, and he was certainly interested in her, but in the curious way of things, it wasn't quite appropriate for him to come over to her house alone. Regretfully, he begged off and she accepted the situation easily enough. But on the way back into Butte with Jacky, Mulheisen pondered the moral climate that made it possible for a woman to shuck off her clothes in the presence of a complete stranger and hop into a hot springs, but problematic for this same stranger (now rather more familiar to her) to come to her house for dinner.

"What is side meat, anyway?" he asked Jacky.

"Oh, that wasn't really intended for you," Jacky said. "Side meat is side pork, it's uncured bacon. I don't think you'd like it. But the thing is, see, me 'n' Sally had a kind of thing once, but since I got married she's been acting kind of funny. Some guys say 'side meat,' meaning a woman on the side. It's crude. I wouldn't say it, but I think Sally was just getting in a dig at me."

Mulheisen didn't think that was it at all, but he wasn't sure, and so he kept his own counsel.

13

Helen-A-Go-Go

Helen had no idea how much money she had. She had counted at least half a million dollars, and she knew it was very much more than that. Joe had always stressed the notion that they had too much money, that its very abundance was the primary problem. This had seemed a laughable premise: How could you have too much money? Now that it was all sitting in the back of the little yellow pickup truck, however, it seemed an enormous problem. In Salt Lake City she had contemplated putting it in a bank, but she soon gave up that idea. It couldn't be done, not even simply in the sense of storage, without interest—a deposit box, or boxes . . . too many boxes. Nobody is going to store that much money for you without asking who you are and where you got so much currency, questions that Helen could not safely answer. Anyway, the thought of money simply being stored, not earning anything—wasting away, in fact—was too galling for contemplation.

Joe had been working on an amusing plan, but he hadn't explained it thoroughly enough for Helen to grasp the essential details. He called it his "Gogol Scam." When he'd first mentioned it, she'd thought he said "Go-go" and he had laughingly taken that up, afterward describing his occasional absences as "Gotta go go-go, for a couple of days." He'd been on a "go-go" trip when he got hit. The Gogol joke still puzzled Helen, although he'd tried to explain it. "It's a variation on 'Dead Souls.' I'm buying dead uncles," he explained cryptically, "for the enrichment of their impoverished heirs . . . and, of course, for the even greater enrichment of us." This had something to do with the fact that the Reagan administration had generously increased the amount of tax-free inheritance to $600,000. As best as Helen could figure it out, Joe was finding heirs who had inherited little or nothing and then striking a deal with them so that they would "inherit," say, $50,000 while Joe "inherited" $550,000, or so. How he retroactively enriched the dead uncle was not revealed, but she assumed it was as clever and secure as most of his schemes.

"Foolproof," Joe assured her, "at least, pretty foolproof. The heir is discouraged from ratting to the IRS, or whomever, since they have been party to a felony. In addition, they continue to enjoy a modest annuity from the trust fund, providing they don't make a fuss. Still"—he sighed—"there are fools who will take a hatchet to the golden goose. Nothing is really secure. But I've built in a couple of cut-outs that should insulate us from investigation."

At any rate, in the few months since they had acquired the money (which was how she saw it: *they* had *acquired* . . . although she'd had no part in stealing the money), Joe had not managed to place more than a couple of million into these seemingly legitimate accounts. This hadn't bothered him: "I've got the rest of my life to lay it out." Helen's problem was more pressing: she had something like twenty million dollars sitting in the back of a truck on the street. She finally hit upon what she thought was at least a reasonable solution. She considered that as long as she and Joe lived in Tinstar, they weren't too concerned about so much cash lying around. They'd simply stashed it in convenient places: a few handy thousand in a drawer; a hundred thousand in an artfully incised and relabeled plastic anti-freeze jug that sat on the floor of the garage among similar windshield-washer-fluid containers; lesser amounts in plastic bags in the bluebird houses (bluebirds crowded out by millionaires, alas) that Joe had mounted on trees and posts. Of course, the bulk of it was stashed in the abandoned mine that Joe had fixed up, up behind the cabin.

What she did now was go to a rental agency in Salt Lake City and lease a house. It was a nice house—two bedrooms, half-basement, a small garage—on Main Street, about a mile and a half south of the city center. She spent a restless night at the hotel, constantly reassuring herself that the little pickup truck and its fabulous cargo (approximately that of a seventeenth-century Spanish treasure galleon) would be safe in the hotel garage. She had taken the trouble to purchase and have mounted a simple, lockable pickup campertop, but she knew that wouldn't survive even a modest attempt at burglary if left on the street overnight, even in Salt Lake City, which was no Detroit. The very next day she found the house by midmorning and obtained the key. That same afternoon she unloaded the money into the half-basement and had a locksmith install some formidable security. By grossly overpaying a couple of carpenters, she got them to drop their current projects and immediately set to work to further secure the house with some unobtrusive window barriers and steel doors. "I can't help it, I'm just paranoid," she said, easily emulating a woman-alone-in-a-strange-city. In the small half-basement they had constructed a vault remarkably like the one that Joe had constructed in the old mine.

So here was at least a measure of security. It still didn't answer to the nagging anxiety of money that was idle. This was a genuine anxiety for Helen. She had never encountered this problem before. As the child of a well-placed mob figure she had never wanted for money, even when Big Sid was being punished for overly sticky digits. Later, as a young woman running her own consulting business, she had done quite well (with, admittedly, occasional donations from Sid when cash flow waned), but she had no capital, and so she had never given much consideration to what happens to capital when it isn't invested. Now she viewed capital in fairy tale terms: the golden goose versus the sack of grain with a hole in it, on the back of an ass, en route to market. Even the tiniest hole makes of the sack an hourglass, with its ceaseless flow of sand. Yes, that was it: It was a kind of philosophical juxtaposition, life versus time. It made her uneasy, even a little ill, to think that she couldn't stop those grains trickling out— one had to eat, one had to live. But there must be a way, if only she knew what it was. Why hadn't Joe told her? Was it part of the old plot, how men keep women down? She tried to console herself with the notion that this was only temporary, that soon she'd get on with the business of making this money work, once she figured out how to keep it safe and also take care of such obligations as Joe's medical care.

It was here in Salt Lake, involved in this busywork, that she read about what had befallen Joe, in the Butte paper that she picked up every day at the newsstand downtown. She was greatly relieved to hear that he wasn't dead; she realized that she had been masking a considerable measure of grief with anger and resentment. To be sure, it didn't sound like he was likely to ever recover his amazing energy and delight in life, and she was sorry to think that he would be a kind of vegetable henceforth, but at least he wasn't dead. Nonetheless, it imposed certain obligations on her and the resentment revived.

She made her first payments to St. James Hospital from Salt Lake City, to secure Joe's treatment. This act was an eye-opener in itself. She walked into one of the large banks downtown and simply asked one of the ladies sitting at a desk for a cashier's check for $50,000. She carried a vanity case, part of a complete set of luggage that she had just purchased, filled with small bills. She was taken aback when the woman, an officer of the bank, pointed out that not only would she have to identify herself, but she would have to file a Currency Transaction Report with the Internal Revenue Service for any—*any*—transaction over $10,000, even the purchase of a simple money order.

Helen was appalled. "But how can this be?" she demanded. "I have all this cash. I have obligations in other states. How am I to take care of them? I can't send fifty thousand dollars in cash through the mail!"

"What is the source of this currency?" the woman asked, clearly very interested.

"None of your business," Helen retorted.

"Actually, it is my business," the bank officer replied. "This bank would be subject to severe penalties if we accepted undocumented currency in amounts of this sort."

"Well, what amounts can be accepted?"

"You can purchase a money order or cashier's check in an amount less than three thousand dollars, without any report, but not more than one in a day."

"Jeez," Helen muttered, counting out $2,995 in small bills. As she left the bank, the woman stood at the window and watched her walk across the street to their competitor. She called her superior. "I think I just encountered a smurf," she said, referring to the well-known practice of drug-related money washers. They stood at the window for several minutes before they observed Helen leave the other bank, swinging the vanity case lightheartedly as she proceeded down the street toward the Zion National Bank.

"Well, you can call the FBI or the DEA," the boss said, "but she hasn't done anything illegal."

The following day Helen returned and the woman saw her purchase another check for $2,995 from a different teller. This time she did call the FBI. An agent arrived in time to see Helen leave the bank across the street. He thanked the officer for identifying her and set off in pursuit. The bank officer never heard from the FBI again.

After a few days, the house having been secured, Helen loaded $500,000 into two suitcases and checked them as baggage as she flew to Los Angeles. She had never been to Los Angeles before and she was thrilled, at first. She spent a few days smurfing the money and shopping in Beverly Hills. By that time she had decided that Los Angeles was not as pleasant as she had initially thought. It was warm and the sky was milky, but it was expensive and not really nice. It seemed about as fragile a place as Detroit. In fact, it was Detroit-by-the-sea, in many ways—sprawling, frenetic with cars, not really visible except from a low-flying airplane: No part of it seemed to stick up much above expressway level. There was a terrible juxtaposition of poverty—shattered buildings and automobiles, people standing about idly—and sheer glitz, a chromed approach to luxury. She flew to Denver.

Now her main project was to find a better way to turn her money, so it could begin to be put to use. She had already smurfed $100,000 for her own use and had invested it with a brokerage (plus another $50,000 for Joe's medical bills), but it was really a lot of work, accumulating that much money in $3,000 increments—visiting some fifty banks and savings and loans. It wasn't an easy life. She wanted to contact someone in the criminal world who could help her, but not in L.A. She had in mind just walking up to, say, a crack peddler on the street and saying, "I've got quite a bit of money, in cash . . . do you think you, or perhaps your boss, could give me a little advice on what to do with it?" But after thinking about it for a couple of minutes she realized it was too dangerous. Maybe it would be easier in Phoenix. It wasn't.

In the end she called Roman Yakovich, the Yak. He told her everything that Humphrey had told him.

"Roman, that's great! It just happens that I've been having a little problem, about money. I'm sure he could help."

"I dunno," the Yak said. "Mr. Diablo has always been okay to us, but I dunno. You oughta be careful."

"Why? Whatever for?"

"He says he forgives you for everything, but I dunno," the Yak insisted. "He's pissed off about Joe."

"He doesn't blame me for Carmine, does he?"

"He says he don't, but I dunno. He says you should call him. 'Tell her to call Uncle Umberto,' he says."

"Thanks, Roman. I know it's late, so I won't ask you to wake Mama, but tell her I'll be home for Christmas. Maybe even Thanksgiving, if I can."

The next day she flew to New Orleans and checked into a fancy hotel. It was about ten P.M. when she called Humphrey.

14
Northern Tier

One of the three other detectives at the Northern Tier Task Force meeting at the courthouse in Butte claimed to know Mulheisen. His name was Larry Edwards and he was from Missoula. He had grown up in Detroit and had gotten his start as a patrolman in the Thirteenth Precinct, he said, before he'd moved to Montana. "I'd probably be dead now, if I still lived there," he said. "As Yogi might put it," he added with the faintest hint of a smile.

Mulheisen didn't remember ever meeting Edwards, but he recognized him as a Detroiter all right—the cynical humor, the implacable face. Edwards was amusing, but he didn't let it get in the way of business. Evidently Edwards was familiar with Mulheisen's career and had spread some tall tales. The other detectives greeted Mulheisen with exaggerated respect. Even the other prosecutors and Judge Leahy seemed to share this deferent attitude, as if Mulheisen were some kind of super detective who was here to set them all on the right path. It was annoying, but as soon as they got down to business, he was gratified to see that the attitude modulated toward simple respect. After a while, however, he realized that all comments were directed toward him, as if this were a briefing of a newly appointed cabinet minister.

Mulheisen forced himself to interrupt, finally, with a little speech. "Ladies and gentlemen," he said, "I don't know what my friend Johnny Antoni has led you to believe, but I have not signed on for this task force. I'm in Butte as part of the investigation of a murder that took place six months ago in Detroit. I was also asked to attend this meeting, as an observer. I don't know anything about this 'invasion' that you speak of, but I do know a little about the mob in Detroit. This is the old mob. It's not what you're up against, if I read you correctly, but if my experience can be of any help, I'm glad to . . . well, to be of any help," he ended lamely.

Johnny Antoni leaped to his feet, smiling, his voice ringing. "Aw c'mon, Mul. You know more about this kind of stuff than we do. Hey, don't you like it here?" He gestured toward the large windows, through which one had a view of some mountains. "Didn't you catch a trout the other day?" After the laughter died, he said, "You don't have to sign on today, but just let us put forward a little bit of what we've observed and what we're looking at in the future. If you want to go back to Detroit, fine, no strings . . . but I've got an idea you might have been hooked yourself."

The meeting resumed, with reports from investigators from Spokane and Boise, from a Kalispell sheriff, an investigator from Medicine Hat, and so on, detailing an increase in gambling interest from "outside." Apparently, someone was buying real estate, trying to muscle into existing taverns that had a substantial gambling business, and making offers to state legislators to support a broadening of state laws regarding gambling. In addition, there was increased prostitution along the interstate system—truckers' plazas now had nude dancing bars and massage parlors where allowed—and an increase in drugs, especially cocaine. In just about every case the trail, admittedly faint, led back to the West Coast, to Orientals, or to people who spoke of Oriental interests.

Mulheisen listened to all this as attentively as he could, although he longed to be out of this meeting room, perhaps out on the river, or at least in a barroom talking to a suspect. What he was hearing, it seemed to him, was not a really great increase in crime or suspect behavior, but just the rumblings of it. He thought it sounded like a normal increase of business that attends an increase in population. He wondered what the demographics were. And then some woman got up with a flip chart and began to show them what the demographics were. Basically, what they showed was population growth—not a very significant population growth overall (Montana had just lost one of their two congressional representatives because their population growth had not kept pace with other Western states), but a different kind of growth. Traditionally, the state had grown through immigration from the east and the south; now it was growing from the west, and the westerners were not arriving in covered wagons, they were arriving in Jet Commanders and BMWs. They were looking for retirement homes and vacation property. They weren't coming to work, they were coming to play. The average income of this group . . .

At this point Mulheisen began to fade. He found himself turning more and more to the vision of the mountains beyond the windows and he felt a bit sleepy. At last he roused himself and said, "I haven't seen anything that strongly suggests an Asian invasion. Now I'm not about to say that it's a phantom, although there is a history in this country of periodic 'Yellow Peril' scares, but I'd like to know if there are any more specific instances, something we can really glom onto."

The Missoula detective, Edwards, said quietly, "I have a snitch who says that a meeting took place on Flathead Lake between three people. One of them was a Mr. Lee, who is supposed to be a Hong Kong businessman. Another was a Mr. Service, who was described to me as a Mafia figure. The third was a Montana businessman, Thomas Shivers, who owns the house on the lake. Mr. Shivers used to be a rancher, but he long ago moved into investments. My informant says the conversation was mainly about gambling and investment. The idea was to set up some kind of money-washing system. Gambling was seen as a good way to do this. Money can be washed through gambling machines, the kind you see in practically every bar in Montana. These machines accept nickels and dimes and quarters, but when the customer scores, he has to collect from the barkeeper. These countless little payoffs have to be reported, but it's easy to fudge. It can be a lot of money, when you consider how many bars there are, how many machines. Now, you can say this is only hearsay, nothing is certain, but my feeling is that if Mr. Lee meets Mr. Shivers, or Mr. Shivers meets Mr. Service, or Mr. Lee meets Mr. Service . . ." He shrugged as his voice trailed off. "But when they all meet together, then I sit up and take notice."

Mulheisen agreed that this was worth notice, but he pointed out that it was mostly conjectural, dependent on a single informant. Were there some other significant instances? Nobody, it seemed, could really provide anything concrete, just this growing awareness of an impending problem. But they were all quite adamant about the need to prepare for a crime wave. It went on in this vein for some time, but eventually the meeting broke up.

Afterward, at lunch with the judge and Johnny and two of the prosecutors, Johnny pressed Mulheisen very hard not to close his mind about joining the task force. The problem was real, he insisted, and the task force was going to happen—the money had been appropriated. Mulheisen began to see that it was politically important to Antoni. He didn't want to let his old friend down, and he ended by agreeing at least to consider joining the task force. For now, he was going back to Detroit. A decision would have to be made soon, though.

Mulheisen went back to the Finlen and met in the lounge with Larry Edwards and Jacky Lee. They went for a drive in Lee's Blazer.

"I've gone over all this with Jacky," Edwards said. "I haven't spread this info around too much because I've had some problems with other enforcement agencies blabbing. Jacky I trust. I don't know anything about this Service guy, but Jacky tells me you do."

They had stopped near a park down on the Flat. The three

men got out and strolled around through the rattling autumn leaves. The sun was shining but it was brisk out. A beautiful day. Mulheisen said that he'd been giving a lot of thought to Service lately. "It seems pretty certain that Service is the guy who's up there in the hospital. I never paid enough attention to Service in the past, but now it seems to me that he's been involved in several cases that came my way in Detroit. He was never a suspect in any of these cases and, as far as I know, he has broken no laws . . . but he was always there. I missed something, I think. There were frequent rumors about a guy from the West, someone the mob had called in to straighten things out. Sometimes they called him a hired gun, but generally he was just a troubleshooter. It was never solid enough to pursue. But lately our investigations of the deaths of some mob figures in Detroit have turned up this name, Joe Service, again. We think he might have been involved in at least three killings, one of them in Iowa City. We have fingerprints from the Iowa City killing, and when I get back to Detroit, we'll try to match them with Jacky's 'Deadman.' There was also an eyewitness in Iowa City, but we don't have any pictures to show her, and we can't justify bringing her out here to look at this guy, at least not yet. But it's enough to pursue."

Jacky Lee said, "Let's call him Joseph Humann. That's the name he used down in Tinstar. It's the same guy. He's been around the Mountain West for a while under that name. No criminal activity that we can see, but there are hints. His medical bills are being paid by some woman who sends in cashier's checks from all over the West—Salt Lake, Denver, Phoenix, L.A. From what Mul tells me, this could be Helen Sedlacek, a woman last seen with Humann—or Service—in Detroit."

"We figure she may have killed Carmine," Mulheisen said. "The point is, they seem to have a lot of money, and the indications are that she is smurfing this money to pay for this Joe Whoever's care, and for her own needs. But she moves fast. We don't have any kind of line on her. I don't think a bulletin to every bank in the West is going to alert people to someone just walking in off the street to buy a cashier's check. But if Joe was trying to make a deal with this Lee and Shivers, that might be something. And then we have this other body—Mario Soper, found on the Humann property."

Mulheisen sketched for them a possible scenario in which the mob had put out a contract on Joe Service and/or Helen Sedlacek. Somehow they had tracked them to this place, Mario Soper and possibly one other man had been sent, but Soper had been killed, probably by Joe. The other killer had apparently been more successful, and Joe's body was left on the highway by this unknown killer, who had then gone on his merry way.

"Could the second killer have been the woman?" Edwards asked.

"Helen? Why would she attempt to kill Joe, and then why would she be paying his hospital bills?" Lee replied. "We've talked to banks all over the West and they give a pretty good description of this woman, and she is always unaccompanied. No, we think there's another killer."

The other question was, Who was the Joe Service who had talked to Shivers and Lee at the Flathead Lake meeting? Mulheisen said, "Say it is Joseph Humann. He has a lot of dirty money, a lot of cash, and he's looking for a way to get it out into legitimate uses. This thing about gambling machines may be just the ticket for him. The problem now is, of course, that he's laid up in the hospital for the foreseeable future."

"The doctors tell me that he's responding to therapy," Lee said, "but he's still disoriented, can't talk, can't take care of himself. He'll be out of it for weeks, maybe even months to come—if he ever really recovers. Let's face it, the man took a bullet in the head. He's lucky to be alive. Hell, I thought he was dead when I found him."

Mulheisen knew it was pointless to go see Service again, but he wanted to. There was very little any of the detectives could do at this point, just wait and watch—particularly watch for Helen Sedlacek.

"And watch for another killer," he warned. "By now the mob must know where Service is. If they went to the trouble to send someone after him in the first place, they'll still be interested. Perhaps even more so. Whether they'd send the guy who failed to get him the first time is a moot point."

Jacky Lee said that the Butte–Silver Bow police couldn't keep a guard on the patient. They simply didn't have the resources.

"Then he's lying up there exposed," Mulheisen said, shaking his head. "Maybe he is a dead man, after all."

"Mul, what can I do?" Lee said. "I can talk to the sheriff, maybe he'll let me have a man, but I doubt it."

"Maybe the Northern Tier could help out," Edwards suggested. "They seem to have money. We've identified Service as a guy who might be involved in this so-called Asian invasion. Maybe they could pay for a guard."

Mulheisen agreed to press Antoni on the subject. "The trouble is, it gets me involved in their operation," he said, "and at this point I have no intention of joining the task force. I've got plenty to do back in Detroit. Besides, I'm running out of cigars. There doesn't seem to be anyplace you can buy a decent cigar around here."

With these halfhearted, minimal gestures the three men parted. Mulheisen said he would keep in touch, and he would be back out in Montana if anything developed. By this he meant if Joe Service ever came around and could be properly interrogated, or if Helen Sedlacek should make an appearance or was apprehended.

He did return to the hospital and was able to speak to the brain surgeon, who, as he expected, could give him no assurances or even any solid indication of what might happen with Joe Service's recovery.

"I see people who fall out of an apple tree and they never remember a thing," the doctor said. "Something happens inside, but we can't see what it is. The person is a vegetable, never recovers. Another one, like Deadman, he gets shot and we can see the damage—I was in there for hours, I saw brain damage—and we think, 'Vegetable, no chance,' but then he's recovering. He hasn't recovered to the point of talking or indicating that everything is going to be all right, but he has made amazing progress already. He recognizes things, he responds to stimuli, and he's guarding himself."

This was interesting to Mulheisen. He wanted to know more.

"I'm observing him," the doctor said, "and I get the impression that he has recovered more than he lets on. Little inadvertent responses that are hard to describe, and a certain look in his eyes at times that seems to indicate that he understands something you say, but then he doesn't respond, as if he were willfully holding back. It isn't too unusual. Most patients are eager to respond, they sense that they are helpless and they want to recover. Mr. Deadman sometimes seems to want to keep it to himself, to husband his successes, to reserve a margin of privacy." He frowned thoughtfully. "Maybe I am all wrong. Maybe he is doing nothing of the sort. It's just a mannerism, perhaps, something he is not conscious of doing.

"The brain is so enormous, you see. It is a large organ, but its extensions, through thought and memory and so on, are as vast as the universe. We have mapped the physical brain pretty well, by now. If there is injury here"—he tapped the left rear of his skull, approximately where the major injury had occurred to Service—"we know that it affects the motor capability here." He lifted a presumably dead right hand with his left and waved it. "It should be gone forever, but it recovers. Sometimes. Whatever was in this region"—he tapped his head again—"is presumably destroyed when the tissue is destroyed. But is it? No. So the information is spread out throughout the brain? Hmm. Maybe. Like every other field, in brain studies there are contending factions. One group says the brain is like a complex mosaic. Another says it is more like a field, a gestalt. The mosaic concept is useful, but so is the field. Me? I don't know. I'm watching Mr. Deadman. He makes remarkable recoveries, but he is holding something back, I think."

Mulheisen went in to see the patient. He was sitting up, staring at nothing. As usual, the pretty little nurse was there. She had been talking when Mulheisen entered, but she stopped in midsentence and after puttering about for a few seconds, she left. Joe Service shifted his eyes to meet Mulheisen's. He seemed to smile. His head was still well wrapped in bandages, but more of it was exposed, and clumps of hair were beginning to hang out through apertures. He looked forlorn, as gormless as a wet hawk, but the eyes still shone brightly.

Did this man have memory? Mulheisen wondered. And if he didn't have any memory, or only imperfectly remembered his crimes, was he still culpable? If he couldn't remember killing a man, could he be held accountable? The act was not altered, but the actor was. What then? It was something to think about.

"Have you ever been in Iowa City, Joe?" Mulheisen asked. He watched the eyes carefully. No apparent response. "Did you ever meet a man named Hal Good? It wasn't his real name. His real name was—" and Mulheisen drew a blank. He couldn't remember the real name of the man from Iowa City, who had been a contract killer for the mob, a man who had been a respectable lawyer in that small city in Heartland, U.S.A., and had misused his position to become a heartless killer. It was embarrassing. "Well, it doesn't matter what his real name was. You would have known him as Hal Good. Somebody tracked Hal Good down and killed him, Joe. Hal Good killed Helen Sedlacek's father. Somebody killed Hal, then somebody—probably Helen—killed Carmine, the man who hired Hal to kill her father. It's like an endless series—A leads to B, which leads to C . . . But it has to stop sometime, Joe. I mean to stop it."

Mulheisen stepped over to the window and looked out. There was a pretty decent view of the mountains to the west. He gazed out at the scattered fluffs of clouds that drifted toward them from beyond the mountains. He felt that he could watch this scene for a long time. Without looking at Joe, he said, "What is the nurse always talking about, Joe? Does it bother you?" He glanced sideways at the bed. There was no response from Joe. "Talk, talk, talk. I hate hospital rooms. You must. You've got to get out of here, Joe."

On his way out, Mulheisen stopped to talk to the nurse. He explained to her that her "Deadman" was still in danger from the same people who had put him in the hospital in the first place. The police were not capable of guarding him, he told her, so it fell to her and the rest of the staff to keep their eyes open, to report any suspicious behavior around Deadman, any unusual inquiries about him, any visitors. He advised her to contact Jacky Lee if anything happened.

Cateyo accepted all this warning with great seriousness and gravity, Mulheisen was pleased to see. But then she smiled and said, "I'll take good care of him, Sergeant Mulheisen. Nothing can happen to him."

"What do you mean?" Mulheisen said. "You know nothing about this man, Miss Yoder."

"I know quite a bit about him, Sergeant. He's a good man."

"Joe?" Mulheisen gestured with his head toward the room he'd just left. "You don't know Joe Service. This man is a thief, a spy, a betrayer. I think he has killed other men, but I can't prove it. His friends, his associates, are drug peddlers and murderers and corrupters. They aren't good people. And now they're mad at Joe. They want to kill him. They have unlimited resources. They will kill him, eventually. But not on my watch."

"And not on mine," she snapped back, the color rising in her cheeks. "And you're wrong about Pau—Joe. He's a good man. Christ was hung with thieves. He associated with people everyone thought were bad. Saul of Tarsus was a persecutor, a spy, a betrayer."

Mulheisen wanted to laugh, but he didn't. Instead, he just looked at the young woman for a long moment, then nodded and walked away. He stopped at the work station and asked for the head nurse. He tracked Nurse Work down a few minutes later and waited while she finished talking to another young nurse before he drew her aside. "What's with Cate Yoder and Deadman?" he asked.

Nurse Work allowed that Cateyo seemed inordinately attached to the patient. "It happens, sometimes," she said, "but Miss Yoder is a good nurse, one of our best. I'm confident that she won't let her feelings interfere with her care of the patient. In fact, it may help."

Mulheisen told her Cateyo's remarks.

"Religious people see everything in terms of their religion," Nurse Work said. "It doesn't mean anything, any more than . . . well, than a doctor using sports metaphors in describing a patient's prognosis."

"I hope you're right," Mulheisen said, "but I'm going to give you my card. If anything unusual happens I want you to call me collect, in Detroit. Will you do that?"

She took the card and slipped it into her uniform pocket, saying she would call. Mulheisen left. He felt uneasy.

15

The Gates of the City

Flying east out of Salt Lake City, Mulheisen realized a simple truth: The modern city is similar to ancient cities. He had taken this route for no particular reason, except that it happened to be quicker in this time slot, and anyway, he thought it would be more interesting to take a different route home, instead of the Billings-Minneapolis route he had come out on (it had nothing to do with the gut-wrenching fighter-jet take-offs and landings on the Butte-Bozeman-Billings run, he told himself). Out of Salt Lake, a much bigger jet climbed out powerfully and majestically over the Wasatch Front, nonstop for Detroit. Mulheisen settled back with his insight about ancient cities and soon recollected a visit to Mexico City, many years before.

In those days he always took his vacation. He had long since quit doing that. He might take an occasional day or two, if he were out of town anyway, and sometimes he took a few days to visit an old friend who had moved to Reno. But he rarely took a formal vacation anymore. But someone had told him that Mexico, D.F., had purchased the old Detroit Street Railways trolley cars, and it occurred to him that he would like to see the Gratiot Avenue car that he used to ride with his father when they would go to a ballgame downtown.

This was a very special memory, involving straw hats and men smoking cigars and the first sight of the green field within the tiered walls of Briggs Stadium. So he flew to Mexico City.

He liked it very much, although it was a mess, of course. There were already many too many people. But the city seemed quite livable in the regions that he explored. And he did get to see the old Gratiot Avenue car and ride on it. Unfortunately, it did not go very fast, as it used to do when the motorman got out toward Seven Mile Road and Eight Mile Road. In Mexico City it stopped on every block and it was loaded with people. But he rode it a couple of times anyway and enjoyed it. They hadn't bothered to paint it, apparently. It was still the same pale color with dark green trim. They had painted over the lettering, but "D.S.R." had bled through, faintly.

One day he got off the trolley and was walking along a big street (he couldn't remember its name) when a voice called out, "Hey, Yank." He turned and confronted an old Mexican man sitting on the steps of a very large building that housed the national health insurance agency. The old man was dark and wrinkled but dressed in a neat and clean suit of yellowed linen. He had evidently taken off his shoes, but now he slipped them back on. He had no socks. He stood up. He was about five feet four inches, including his panama hat. "I knew you were a Yank," he said, in very good English.

"You must have spent some time in the States," Mulheisen said. It was very bright here in the street and hot. He wondered how long this conversation would take and if it meant only handing over a few pesos (the peso was worth much more at this time).

"Yes, I have been in many cities of the United States," the old man said. "Not just Texas cities or California cities, but also in Chicago, Illinois, and Dayton, Ohio, not to mention Pittsburgh, Pennsylvania. Have you been in those cities?"

"Yes," Mulheisen said, "but it is hot. Would you like to go to a *cervezeria?*"

"No, I can't leave here, but I would appreciate something to drink, if you don't mind." He gestured at a vendor of soft drinks, not far off. Mulheisen went to get the old man a bottle of warm citron drink.

"Why can't you leave here?" Mulheisen asked when he had brought the drink.

"My daughter works here. I need to see her."

Hundreds of people were entering and leaving the building constantly. The old man watched them out of the corner of his eye while he talked to Mulheisen.

"How long have you been here?" Mulheisen asked.

This was the fourth day, the old man said. He said he had been a schoolteacher. He taught English. He was also a poet and a short-story writer. He had a collection of his short stories and poems with him, in an old and cracked leather briefcase. They were typed with a very faintly inked ribbon on blue-lined school exposition paper for a three-ring binder, with many "xxxx" markings on several words in each paragraph. They were written in English and had titles such as "The Aged Crone at El Pastor Fido Home."

"That's where I live," the old man pointed out. "It is a retirement home, as you would say. It is an infamous place." The home was located outside the city. The old man had gotten a ride with a market farmer part of the way, then walked the rest. He walked home each evening, after the offices closed.

"Some of these stories have been rejected by *The New Yorker* and *Esquire*, even by *Playboy* magazine." He showed Mulheisen the printed rejection slips. "The stories are too risqué for Mexican magazines. They are about prostitution, one of the greatest evils in the history of civilization. This is a terrible country for censorship. Sometimes the American editors send me five dollars, which I have told them to hide within the sheets of the story, for there are thieves in the post office."

"Does your daughter know you are waiting?" Mulheisen asked. "Did you call her to tell her that you were coming?"

The old man smiled forbearingly. "You Americans." He chuckled. "Not everyone has a telephone. The home would never allow me to use their telephone, even if I could pay and if Daisy had a telephone."

"You could have written to her," Mulheisen pointed out.

"I don't know which office she works in, or where she lives. She won't tell me. But I will see her today. This is the last door where she could go in."

Mulheisen didn't know if the old man had ever intercepted his daughter, but he had seen Helen Sedlacek this morning at the Salt Lake City airport. As a policeman he was used to the drill whereby you monitor airports, bus stations, and train stations to intercept wanted criminals, but he also knew that the tactic didn't often succeed, since most people drove cars. Modern cities were too porous when the police were dealing with auto traffic. But he realized now that when it came to air travel, a great hub such as Salt Lake City was like the walled cities of yore. They had just a few gates, and one could watch for travelers there, in just the way that the old man waited patiently for his daughter to go in or come out of one of the four great doorways of the national health building in Mexico City.

At Salt Lake he had just caught a glimpse of Helen on the conveyor system. She was going in the opposite direction. By the time he hopped off the conveyor bearing him toward a different wing of the huge complex, the wing where the gateway to the east was located, and doubled back, he could not find her. But what he soon learned, however, was that she must have gotten on a plane to the north. That was where that gateway lead, the same one he had come in on. She was flying to Butte, perhaps, or Spokane, even Seattle.

Mulheisen found the gate where the next Butte-bound flight boarded and showed his identification. A helpful young woman from Delta Airlines checked the passenger list and found no "Helen Sedlacek" or any similar name. The plane hadn't boarded yet. Mulheisen cruised the other gates without success. He didn't see her in any of the little shops or snack bars, either. So, he had missed her, this time.

For several minutes he wandered about, wondering if he should interrupt his flight to make a more protracted search, perhaps with airport authorities. But he realized that it would take too much time, and anyway, he didn't have a warrant. Indeed, he had no grounds whatsoever for detaining her if she were unwilling to be interviewed. She was a suspect, that was all.

On the plane east, he pondered the situation and decided that she was probably not just passing through Salt Lake. That would be a mere coincidence. If a person were starting out from any place in the United States, the chances that they would pass through Salt Lake City and have to change planes there were not high. Not remote by any means, but not high. On the other hand, if she were staying in the area, she would be bound to travel in and out of a handful of gates that served an enormous region. It seemed to him that the odds were quite good that she was in the area. The question was, how long would she remain?

Jimmy Marshall was at Detroit Metropolitan to pick him up. When they got past the preliminary foolishness—"Where'd you leave your horse?"—Mulheisen explained his notion about watching for Helen at Salt Lake City. Marshall thought it was a total waste of time. The region served by that airport was larger than Europe. If Helen Sedlacek were using a different name, it would be a matter of physically monitoring the gateways. Jimmy Marshall couldn't imagine that the Salt Lake City police, or any other agency, had the personnel to spare on this scale to aid the Detroit police, particularly since they had no arrest warrant.

"Not yet, anyway," Mulheisen said. He explained about the shotguns Jacky had retrieved from the cabin on Garland Butte. Mulheisen had brought the guns back with him, along with ample latent fingerprints from the house, which could be compared with known prints of Helen Sedlacek and the prints found in Iowa City. As for Joe Service, he had no prints on record, as far as they knew. But if Joe Humann was Joe Service, he would now.

If there was any kind of forensic evidence linking Helen to any felony, Mulheisen felt that the airlines—there were only a handful—could be pressured into at least a computer monitor of their reservations system, a kind of flag on the name "Helen Sedlacek," maybe even any "Helen S——" flying into or out of Salt Lake City. When people used a false name, they didn't usually falsify it much, especially amateurs. "Let's find out what Helen's mother's maiden name was," he suggested. "Also, wasn't she married once? I seem to remember something about that. What was her married name? It doesn't seem likely—I suppose divorced women don't like to use the name of a man they rejected, or who rejected them—but a running woman may be desperate enough."

Back at the precinct—more greetings of "Where's your boots, podner?"—the file revealed that Helen had been married before, but the name wasn't indicated. A check at the Wayne County records produced a birth certificate and Oakland County found a marriage license. She was born to Mary Kaparich and Sidami Sedlacjich. She had been licensed to marry Ara Koldanian.

Mulheisen was intrigued. A Serb marries an Armenian? It seemed unusual. There were a lot of Armenians in the Detroit area, mostly on the west side, he thought—Dearborn, the downriver communities. They were hardworking, enterprising people, in his experience. Like the Serbs, they were Eastern Orthodox, but he assumed there were significant differences in the two churches. Marshall agreed to run the two names past the airlines and also to set up an interview with Koldanian: He might have something useful to tell them about Helen.

There was also about two weeks of phone calls to return and reports to be updated, developments on old cases to review, and . . .

About five o'clock, he looked up to see Jimmy leaning against the doorjamb, smiling wryly.

"So, Mul," Jimmy said, "you ready to move to Montana?"

Mulheisen shook his head. He was tired and ready to go home. "It's all right," he said. "It's fine. I liked Butte. It's kind of a cranky, interesting old industrial town. But to live there or work there? Nah. Everything's so open, you're so exposed to the elements. I don't think so. It'd be colder than a brass jockstrap in the winter, I bet. Also, the newspaper is a pretty decent rag, but it doesn't cover the Tigers much, and it's hard to get good cigars. Nice country, though."

"What about the women?" Marshall wanted to know. "What'd you think of those cowgirls?"

"Cowgirls?" Mulheisen laughed. "I'll tell you one thing, though, it seems like those women are a lot freer than around here. They're ready to jump out of their clothes at the drop of a hat." He recounted the incident at Antoni's sauna and Sally McIntyre's cheerful shucking of her jeans at the hot springs. Marshall was deeply impressed.

Sometimes when Mulheisen looked at his mother, he just about didn't recognize her. It seemed to him that she had once been older, fatter, bulkier. She wore flowery dresses once upon a time. She had a bosom once. The name Cora didn't seem odd, in those times; it seemed normal among her friends, Hazel and Grace and Mabel.

He had been only a little boy, of course. His father was still alive, still going off to work every day in his brown or blue or gray suit, wearing a fedora and an overcoat. A pleasant man, he wore wire-rimmed glasses and smelled faintly of Old Spice aftershave lotion. He was the half of the salt-and-pepper shaker set that had disappeared. A grandma-and-grandpa set. He would be salt, maybe. His mother would be pepper, though evidently not a very hot pepper, just darker than salt.

She was thicker then, and not only did she wear a flowered housedress but even, and always, an apron. Her hair was longer then, but already gray, in a bun on the back of her head, and she wore wire-rimmed glasses, too. She smelled of talc and a perfume that he believed was called White Shoulders, though perhaps it was just lilac water.

In the intervening years, his mother had become younger while undeniably getting older. Her face was more lined, but she had become leaner, tanned, her bosom had disappeared, and her hair was quite short and a more steely gray. She wore contact lenses most of the time, but when she wore glasses, they were one of several pairs in Italian frames and never, never wire-rimmed. It appeared that she spent quite a nice sum on sunglasses. She wore slacks, bulky sweaters, boots (usually colorful rubber ones, or sturdy hiking ones), running shoes, a startling variety of stylish but clearly sturdy and protective jackets, anoraks, and parkas. She seemed to have a lot of gear: bicycles, binoculars, helmets, special gloves, backpacks, cameras. And she talked knowledgeably and interestedly about all of it.

How all this had happened, Mulheisen didn't know. It had been gradual. Her round face had leaned into this finely wrinkled but leathery one so slowly that he hadn't noticed how. For one thing he didn't see a lot of her, generally speaking. For days, even weeks, their only communication was via notices attached to the refrigerator with magnets. Even these magnets had changed; where once they were bunnies and ducks, now they were embossed with old railway emblems, or the logos of environmentalist organizations.

They did have a memorable conversation on the evening that Mulheisen came home from Montana. He got home about six. He was surprised to find her there. He had gotten used to not seeing her, to communicating on the refrigerator. She had just come back herself a few hours earlier, from the Gulf Coast. She had been following the migration of cranes. She was delighted to hear that he'd been to Montana. Butte, she said, wasn't far from Red Rocks Lake, where the trumpeter swans were. If he went back, he ought to take a run down there and also check out the possibility of wolves on the Idaho-Utah border.

She observed that he looked tired, but also refreshed. He did feel refreshed, he said. It had been nice to get away. She watched him with interest and then said that he ought to get away more often, maybe permanently.

He'd been thinking about that, he told her. He had been wondering if he ought not to make a change. But . . . it was hard.

Usually for the good, though, was his mother's observation. Then, apparently lapsing into a reflective mood, she said that she had experienced three or four major changes in her life, and every time she had been afraid, fearful that the change was not going to be for the best. Marriage was one of those times. Giving birth was another. In a conventional way, of course, one was supposed to think of these changes as positive, but when it was happening to you it didn't always seem that way.

The biggest change, she supposed, came when his father died. But that too had turned out to be liberating. And then discovering the birds—that was a real liberation.

She was thrilled to discover birds . . . and also shocked. Having lived for a good long time, she had not been prepared to find that she knew nothing about the hundreds of beautiful, colorful, even spectacular birds that just ordinarily surrounded her. She didn't know how this could have happened. One day she had been aware, if she had been asked, that there were sparrows, robins, chickens, ducks, and maybe eagles. Within another day or two she had discovered a rose-breasted grosbeak (an incredibly gorgeous bird, not imported, but sitting in the plum tree in her own yard), then a yellow chat, several warblers, and a golden-crowned kinglet, a green heron. Most important, she realized that her life had always been surrounded by creatures of surpassing beauty, elegance, and mystery. It still shocked her to think that these fabulous beings had been invisible to her, simply because of ignorance and an inability to see.

All it had taken was a single walk around her own yard and down to the St. Clair River with a woman she had known for many years, a fellow past matron of the Eastern Star, who happened to be a birdwatcher. From that had come an incredible sequence of discovery, enchantment, and finally devotion to the causes of the environment and ecology.

She was silent for a good long time, evidently reflecting on this remarkable transformation. Suddenly, she said, "Not all changes are liberating, of course. I never told you—we thought it was better not to—that I had a child long before you. She didn't live very long, just a few days. Her name was Mary, after my mother. After that, things were"—she hesitated—"difficult between your father and me. But, we got over it and ten years later you were born." She smiled.

Mulheisen was thunderstruck. A sister he had never known about? Years of his parents looking at one another in a special way, of saying things in a special tone, and he was not privy to it! He would be unable now to recollect some of these moments, to reconstruct the situation. His father was gone, his mother would be gone before too much longer, and only now he was learning that there was a whole aspect of life in the house where he had grown up to which he had no access. He wanted to ask a million questions, but as he looked at his mother she just shook her head. "Don't spend even a minute thinking about it," she said. "Your father and I were stupid enough to let it bother us for years, until you came along. It was a waste of time. We never figured it out."

There was, of course, yet another change awaiting her, she said. This would be the big one. She had every reason to hope that it would be as liberating and exciting as the changes that had gone before.

16
Vetch

"**T**hese people have no culture," Victor Echeverria explained to his associate Hernan as they drove to a meeting with Humphrey. It was an evening meeting, at Humphrey's home in Grosse Pointe, not at the Krispee Chips factory.

"The Italians?" Hernan asked. It was Echeverria's Mercedes, but Hernan drove. He liked to drive nice cars, and Echeverria wanted to indulge him. They drove out along Jefferson Avenue and then turned down toward the lake.

"The Fat Man isn't Italian," Echeverria retorted scornfully, "not really. He is Norte . . . a Yank. The Italians have culture, certainly—cathedrals, the great artists, music—but these pigs, they have been in Detroit too long. Their culture is Cadillac culture." He laughed, they both laughed.

"Now he wants to be called Humphrey, or Mr. DiEbola," Echeverria went on. They crawled along a quiet street, the bare limbs of the oaks and maples rattling in the wind off Lake St. Clair, which was not visible beyond the walls and gates of these exclusive estates. They were looking for Humphrey's gatehouse. "I will call him Diablo, the devil." He appreciated Hernan's low chuckle.

The gate man did not wear a uniform. Humphrey didn't like uniforms. This man was young and athletic. He wore dark slacks, a dark and warm jacket, and a baseball-type hat. A holstered automatic was strapped to his hip, and he carried a cordless telephone and a clipboard. The visitors sensed rather than saw at least two other men nearby, who presumably were more heavily armed. The gate man checked their names against the clipboard and repeated the names into the telephone. He told them to drive on, but warned that they must stay on the main drive and not stop.

"To the Fat Man we are all Mexicans," Echeverria remarked as they rolled slowly along. It was at least a half minute to the well-lit front door of the house. Before they reached it, Echeverria insisted that Hernan stop.

"He told us not to stop," Hernan said nervously, but he stopped.

"Fuck El Gordo," Echeverria said. He got out and unzipped his pants. He pissed calmly while staring up at the ragged clouds that scudded off the lake, hauntingly lit by the half moon. He zipped up quickly when he heard what sounded like a small herd of ponies galloping, and he jumped back into the car. Three huge dogs arrived seconds later and placed their monstrous paws on the rolled-up windows of the Mercedes. They barked loudly, their foot-long tongues lolling out. They were Dobermans.

"Get away!" Echeverria shrieked at them, wincing at the scratching of the dogs' claws on the metal of the car. Someone came running and called the dogs off as Hernan pulled away. At the door there was no sign of the dogs, and another darkly appareled young man, armed with a shotgun on a sling, stepped forward from the lighted portico and opened the car door to let Echeverria out. The young man made no mention of the dogs or of their stopping. Echeverria walked quickly into the house. A pretty young girl in a conventional maid's costume led them along a carpeted hallway lined with finely upholstered chairs, a silk-clad couch that appeared to be Renaissance Italian, past a small, graceful table on which there was an intricate old bronze statue of intertwined figures, a man and a dragon-like snake. She stopped at a large door and knocked once, then opened the door. She closed it behind them.

Humphrey DiEbola sat on a high teak and leather chair, almost a bar stool, one elbow on a marble-topped bar. He wore a navy blue jumpsuit and slippers, and he was eating from a bowl with a plate of Italian bread at hand.

"Vetch!" he cried out, beckoning to them. "Come in! Come in! So nice to have you here. Have some menudo. You like menudo? Sure you do. Everyone likes menudo."

"No, thank you," Echeverria assured him. He turned to his companion. "Mr. Diablo, this is my associate, Mr. Ghittes."

"Mr. Ghittes," Humphrey acknowledged. "Have some menudo. You guys like menudo. You must. My chef is a genius with menudo, but this recipe I got from a guy upstate, from Traverse City. The poet Harrington. He's very famous." The name meant nothing to Echeverria. "I never heard of him neither, till I met him at a party," Humphrey admitted, "but he sure knows menudo. 'The holy Mayan menudo,' he calls it. You don't want some? No? Too bad. Your loss." He mopped up the remainder of the stew with a hunk of bread and devoured it, then mopped his chin and slid off the stool. "Well, let me get you a drink. Whattayou have? We got everything. Marco!" he bellowed and a young man instantly appeared. "Get these fellas what they want to drink."

The room was large with French doors that looked out onto a terrace and beyond a broad dark lawn to the tumbled waters of the lake, gleaming under the moon. A fire burned in a marble-framed fireplace. DiEbola sat down heavily on a large couch. Marco brought him a large glass of carbonated water with ice and a twist of lemon. He brought the others whiskey. When the weather had been disposed of and the compliments on the beauty of the house given and accepted, Humphrey said, "Ghittes? You must be the son of Hector Ghittes, out of Cali?"

The young man admitted that he was the son of the man who was, if not the absolute czar or generalissimo of cocaine in Colombia, then at least a principal member of the inner circle. In these days it was hard to keep track of who was currently on top. But Ghittes senior had been at the top, among the chiefs, for a very long time.

"My regards to your father," Humphrey said. "We have been good friends and we have done business, with pleasure."

"My father sends his compliments," young Ghittes responded. "He will be pleased to hear your regards and my report that you are looking well and in good health."

"Thank you," Humphrey responded. "I am feeling very well."

"You have lost weight," Echeverria said.

It was true. Humphrey had lost as much as fifty pounds in the six months or so since he had ascended to power. Perhaps it was worry or the stress of holding together the organization, but he didn't admit it to his young guests. Humphrey privately attributed it to habanero salsa. He said he was working hard but he felt good, and he was getting regular exercise, long walks along the lake, and his diet was good and regular. "But," he said to Ghittes, "I'll never be as dashing as you, my young friend. You must keep the señoritas dancing at a furious pace!"

Echeverria was clearly impatient with this focus on Ghittes. He was a tall, slender man, hardly older than Ghittes, with handsome features and a very assured manner. "We have come to talk about business, Diablo," he said.

"I was sorry to hear about your brother," Humphrey said. "Ray Echeverria was a valued friend. I was pleased to hear that his assassin was himself killed."

"My brother was killed by a man in your employ," Echeverria pointed out, sniffing and raising his chin pointedly.

"Technically," Humphrey conceded, his fat hand tipping back and forth. "This man, Lande, was crazy. He had lost his wife to cancer. These killings he undertook in the madness of his grief. They had nothing to do with us. Many others, our own people, were slain. Your brother was unfortunately caught in the crossfire. I am deeply sorry for this, and I hope it doesn't strain our friendship. Ray Echeverria was avenged by one of our people, as you know."

Echeverria wasn't buying this. "This man who killed the cur Lande—where is he? Joe Service is his name? He was actually commissioned to kill this, this loco?"

"Yes, it was Joe Service. No, he wasn't commissioned to kill Lande. We wanted Lande alive," Humphrey conceded, "but the man was crazy, as I say, and wouldn't have it any other way. Joe was forced to kill him."

Echeverria looked angry. He drank his whiskey too fast, almost choked and then said, "Do you mind if I smoke?"

"Have one of these excellent cigars," Humphrey said. He leaned forward with an effort and flipped open the lid of a silver humidor.

Both the young men took a cigar and busied themselves with clipping and lighting them. When the puffing had settled and the drinks were replenished, young Ghittes said, mildly, "We have heard that the policeman, this Mulheisen—they call him Sergeant Fang"— he laughed—"was the one who actually killed Señor Lande, although the police called it suicide, of course. No?"

Humphrey shook his head. "It was Joe Service. Mulheisen was the one who found Lande's body. They called it suicide, but nobody believes that."

"And did he also find our money?" Echeverria asked.

"Your money?" Humphrey raised his thick eyebrows comically. "I didn't hear that you lost any money, Vetch. Anyway, the police didn't find any money."

"Not me personally," Echeverria said. "And I'm not concerned with the money that Señor Sedlacek and Señor Lande and their friends stole from you. But did you know that Señor Lande was also handling money for Señor Ghittes? Yes, it is true. My brother Ray was impressed with Señor Lande's ability to—how shall we say?—*recycle* money. He had given him . . ." He delved in the pocket of his splendidly tailored blue silk suit coat and withdrew a piece of paper that he extended toward Humphrey. " This."

Humphrey lunged forward and took the paper, unfolded it and read, "To Eugene Lande—$5,342,265.00." It was dated and signed by Ray Echeverria and countersigned by Eugene Lande. Humphrey flipped it back onto the coffee table. "So what? He gave some money to Lande . . . I guess," he added pointedly. "He didn't give any money to Carmine, or me."

"Señor Lande's operation was, shall we say, sanctioned by Carmine. We received only one million of these dollars in our account in Panama, in Colombian pesos," Echeverria said. "Four million—and change, as you say—is still owing to us. We like to be fair. We will ignore the 'change.' "

Humphrey laughed, a thick, gurgly laugh. "That's good of you, Vetch, but I don't know anything about your money. You made a deal with Lande. If Carmine okayed it, I never heard anything about it. And now Carmine is dead. We aren't in business with you. Maybe in the future, who knows?" The eyebrows bobbled.

"The police did not recover this money," Echeverria said severely. "Your man, Joe Service, got this money."

"Don't know a damn thing about it," Humphrey said.

A long silence settled on the room. The wind buffeted the French doors, the fire crackled. Echeverria stared intently at Humphrey, who stared blandly back. Finally, Humphrey said, "Maybe you should talk to Joe about this."

"Where is he?"

Humphrey thought about the woman Heather. Rossamani had talked to Smokey Stover a few days earlier. Smokey had said that

Heather was making progress, but there was no indication of when the job would be done. At the time, of course, Humphrey had known nothing about any money that Lande had taken from Ghittes. Carmine had led him to believe that Big Sid had accomplished his skim, and the money had been shifted to the Cayman Islands. They had made inquiries but had concluded that the money had simply gone. For a while they had tried to recover it, or Joe had tried to recover it, but nothing had come of that. Personally, he had supposed that Joe might have found some of it, but how would they ever know how much it was? He had concluded that the task at hand was to find Joe, try to recover whatever he had absconded with, and close the case with Joe's death. He still had hopes in this direction, but lately his focus had been on little Helen. Now she might have the money, but he was damned if he wanted a bunch of Colombians poking around in the bushes while he dealt with her. He had never heard anything about Lande washing money for the Colombians, but he supposed it was so.

"We've got someone on Joe's trail," he said, "and it looks promising, but . . ."

"Where is he?" Echeverria demanded.

"I can't tell you, right now. We've got a good lead on him."

"Who is on the job? What is his name?"

Somehow, Humphrey couldn't bring himself to say it was a woman. These awful macho Colombians—well, Echeverria was a Basque, but that was worse, perhaps—would be incredulous, horribly mocking. He wished he had never heard of Heather. This is what happened when the empire failed, he thought. He wished he had Rossie here, to kick in the ass for hiring Heather.

"I'll tell you what," he said. "Things are in a delicate state. I'm not gonna fuck it up just for your lousy four million—which I never heard of till this minute, and which it ain't my responsibility anyway—but I can see that you got a stake in finding Joe." Humphrey was thinking fast. He didn't give a rat fuck about the Colombians, but who knew when he might have to do business with them? It wouldn't do to simply ignore their claims, and they might prove useful, yet. "How 'bout I get back to you in a coupla days?"

This was hardly agreeable to Echeverria, but there was nothing he could do. At least the mob hadn't simply thumbed their noses at him. He put up a lot of bluster and heaped some more contumely on Humphrey's head—"Diablo" he persisted in calling him—but ultimately he backed off . . . for a week. The two men left under outwardly amicable terms.

These discussions were very much in Humphrey's mind when Helen Sedlacek called two nights later.

"Unca Umby!" she squealed, and he couldn't suppress a flood of joy in his heart.

"You little scamp," he said, laughing, "where have you been? You're driving your mama—and me!—crazy."

"Oh, Unca Umby, I'm so sorry. I am crazy. It's been a crazy, crazy time. But I'm so sorry. I want to make it up to you."

"Then come home," he said, promptly. "Come home right now. Your mama needs you. She isn't well."

"What's wrong? Is she sick? What's wrong with her? Is she in the hospital?"

"Noooo, no, no, no. She's not that ill. She's not in the hospital. I shouldn't have said such a thing." He waved at Marco and gestured toward his glass. He was sitting on the couch in the same room where he had entertained Echeverria and Ghittes. Marco poured more Perrier into Humphrey's glass. "Her health is not good, but she gets around. Roman tells me she spends too much time in bed, though. You've got to come home, get her up and cooking. Come for Thanksgiving. We'll have a big feast. You come to my house."

"Mama will never come to your house," Helen said. Her voice

was very calm now, more businesslike. "But maybe I will come home for Thanksgiving . . . if things work out."

"What's to work out? Tell me, sweetie, and your Unca Umby will see that it's done. What's the problem? It's Joe, isn't it? What's that crazy bum up to? I should of known he'd steal you away from me. Hey? What's Joe doing?"

"Oh, Joe? Joe's all right," she said. "You know Joe. He's got a million scams. He's off somewhere right now."

"He's off? This crazy guy steals our Helen and now he's off? Where?"

"You know Joe, Unca Umby, he doesn't tell anybody anything. I don't know if he even tells himself. But he's fine, he's fine. He's just off, somewhere, taking care of business."

Humphrey's voice took on a mock sternness as he said, "Is that bum treating my little Helen all right? C'mon, sweetie, tell Unca Umby. Is he treating you all right?"

Helen laughed. It sounded genuine over the line. "We're fine. Honest, we're fine."

"Tell me something, sweetie. Did you guys get married?"

There was a pause. "Uh, no. Did Joe say something about getting married?" For a moment, lying on a huge bed in a hotel in New Orleans, Helen found herself speculating about marriage with Joe, just as if nothing had happened. It was amazing. In the course of just a few minutes of conversation, all of it profoundly fictional in text, she and Humphrey had conjured up an elaborate edifice in which they could both participate, and pleasurably. She was reluctant to abandon it.

"Where are you calling from?" Humphrey asked casually.

"Seattle. It's great! Have you ever been there?"

Humphrey smiled, noting the "there" instead of the "here." "No," he lied, "but I have some friends there, old friends. You should call them. Your papa knew them, too. Connie and Al Munsch. Remember them? They both worked for your papa at one time." This was a fond memory, in a way: Connie had been one of Big Sid's girlfriends, and Al was her husband, a pimp. Great-looking girl, Connie. And Al was a gambler, a guy who would bet on anything from one minute to the next—whether that bus up ahead would make the light, whether there would be a man on the next block who was baldheaded and not wearing a hat—bets of a dollar, or a hundred dollars. Humphrey missed Al, and Connie.

"So you'll be home for Thanksgiving, that's great," he said. "I'm so glad you called, sweetie. Was there anything special, or did you just wanta say hi to Unca Umby?"

"Well, I wanted to talk to you. It's about money."

"You're short of money? What's the matter with that bum, Joe? Listen, honey, if you need money I can—"

"No, no, Unca Umby," she interrupted, "I've got money, plenty of money, but my situation is, well, you know . . . changed. I don't feel very good about banks and the I.R.S. and investing. You know what I mean?"

Humphrey understood immediately. "You're a little too liquid, maybe?"

"I'm not sure I understand."

"Too much cash," Humphrey said. "It makes you vulnerable. You need a return on your money and you need security."

"Yes, that's it," Helen said, pleased.

"And Joe isn't helping you?"

"Well, he's not around. I don't think I can count on Joe for much . . . at the present, anyway."

"Ah, I see," Humphrey said. "You need to take care of this on your own. Hmmm." He thought for a moment. "Of course I'll help, sweetie, but it's not something that we should discuss on the telephone. Can we meet?"

"Couldn't we just handle it on the phone?"

"If it's just a few bucks, sure," Humphrey said. He waited.

"I'll have to think. I'll have to call you back."

"That's fine, sweetie. You call me back. Unca Umby'll be here. Otherwise, maybe I'll see you at Thanksgiving, eh?"

After she hung up, he called in Rossamani and discussed the situation.

"She must of took off with Joe's stash," Rossamani opined. "How much do you think it could be?"

"Lande had plenty, that was Carmine's theory," Humphrey said, "but who knows how much? He was washing it, getting it out of the country, so him and Big Sid could use it when they bolted. That's why we put Joe on it. But then him and the broad bumped Carmine. Who would of figured it? To me, Joe was always straight. I could count on him. If I hadda guess, I'd say Lande had maybe a coupla million set aside, but it could be more. Lande was never anything but a small timer. The deal he was in with Big Sid, though, that was a pretty big deal. They put a lot of it into a legitimate deal in the Caymans, on a resort, but they wouldn't of put it all in. And then there's these Colombians, Vetch and his pals." He had told Rossamani about this, not that Rossamani hadn't already heard all about it from Marco. "Maybe there was more to Lande than I thought. Carmine always believed the take was in the ten mil neighborhood."

"Sounds like she's got Vetch's four bucks, anyway," Rossamani said. "What do you want to do when she calls back? She'll want to meet somewhere neutral."

"Helen don't know from neutral," Humphrey said. "To her, Disneyland is neutral. The thing is to find out where she put the money she took from Joe. That's the whole thing. 'Cause it ain't with Joe anymore, you can bet on it. So I go talk to her, in some place where she feels safe, and you go where she has stashed the money, once I find out."

Rossamani nodded. He thought this was just like Humphrey, and it was what he saw as Humphrey's weakness. Carmine, he thought, would simply have snatched the woman and then pounded

her until she told him where the money was. That was what they had
done with Big Sid's girlfriend—he couldn't remember her name now.
He had been one of the guys who worked on her. They had done a
good job of it, took their time, three days of it. He'd liked her a lot. In
the end she didn't tell them anything—she didn't have Big Sid's
money—and they had to let her go. Humphrey's orders. They should
have zipped her, Rossamani thought. Big Sid was dead, he couldn't
complain. But, as it turned out, she kept her mouth shut. Still, you
never know. She knew too much, and all they had on her was fear,
fear of the fist and fear of being fucked to death. That isn't always
enough. Now Humphrey wanted to go talk to this broad, this bitch
who had actually crawled into Carmine's fucking limo and blasted
him! Rossamani couldn't see it. You don't talk to a cunt. She don't
have no say in this. Grab her and pound her and let the boys have a
little fun, and she'll tell you what you need to know. And then get rid
of her, for chrissake!

Helen called back less than an hour later. She was willing to
meet with Humphrey. A neutral place. Butte, Montana.

Helen didn't know why she had said Butte. She had considered
Salt Lake City, but that was where the money was. Then she thought
of L.A., but she didn't know L.A. Humphrey would have plenty of
people he could count on in L.A. It would be the same anywhere,
probably. And then she had thought of Butte. She couldn't imagine
that the mob had anyone in Butte, and Joe was there. He wasn't in
good shape, but she reckoned he was getting better. Hell, he might
even be in good enough shape to get her out of this.

She realized with that thought that she had made a mess of
things. She hadn't handled the money right, and now she was simply
going back to square one. Well, at least the money was safe in Salt
Lake City. No problem there. She would go out tomorrow and smurf a
few more thousands and then head on over to Butte to meet with

Humphrey. She had warned him to come by himself, no bodyguards. At Butte she would see him walking from the plane—there was no skyramp, or whatever they called it—and if he wasn't alone, she wouldn't be waiting for him. She'd be long gone and that would be the end of it.

Humphrey had protested mildly. "I thought you wanted my help," he pouted, "but now you sound like you're afraid of me."

"It's a delicate situation, Unca Umby," she said. "Joe doesn't know and I don't want him to know. This is just between you and me. Let's face it, some, uh, difficult things have gone down. I can't be sure of anything, anymore. I made some mistakes, but I want everything to be straight between us from now on. Okay?"

"Honey, you took the words right out of my mouth," he assured her. "Listen, we're family. A family is gonna have disagreements, but a family works it out. You can count on me, sweetie."

As soon as she was off the line, he said to Rossamani, "Get the plane ready and get onto Stover, in Butte. I want him to meet me at the airport there before noon tomorrow."

Smokey Stover was not thrilled. He never liked to see the bosses in town and, to be sure, he almost never did, unless they took it into their head to do something weird, like go elk hunting, or fishing. But they weren't fishing for trout now, he was sure. "Mr. Rossamani, our gal Heather seems to have everything well in hand. Is there a problem?"

"Yeah, there's a problem," Rossamani told him. "You get hold of her, now. Tonight. Not tomorrow, but now. Tell her everything's on hold. This is very important, Smoke. She don't make a move. I'll talk to her when we get to Butte."

17

Philosophy 101

It occurred to Joe Service that now there were two parts to his life. This could be called "Service II," perhaps, like one of those endless Rambo or Rocky movies. Maybe, like the Super Bowl, he should aspire to Xs and Vs. Anyway, in Part Two, he thought, Joe Service comes back to life and astounds everyone with his incredible exploits. Is he different? Is he truly "born again"? Is he really a new man? The New Man? An inquiring public wants to know. Hell, *he* wanted to know.

It could never be said by anyone who knew him that Joe Service was a contemplative man. Still, he was a man who was fascinated with everything about him, wildly curious, and naturally given to speculation. No human being, after all, is not thoughtful; it is a defining characteristic of the species. In his present circumstances, of course, he was bound to be contemplative. Although he was doing well in physical therapy, almost back on his feet and even making a few intelligible noises, he still had a long way to go. He spent long hours doing little more than sitting and looking. He couldn't read yet, it was too confusing—he could never get beyond the first few words before all the possibilities of meaning assaulted him, tying him up in knots. He didn't watch television; for some reason it seemed alien and irrelevant, so he ignored it. When Cateyo was around he enjoyed listening to her talk, particularly her rambling discourse on the nature of the new man. He understood, by now, that she half-believed that he was the new man, himself, the one who was coming to straighten everything out that had gone so wrong in the world. Joe encouraged her in this belief, although he couldn't really believe it himself. But anything to keep her bound to him. He felt exposed and fearful when she was gone.

Still, he longed to set her right on a few things, and he had tried a couple of times, but it was difficult for him to organize his thoughts properly. For one thing there was an abiding concern with memory. Everyone wanted to talk about his memory. The doctors were positively pests about it, particularly the brain surgeon. What did he remember? What was the last thing he remembered before the curtain (as he'd come to think of it)? What was the first thing he remembered after the curtain? They were all after him about it, including the detective, Mulheisen, who had been to see him a couple of times. This guy made Joe nervous. He sat there looking at him with those slightly hooded eyes, not saying anything for long periods of time. Joe thought he might be looking into his brain. Anyway, he had decided that memory wasn't so important. He had a feeling that if he just left it alone, it would come back. In fact, it was always there. He sensed it, not as a body of knowledge but as a kind of field, a network or web that was pervasive and always present but not presently . . . well, not presently retrievable. Or, at least, not readily retrievable. But he believed it would be, eventually. Of course, nobody's memory is 100 percent retrievable, not at will, but Joe didn't know that.

Some things, actually a lot of things, he did remember with no difficulty whatsoever. In fact, it wasn't so much that he remembered them but that he knew them without having to remember. Thus, he knew who he was: He was Joe Service, and he was twenty-nine years old; he lived in Montana, but often traveled to other places; he had a house and there was a woman named Helen who lived there with him and was very important, but he wasn't sure in what way. He knew how to shave, how to walk—he was amazed that he couldn't walk better, but it seemed that parts of his right leg, right foot, right arm, and right hand were missing. They were not, in fact, missing. He could see the "missing" parts but he couldn't figure out what they were doing there, as he was sure that they weren't there. He had learned that he had been injured and he gradually began to understand that the use of his body would return to him—how to talk, how to learn. Important things.

One day he remembered, without trying (See? he told himself, just be patient), meeting a man who was some kind of biologist. He couldn't remember the man's name, but he suspected that it wasn't important or that he had never learned it in the first place. He had met the man on a train. This was about three or four years ago, he thought. (He still wasn't secure with the notion of time: A day he knew, and thus a week of days and a month of weeks and days, but a year was still a little nebulous—it was a long time, but not a terribly long time, he thought. He'd learned that a year was twelve months and that it had been almost three months since the curtain.) He was on a train, sitting in the lounge, talking to the biologist. The biologist explained to him a theory that life requires adversity, struggle, difficulty. According to this theory, without adversity the organism falls into complacency and then stasis, or death. The whole principle of life is at odds with the basic status of the inconsiderate universe; every cell quivers with the need to pit itself against an indifferent force. Thus, the most dangerous moment in life is the moment of triumph, of accomplishment, satisfaction, and happiness.

This was all very fascinating and amusing when one is sitting in a club car sipping whiskey, with no greater goal in mind than the end of the journey, hours or days ahead, aboard a train that is going there whether you want it to or not. But he'd thought about it a good deal, later, when he was living with Helen in his little cabin in the mountains. (He thought of that now, recovering it more or less completely in the process.)

They had driven from Detroit. They were deliriously happy. They had stopped to see all the sights en route: the Mississippi River, the Badlands, the presidents on the mountain, the Missouri River, the mountains. They had made love frequently and furiously. At the cabin they had devoted themselves to little more than playing. They shopped for things for the house. They went fishing. They went down to the hot springs. Helen was wildly happy and so was he. And then the problems had started.

He couldn't recall (and suspected that he would never be able to recall) the moment when it all started. The moment when it wasn't enough to play and be happy. He had to be doing something. Something worth doing. Something that would mean more than just being happy. Sex was an excellent antidote, for a while, to these moments of unease. And these moments of unease were railed against: Why should one's pleasure be spoiled by this vague and nagging unease? And then he had begun to understand what the biologist was talking about. Why a person would put himself in danger, would flirt with danger, to make life more bearable. Presumably, there were people who had learned to get over this unease, but these people were truly in danger, if one believed the theory of adversity. As for Joe, he was uneasy, but he was happy. He was alive.

He had to leave the hospital soon, he knew. He had to recover his old life, so he could get on with Joe Service, Part Two. There was a lot at stake, although he wasn't sure what it was. He was bothered by the woman Heather. She had become a close friend of Cateyo's, but he was afraid of Heather, and he couldn't explain it to Cateyo. He had to get back to the cabin and find out about Helen, whom he had also been unable to discuss with Cateyo. Anyway, the hospital wanted him to leave. He didn't need to stay in the room. Apparently, he had enough money to hire Cateyo to stay with him. In fact, he knew that he had plenty of money at the cabin, although he wasn't sure how much. But the money was important, he knew that.

For some reason, Cateyo had not told Joe that Heather had moved into her house. She never talked about the house, anyway. But as the time came closer for Joe to leave the hospital she began more and more to regret having offered Heather the spare room. She enjoyed Heather's presence, despite the fact that she often barged into the bathroom at embarrassing moments. The woman took a lot of the day-to-day tasks off Cateyo's hands, shopping and keeping house. And it was a comfort to sit and talk to her in the evenings. Sometimes, in fact, when she came home, dead-tired, it was a treat to allow Heather to bring her tea and bakery goods, tucking her up on the couch while she recounted the day's events. Mostly she talked about Paul—she still called him Paul, although they had learned his name was really Joseph Humann. It was very comforting to explain to Heather what a remarkable man Paul was and how she felt called to serve him. "It's God's purpose," she said. "God doesn't do anything without a purpose, so there must be a reason he sent Paul to me."

Cateyo had two additional reasons not to feel bad about Heather's presence: One, Heather would be leaving soon. Her job, which didn't seem to take too much of her time, would soon be ending, and she had another lined up in Seattle. And two, Cateyo had agreed to take a leave of absence from her nursing job when Paul was discharged. They would go to his cabin to live. This was an indication of how much Joe's condition had improved: his ability to make these kinds of plans and decisions with Cateyo and the doctors and counselors. They all agreed it was a terrific sign.

For Joe, however, as his memory improved and plans were being formulated, the cabin became not just a hopeful destination but also a focus for anxiety. Helen was there, or should be there. But he hadn't heard from her. She hadn't come to visit him. He had bought her a new truck, he remembered that. He'd gotten it in Missoula. And on the way back . . . it was a beautiful day . . . hawks, deer, mountains, the shadows of clouds drifting across a valley floor . . . the irritation of the Superfund project site . . . and then the curtain. Oh yeah, the dead man. Then the curtain.

He could walk now, a little. He could be alone and take care of himself for short periods of time. They would leave soon. First they would take a day trip to the cabin, to see if everything was all right. Cateyo was arranging it with Big Face, the guy who came by nearly every day and just looked at him, standing at the foot of the bed in his boots and khaki shirt with the badge. Some kind of cop. Why Big Face controlled the cabin, Joe didn't know, and it annoyed him, but he didn't think it was too important. Not as important as Helen or Heather. She was going too, to help out, Cateyo said. Joe didn't think that was right, but he couldn't get it across to Cateyo.

Cateyo was talking about the World. It was a very bad place. There was a better place, Heaven. In the beginning, Joe didn't get this, but soon it all came back to him. She was talking about some imaginary place where everything was all right, where it was okay to be happy and do nothing—a concept that the biologist's theory had blown once and for all. Joe never objected. He just listened. In the World you had taxes, schools that ignored Jesus, pornography everywhere, unutterable obscenities, people who walked around pretending that Jesus and Heaven didn't exist. The fact was, it was the World that was just a shadow. This seemed a little uncertain to Joe. The World existed, sure, but its existence was somehow unreal, only a momentary existence, at least in comparison to Heaven, which was eternal. This was why the new man was required: to reawaken the people to the existence of God's Heaven, where real life would commence, outside of Time, once this shadow world was destroyed. It couldn't be long, the signs were everywhere: the Soviet Union destroyed—self-destructed!—a clear sign of God's wrath. There were plenty of other signs, but one had to be careful how one interpreted them.

Cateyo laughed about her father's folly: He had almost gotten it right, but he'd been too fascinated by ridiculous details that were mere distractions. He'd believed that Jimmy Carter was the anti-Christ, for instance: The initials J.C. had confused him. True, the anti-Christ would seem to be a kind of savior, a religious man, but he was really a devil, and Jimmy Carter had been, deep down, a liberal. Liberalism was a genuine evil. Anyway, Jimmy Carter had tried to make the Jews and the Muslims lie down together, which would have been an act of the anti-Christ, all right, but it hadn't worked. Now, Saddam Hussein, there was a potential anti-Christ! Her father would have reveled in the rise of Saddam, and no doubt he would have seen in Desert Storm the makings of Armageddon, but Cateyo hadn't been fooled for a minute. What was needed was a truly new man, a man resurrected from the dead, like Christ. This new man would not be an anti-Christ. She was understandably leery of anti-Christ theories. No, the new man wasn't something out of prophecy, but out of the Gospels themselves. Why, St. Paul himself might be considered a type of new man, which was why she had taken to calling Joe Paul, although that was really just a joke . . . and on and on.

Over a period of time, literally weeks of hearing this notion explained and elaborated, sometimes self-mockingly ("I know folks think I'm crazy, but . . .") but generally quite seriously, Joe had gradually recovered his own memories about all this, about Heaven and Jesus. He couldn't take it seriously. He looked at Cateyo and saw a lovely young woman, healthy and happy, bright and bubbling. The world was a fine place if it had such people in it. He was happy to be alive, and he'd literally had his brains blown out. He wanted to say, "Babe, wake up. It's a great world. You're young, you're on top of it. I'm lying on my back, trying to recover my scrambled wits, and you're dreaming about playing a harp."

In the meantime he was thrilled by her almost daily baths that ended with her stroking him until he ejaculated. On two occasions she had even applied her mouth. Talk about heavenly! He wondered how she squared these seemingly lewd activities with her disgust for pornography and immorality. Obviously, he thought, she just didn't think about it. Clearly, she was happy, her ramblings about the evils of the World notwithstanding. She told him so. In fact, she came very close to telling him that she loved him. He knew she loved him. He was glad.

Love is such a wonderful thing. It not only makes happy those in love, or loved, but even the ones around them are affected. For that reason, Cateyo's supervisor, Head Nurse Work, could not bring herself to do any more than warn Cateyo about "unprofessional" attitudes and restrict her access to Joe to normal shift hours. Anyone could see that the patient was responding very well. So, okay, she tolerated a few "extra" hours of attendance. Who can stand in the way of happiness?

The day of the outing arrived at last.

18

Rocky Mountain Rendezvous

There are certain kinds of winter days in the Ruby Valley that are just awful. Ordinarily winter isn't so bad in the Mountain West, particularly in the sheltered valleys. In fact, it can be beautiful. Low temperatures can be a problem, but except when a cold spell goes on for more than a few days, it's not necessarily awful. Snow can be a nuisance or a threat, but generally is quite pleasant and brings with it recreational opportunities and, most important, is like a deposit in the bank, for summer withdrawal—westerners, particularly those outside the towns, appreciate snow.

The hunters like snow because it brings the elk down from the high country and you can track a wounded critter. The skiers love snow, of course; the cross-country skiers because it opens up a vast back country. Field mice love snow because it hides them from the hawks and the owls, and they can tunnel to their hearts' content in the dry grass. For the trout, it closes the streams to the osprey and the great blue herons and it promises summer flows. Trappers and snowmobilers simply love it. The wind . . . well, the wind is never really welcome. The wind is a killer. Cold is tolerable when it is calm. Every knot of wind makes it less tolerable. Fortunately, the valleys don't get much wind.

But an overcast day in November, −10 degrees Fahrenheit, twenty-plus knots of wind, stinging snow . . . nobody loves a day like this. The mobile-home dweller for sure doesn't love it. No mobile home seems quite secure against a day like this. The wind has a way of penetrating through the bales of hay and the plywood skirting to freeze the pipes; the structure rocks in the wind like a sleeping car on the Trans-Siberian Express; it's never quite warm enough, or if you have a woodstove, either it's too hot or—all too frequently—you've got to go out and get more firewood.

That was certainly the way Sally McIntyre looked at it. She got her two preteen kids (Jason and Jennifer) off on the school bus at 7:15, when it was still dark. Then she got ready for work. She was feeding cattle on the Garland Ranch; her ditch-rider job was through for the season. She put on her long johns, an insulated coverall over a wool shirt with hooded sweatshirt and jeans, pulled on her felt-lined Sorel boots and donned a brown duck tin coat. She hauled in more firewood for the airtight stove and set the fire so it would hold for several hours. Her old pickup started readily: She kept it tuned and the battery well-charged (she hauled it inside when the temperature dropped below −15 degrees Fahrenheit); it had an electric engine heater, which she kept plugged into an extension cord. She left it to warm up while she filled a thermos with hot coffee and packed a heavy lunch: two meat loaf sandwiches, an apple, a couple of Snickers candy bars. You burn a lot of calories pitching bales of hay in sub-zero weather.

All morning she hauled hay and spread it in the fields near the ranch house for several hundred cattle to feed on. They looked pretty miserable. It was just damned unpleasant, although the sun periodically broke through, for ten minutes at a time, between snow squalls blowing off the mountains—what she called a dirty sun, its face never really bright. The thermometer never got close to zero, the wind gusted to thirty knots at times and drove the snow like BB shot. But by midday she was finished and she found herself up on the service road below Garland Butte, not far from where she had found the body in the balmy days of goose summer. She was warm enough, in a general way, but still cold in parts. She had eaten her sandwiches and candy bars while driving between haystacks and feed lots. She had lain in the snow and ice to tighten the chains on the rear wheels of the truck, she had nearly frozen her fingers repairing a gate, and she had gotten a sleeve wet breaking ice in a drinking trough. She was tired and dirty.

There wasn't a lot of snow in the fields, most of it swept into ditches and drifts. She decided to walk up to the hot springs. She found a half-pint of Jim Beam bourbon in the truck and slipped it into the pocket of the tin coat. It was easy walking, even exhilarating to hike into the spitting wind up the long north slope to the copse of pines behind the Humann cabin on Garland Butte. There were ravens scudding before the wind, but little other evidence of life in this bitter season.

The springs, however, were wonderful. They were well sheltered from the wind by the huge trees, but the snow howled above, the wind tossing the tops of the ponderosas. The steam billowed, one moment as impenetrable as valley fog, the next swept nearly away. Chickadees and a small gang of juncos yammered and peeped around the springs. A small, oblivious downy woodpecker worked stolidly about the lower limbs, tapping, listening, tapping.

Sally quickly stripped off her clothes and jumped into the hot water. She immersed herself until her body temperature was sufficiently high, then rose out, steaming, while she carefully folded the clothes and found a place in a cleft that wasn't too damp but still warm from the steam, so that the clothes (particularly the boots) wouldn't freeze while she bathed. Then she sank back into the hot water, lying submerged with her head resting against a convenient mossy rock. Her red hair was frozen where it had gotten wet and she lay back, watching through slit eyes the steam rising up among the frosted green boughs and the snow sifting down as it fell out from the wind roaring over the tops. Every once in a while she reached out a parboiled arm and took hold of the whiskey bottle. A sip was about a half-shot and it felt warm all the way down. Then she set the bottle back and sank down, occasionally shifting about, sort of walking and dragging on her back, with her hands on the sandy, stony bottom, pushing herself along, to find a still hotter spring. Once she stood up and walked out of the pool entirely, her naked body glowing in the snow as she walked about, cooling off. Then she plunged back in and swam submerged to the hottest part of the pool, to lie awhile and let her hair freeze.

This was bliss, but not perfect bliss. She did not, on this occasion, think about the cowboy, Gary, who had been an object of fantasy on her first visit to the springs. She hadn't seen Gary since before the visit and she didn't miss him. Nor did she think for more than a second about her ex-husband. He had been rather like Gary, all cock and no brains, to say nothing of his being too fond of booze coupled with a tendency to punch women. She thought instead of her children, scrappy and independent, but still childishly loving and an almost continuous delight. She thought about her own mother, now sitting around a trailer park in New Mexico with her fourth husband, a retired mailman. A pretty nice old broad, actually, quite funny if a little boozy. The doctors had removed a breast a year ago, but she still smoked a pack and a half a day. Sally worried about her, but not much.

Finally, sipping whiskey, she thought about the cop who had come from Detroit. Mul, his name was. The rest of the name wasn't so easy to recall: -lyzer, or some such. Nice-looking man, she thought. A little sad in the face, but he looked competent and not mean. A woman wouldn't have to look after a man like that, she thought, and he wouldn't beat on you. In fact, a man like that would probably be a bottom-line plus. He'd bring more than he took. She had invited him, and Jacky, to dinner that time, but she hadn't been too surprised when they hadn't accepted: Jacky was married now, and he must have realized that the invitation wasn't really meant for him. And if Jacky didn't accept, then it would have been a little obvious if Mul had. She'd been a little disappointed, but not greatly.

She thought about Mul for a good long time, gently scissoring her legs in the warm water. A nuthatch yank-yanked on the furrowed bark of a nearby ponderosa and then a chickadee flew down and landed quite close to her head. For a while she watched a pure white ermine slipping around the gnarled roots that were exposed among the rocks. Mul had asked her to keep an eye on this place, for any unusual activity. She'd heard that the owner, Humann, was still in the hospital. He might never get better, poor devil. That's what they said in the Tinstar Saloon. Got shot in the head by a hitchhiker, they said. Must be pretty tough, she thought, to survive a bullet in the head.

So, when she couldn't take the heat anymore, she got up and slicked the water off her, then dressed before she could get cold. She set off up the trail. She had not actually walked out of the trees when she realized that there was someone in the cabin. She stopped in the trees to watch. Smoke was coming out the chimney and there was a car in the yard, near the garage. It was a blue Ford, and Sally could read the license plate number—the "1" prefix indicated that it had been registered in Butte–Silver Bow County.

Sally stood and watched for a few minutes, but the wind and the snow swirled around the cabin and it chilled her. She was about to go back down the trail when a woman came out of the cabin. From her position she didn't actually see the woman come out, but she heard the front door open and close. The woman, who had blond hair under a wool hat, walked across the driveway toward the woodpile in the shed/garage. She stopped then and turned to look back toward the cabin. After a moment she started back toward the cabin, but Sally heard the front door open and close, and a larger woman soon joined the first woman and they continued on to the shed. The larger woman loaded the smaller woman's arms with wood, then filled her own arms and followed her back to the cabin. Sally waited a short time, but there was no indication that they were coming back out.

When she got back to the trailer, there were a couple of Christmas cards in her mailbox and the telephone bill. It was still a couple of hours before the kids would be home. She built up the fire and made some tomato soup, using canned tomatoes, which she pureed in the blender, plus some of her own vigorous, garlicky vegetable stock. Her kids loved this soup and so did Sally, though she added a spoonful of hot chili sauce to her bowl. When she had eaten the soup and read the Christmas cards—one of which was from Lake Milling and Feed—she called Jacky at the station.

Jacky Lee was very interested in Sally's observations, not least in the fact that she'd been skinny-dipping in the hot springs. It sounded like something worth doing on a bitter Montana day, but he didn't comment on that. "A blue Taurus?" he said. "That'd be the nurse, Cateyo. She stopped by to get the key to the gate, said she was taking what's-his-name, Humann, up there for a day outing. It's all right. Hell of a day for it. But thanks for letting us know, Sally. I don't know who the other woman could be. Kinda big, hunh?" That didn't sound like one of the other nurses to him. He asked her to describe the woman's clothing. A wool plaid coat didn't mean anything to him, however.

"At first I thought it was a man," Sally said, "but I could tell by the walk, and then I realized that her hair was either short or tucked into the hat. It was a woman, all right. She seemed in charge. She showed the other one how to hold out her arms, then loaded her up, then sent her off. Not real bossy, or anything, just in charge. The smaller one, the blonde, didn't seem to mind, or anything."

Jacky nodded, then remembered he was on the phone and grunted. "You still in the same place?" he asked. "I might run out that way, later."

"Not on my account, I hope," Sally said. "Will you tell Mul about this?"

"Why?"

"Because he asked you to," Sally said.

"No, I mean why shouldn't I stop by?"

"Because I've got kids here and they're older now and I don't do that anymore," she said.

After a long silence, Jacky said, "I'll call Mul."

It was well after five before Jacky got through to the Ninth Precinct. Mulheisen was not there, but Jimmy Marshall was. Jimmy was apologetic. "I meant to call you," he said, "but I just didn't get around to it yet."

"What do you mean?" Jacky asked.

"Mulheisen is on his way to Salt Lake City," Jimmy explained. "I put him on the plane a couple of hours ago. We got a call from Delta. They booked a 'Helena Kaparich' on a flight out of Butte tomorrow, for Salt Lake." He explained about Mulheisen's theory of false names.

"So she's in Butte now," Jacky said.

"I suppose," Marshall said. "Delta didn't have her booked in there, but they suggested we check with Northwest. Northwest didn't have anything on that name."

"Did you check Horizon?" Jacky said. "That's a little feeder airline, flies a lot of flights in the Northwest."

Marshall hadn't. Jacky said he'd check. In the meantime, Mulheisen was planning to stay in Salt Lake City, hoping to intercept Helen there. This time he had a warrant for arrest: Frank Zaparanuk in the forensic lab had found traces of Carmine's blood on one of the sawed-off shotguns that Jacky had confiscated from the cabin. This same gun also surrendered some textile fibers that were identical to those used on the upholstery of Carmine's limousine. In addition there were some fibers from clothing. Mulheisen wanted all of the clothing at the cabin seized. With luck, a jacket or a pair of pants would have traces of blood. The shotgun with Carmine's blood on it also had the fingerprints of Helen and Joe on it. This wasn't as conclusive a piece of evidence as it seemed, but you could sure as hell get a warrant with it. Marshall was busy on the extradition papers now.

Jacky suggested it might be better to intercept Helen in Butte, if possible, since he could guarantee cooperation—the Mario Soper shooting was their jurisdiction, after all. He could work up some kind of preliminary charge relating to the guns they had found at the cabin. Or he might be able, at least temporarily, to detain Helen as a material witness in the death of a man discovered on property where she was a resident.

Marshall agreed with that, but it was up to Mulheisen, who would undoubtedly call him as soon as he reached Salt Lake. "Of course, if she shows up there between now and then, use your own judgment," Marshall said. "But it might be best to coordinate things with Mul."

Jacky assented to that and as soon as Marshall hung up he called Horizon. A "Helena Kaparich" had flown into Butte that morning. Kaparich was by no means an uncommon name in Butte, Jacky knew. Ordinarily he wouldn't have remarked it but for the first name and the information from Marshall. But now what? Was the smaller woman at the cabin Helen Sedlacek, and the larger one Cateyo? Sally's observation could have been simply a comparative thing, but it didn't seem like it. Cateyo could never be mistaken for a man, even momentarily, and he didn't recall her wearing a plaid coat. Sally had mentioned blond hair; presumably that would be Cateyo's golden hair. No, the larger woman at the cabin must be a friend of hers, someone helping her with Humann. So where was Helen Sedlacek? Maybe she was on her way up there, or she may have arrived there by now. He supposed he had better go check.

In the event, it was dark and snowing, and he decided to wait until he heard from Mulheisen. The decision proved critical. Mulheisen called within the hour, and when he heard that Helen had arrived in Butte that morning and that Joe was up at the cabin, he decided to take the last flight for Butte out of Salt Lake City. He would arrive around ten o'clock. The prospects looked good for some kind of break in the case.

Several events conspired to blow this well-laid plan. The first was an arson fire at an abandoned house up near the old Anselmo mine. Jacky spent two hours there and thus was unable to make even a cursory check of local hotels and motels, much less the cabin. If he had, he would have discovered that Helen Sedlacek had checked into the War Bonnet Inn, down near the interstate, not far from the airport. Another event was that when he did get to the airport, he noticed Smokey Stover with three strangers, including a rather portly man to whom they all deferred. He didn't approach the party, but he soon learned from flight service that they had just arrived on a private jet, from Detroit.

The third event was that the runway closed down due to a howling blizzard shortly after nine o'clock. The late flight from Salt Lake City was already airborne. It was forced to go on to Helena, the state capital, some seventy miles north, beyond Elk Park Pass. The north-south interstate highway was not closed, but the bus that Delta had hired to carry passengers to Butte would not arrive before midnight, at the earliest.

What Jacky did not learn, because he was no longer at the airport, was that ten minutes before the runway closed, another private jet from Detroit landed.

In the meantime, things were not going well at the cabin on Garland Butte.

Heather couldn't believe her good luck. A perfect opportunity to accomplish all of her goals at once. It was risky being here. Smokey Stover had told her that Humphrey was very interested in some money that Joe Service had taken. This was the first she'd heard of any money, but it rang true: She'd been skeptical from the start about the need for a hit based on simple retribution. Of course, such hits were ordered, but it was money, big money, that caused them to be long pursued. Smokey hadn't told her how much it was and he'd advised her not to meddle, just hang tight and keep an eye on Joe. From that she deduced that it was quite a bit of money, perhaps $100,000 or more. It wouldn't be easy to hide that kind of money, she thought, and why would Service bother to seriously hide it, anyway? She would find the money—probably in a safe—take care of her contract on Joe Service, and have the delectable Cateyo all to herself.

A sensible person, of course, would have seen that all of these objectives were impossible. Heather was not a sensible person. She was driven nearly crazy in her desire for Cateyo. Weeks of being a roommate had tantalized her beyond endurance. How many times had she blundered into the bathroom during Cateyo's baths, devouring with her eyes those luscious breasts, the curve of those hips, that lovely belly, and the golden hair between the girl's tender thighs? It had nearly endangered the whole project. She could hardly keep her hands off the girl. Her mouth literally watered when she looked at her.

Gloomily, she had learned two crucial things: Cateyo was not susceptible to her affections and she was besotted with this crippled vermin, Joe Service. The stupid girl was unbelievably insane on the subject—she seemed genuinely to believe that Joe was some special avatar of god, sent to her especially, to help him achieve his holy purpose on earth! Heather could tell her a few things about Joe Service, and longed to do so, but that wouldn't further her own purposes.

To be sure, she realized that her task was difficult. The weather helped. They had gotten a late start and the Ford had busted through several shallow but hard-packed snowdrifts on the road up to the cabin. It wasn't difficult, but now that they were here and the fire was blazing, it had begun to snow harder. Heather had been outside a couple of times, returning to advise Cateyo that they might not be so lucky trying to drive out in the dark. She could see that Cateyo was not immune to the charms of being temporarily snowbound. The cabin was cozy, they had brought plenty of food, and there were plentiful supplies in the pantry. Getting out in the daylight would be less difficult than attempting it at night. Cateyo had all of Joe's medications, she could take care of him. Heather also saw that Cateyo was intrigued by the fact that there was only one bed. There was also a couch, a large and comfortable one situated in front of the fireplace. Obviously, the patient should have the bed. It was large, king-size. The couch wasn't really big enough for two.

What did she want herself? She wanted to sleep with Cateyo. She wanted Cateyo to want to sleep with her. But she knew better. So, there was nothing for it. If she couldn't have Cateyo willingly, she would have her nonetheless. It seemed fairly clear. This was the moment. If she could find the money, she'd take care of Service and dally with Cateyo. Tomorrow she would be out of here, with the money. And Cateyo could stay with Joe forever. It was sad, but she couldn't see any other way to achieve her desired ends. Take what you can get. In this case, it was potentially a lot.

Heather set about it directly. They got in plenty of wood. Then she suggested they should stay the night. As anticipated, Cateyo fell in with that idea without protest. The telephone was working, fortunately. Cateyo called the hospital and explained the situation, somewhat exaggerating the snowfall—although by dinnertime it was clear that a storm had definitely set in. The wind had risen and the snow was swirling about the cabin. You couldn't even see the shed anymore.

Joe Service was no problem. He was alert and interested, shuffling about the cabin with his cane, eagerly looking at everything as if he were simply happy to be home. Heather wasn't fooled. She knew he was looking to see what the cops had removed, whether his stash had been discovered. She contrived to watch his progress every second. He ignored her. He didn't like her, she knew, but she was confident that he didn't realize who and what she really was. Cateyo followed him around like a doting mommy, or a little girl with a curious puppy. But eventually he seemed satisfied, Heather was glad to see—the money must still be here—and he allowed Cateyo to tuck him up on the couch with hot chocolate while they listened to CDs of old singers, like Judy Collins and the Beatles. Heather volunteered to make dinner. They paid little attention to her. They were flirting outrageously and almost openly scornful of her presence. Unquestionably, they were looking forward to bedtime. Heather was annoyed, jealous, but she kept her counsel and even opened a couple of excellent bottles of wine, Oregon pinot noirs, to serve with the spaghetti she was making.

Then she made a stunning discovery. She went to the bathroom and while she was washing her hands, she matter-of-factly investigated the medicine cabinet. Her eyes locked on a bottle of sleeping pills prescribed by a physician in Huntington Woods, Michigan, for Helen Sedlacek and filled in a Detroit pharmacy. Evidently, the Sedlacek woman had used hardly any of them. The prescription was more than a year old, but they looked okay.

What a find! She had visions of the two young people doped and totally knocked out. She could leisurely search and just as leisurely make love to an unconscious Cateyo. Sometime in the night Joe Service would wander out into the blizzard and perish. By morning Heather would be gone.

The lovebirds cuddled on the couch, watching the flickering flames and listening to sappy music. They ignored Heather as she ground the tablets and sprinkled them among the grated parmesan cheese. Just to be sure, she stirred more ground tablets into their wine. Then she called them to dinner. She had laid the polished pine table with a checkered tablecloth she had found in a cupboard—perhaps Service had enjoyed this kind of meal with the woman whom Smokey had told Heather about, the one who had disappeared.

The lovebirds ate well. Heather was glad she had not relied

upon the parmesan, for neither of them used much of it. They drank the wine, however. And a half hour later, while she was washing up, they were noticeably drowsy.

"Listen, why don't you kids take the bed?" Heather suggested coyly. "I'll be fine on the couch and I can keep the fire going, though we better turn up the electric heat, just to be on the safe side."

Cateyo fell in with this suggestion with alacrity. She was pretty dozy, however, and Heather had to help them to bed. It was especially pleasant helping Cateyo undress and get into a flannel nightgown that Heather had found in the closet. By the time she said, "Night-night, you two," they were in each other's arms and almost asleep. She strolled back into the living room and poured herself a glass of wine, then sat down before the fire to relax and wait until deep sleep descended.

She set to work before long, starting at the kitchen end of the large main room, systematically opening drawers and looking into every cranny, testing for hidden cavities. Periodically, she would look into the bedroom, to be sure that Cateyo and Joe were sound asleep. They were totally out of it. Looking down at the unconscious Cateyo, she could hardly resist the desire to make love to her. Finally, she swept the girl up into her arms and carried her into the living room. She placed her on the couch and removed her nightgown. She gazed down on the girl lustfully, then knelt beside her.

Love is, of course, blind. Not totally blind, however. Neither Cateyo nor Joe had been quite oblivious to Heather's behavior. On the other hand, Heather had not paid adequate attention to their behavior. She hadn't noticed, for instance, that Cateyo the nurse had restricted Joe's intake of wine. Cateyo hadn't wanted to offend Heather, but she didn't like the way Heather kept pushing the wine at Joe. A man with a brain injury cannot be served alcohol, she felt.

Whenever possible, she surreptitiously emptied Joe's glass into her own. The few sips he managed were not dangerous, she felt. She didn't understand why Heather was trying to get Joe drunk, but she suspected that it had something to do with Heather's obvious lesbian tendencies. These had increasingly made Cateyo nervous in the last few days, and she had decided that if Heather didn't soon leave for Seattle, she would have to ask her to move.

Cateyo was deeply drugged. She did not feel Heather's rough hands on her breasts nor her lips on her belly. Heather moved farther down the unconscious girl's torso and buried her face in the softly scratchy hair. She breathed in deeply, relishing the womanly odor. After a moment of this, she stood up to take off her own clothes. She gazed down at the maddeningly abandoned disposition of Cateyo's body, the arms listlessly akimbo, the legs spread. The girl's mouth was open and she snored gently. Heather had no more than unbuckled her belt when the telephone rang. She froze, staring at the machine while it rang four times. Then the answering machine pinged.

"Hi," said a perfectly healthy Joe Service. "You found me. After the long tone you have two minutes to leave your message. I'll get back to you as soon as I can."

Whoever had called was clearly startled. There was a pause after the tone and then a gruff man's voice said disbelievingly, "Joe?" Then, "Okay, okay. I get it. Helen, this is Humphrey. I got here—somehow. Don't ask me. Whew! Awright. Call me at ———," and he gave Smokey Stover's home phone number. The machine clicked and went silent, except for a tiny "peep" every fifteen seconds, to alert the intended recipient, when he or she came home, that there was a message on the machine.

Heather was transfixed, staring at the telephone, her belt loose. She hadn't even realized that the telephone console contained an answering device.

Joe Service was also surprised. At the sound of his own voice, he sat straight up in bed, the first time he had done that since the curtain. It took him a few seconds to figure out what was going on and then he was grateful that he had not made any other sound.

Joe was not drugged at all, at least not in the way that Heather had intended. Cateyo had given him his usual medications for pain, but he had not imbibed a single ounce of the wine that Heather had been so obviously pushing. He carefully crawled out of bed, wondering where Cateyo had gone. He had fallen asleep thinking, regretfully, that she was too far gone to engage in any games that night, despite the build-up of expectations.

He watched Heather from the shadows of the bedroom, through the door that she had left ajar. She was standing near the couch, staring first at the telephone across the room, which had now silenced, and then looking down at the couch, the back of which was turned toward him. It struck Joe that Cateyo must be on the couch. At one point Heather turned and looked directly at the bedroom. Joe started back involuntarily, then caught himself. She couldn't see him. She was obviously in a quandary, uncertain what to do.

While Cateyo slumbered on, the two conscious minds in the cabin pondered the significance of Humphrey's presence in—well, in where? Butte? It would seem so. Joe took an additional moment to ponder why the Fat Man called himself Humphrey. And both of them wondered why the man was calling the cabin and asking for Helen, who not only wasn't here but hadn't been here in nearly three months. Was she coming here? It seemed likely, a possibility that raised both their pulse rates.

Heather looked down regretfully at the couch again, and Joe decided conclusively that she must be looking at Cateyo, who must be out cold, otherwise she would have responded to the telephone. What had been going on? Now he could hear Cateyo's faint snore. Jesus, he thought, this Heather is too much—hitting on a sleeping girl, could you believe it? He looked at her rapt face and he could believe it.

Heather turned away from the entrancing vision of the girl on the couch and went to the telephone. She stood peering at it for a moment, then reached out and punched a button. The machine whirred and then played back Humphrey's message. The peep stopped and the machine rewound, indicating no messages received. She had erased the message by not saving it. She recognized the phone number, though. It was the one Humphrey had given her when he sent her out to Butte. So he was in Butte.

She picked up the answering machine and turned it about, trying to figure out how it worked. She replaced the machine on the stand next to the door. She considered turning it off or disconnecting it, since she had tampered with the message, but she was reluctant to do that. She stood there irresolutely, hands on hips, looking about the room as if for some sign of what she should do. Finally, she turned and looked over her shoulder at the bedroom door again. Something hardened in her face and she slowly turned her body toward the room and began to remove the unbuckled belt from her wool slacks as she walked purposefully toward the slightly opened door.

She was halfway across the room when the telephone rang again. She whirled and stared. As before, it rang four times and then, while Joe's message was played, there came a couple of beeps and then another tone. This time, instead of a caller giving a message, there was only a long, pregnant silence. Cateyo snored peacefully and Heather took a step toward the phone. The floor creaked and she stopped, gripping and regripping the belt tensely. Then came a single peep and the line disconnected. It was eerie.

After a moment she turned again toward the room where Joe waited, her face more determined than ever. She had hardly taken a step, however, when the phone rang yet again. This time she wheeled and snatched up the receiver on the second ring. "Hello," she said huskily.

As he watched Heather walk toward the room, her rough hands gripping and regripping the belt, Joe Service made up his mind.

Up until that moment he had debated what to do. One part of him said, Get the hell out of there. Another part said, *What about Cate?* Cateyo's all right, she's in no danger. The worst that can happen to her is she'll have an orgasm. *This woman Heather is unstable, she could harm Cate. Cate loves you, she takes care of you.* Cateyo is a certifiable loony who thinks you're the Second Coming. Get the hell out of there. There's a back door out of this room. It might not be easy to open, it might be frozen, but you can get right out of there. *Hey! Isn't this supposed to be Joe Service, Part Two? What's the point of a fresh start if you do the same old run-and-hide shit?* You're in no condition to go up against a bull dyke like Heather, you numskull. Beat it!

A seemingly neutral voice suggested that he could go get help. But the howling of the wind and occasional shudder of the cabin as a powerful gust struck it were not propitious. And when the telephone rang the second time, Joe realized from the eerie silence that someone was listening to the room. When it rang the third time and Heather answered it, Joe picked up his cane and stepped out of the bedroom. What the hell, Joe, he said to himself, what's so new about this?

19

Get Outta Town

The bus that Delta had hired was prompt. It was large, warm, and comfortable. Mulheisen got a good hour of sleep, anyway. They made fair time, winding up over Elk Park, despite howling winds and driving snow, but it was still after midnight when the bus pulled into the parking lot at the Butte airport. Jacky Lee was there to greet him. He had already contacted Mulheisen when he landed at Helena, to tell him about the arrival of the Detroit contingent. Jacky had tracked the men to Smokey Stover's house up on the Hill (actually, he had just assumed they would go there, and so he called a patrol car and asked them to check, which they were able to confirm).

It was like Stover not to live down in the country club neighborhood, where Antoni lived among the power company bigwigs and Butte's most famous citizen, Evel Knievel. Stover had been born in the Patch: He aspired to the Hill. To him, even the country club was The Flat, where the workers lived. He had completely refurbished an enormous mansion on Excelsior Avenue, just off Park Avenue. It had been owned by one of the Copper Kings, as they referred locally to the early mining magnates. Nobody remembered now just which copper king, but he must have had plenty of money. The house had more rooms than Smokey had ever visited, counting the servants' quarters on the top floor. That floor was closed off now.

Smokey put Mr. DiEbola in the huge second-floor guest room. It was called the Tower Room, because formerly a spiral staircase ascended a tower in the corner. Smokey's second wife had called in an architect, or maybe he was just an interior designer, who yanked out the staircase and the floor of the tower room on the third floor, and now there were enormous windows, two tiers of them, that provided a spectacular panoramic view, in good weather, of the Continental Divide on the east, the mountains to the south, and even the mountains to the southwest. None of this was visible this evening. In fact, you could barely see across Excelsior Avenue. Smokey explained the view at length, however, until Humphrey stopped him. "Where's the phone?" he demanded.

What's the point of making plans? That's what Helen asked herself. She was ready to believe that plans don't just go awry, they go so wildly awry that there is really no reason to make them. She had arranged for Humphrey to come to Butte, but now she doubted that he had been able to fly in. She didn't know enough to check with flight service, didn't even know such a thing existed. She didn't want to go out to the airport, in case she would be seen, either by Humphrey or the police—she had no idea if she was wanted by the police, but she assumed so.

Her big idea was to have Humphrey call the cabin when he landed. He would leave a message on the answering machine: a phone number in Butte that she could call to give him further information and set up a mutually satisfactory meeting. That is, a place where she could meet him, alone, without danger to herself. The place she envisioned for this was out on the interstate highway. She considered this plan ingenious. Humphrey would be told to wait for her call tomorrow. He should be ready by eight o'clock (or, if he objected, nine o'clock or later—she had no desire to be unreasonable). At the appointed hour she would call and tell him to drive, alone, out the westbound interstate highway. When he got to the first rest area he should pull in and wait by the telephone. Someone would call him with further instructions.

Terrific plan. She would be parked all the way across the median, off the eastbound lanes. She had driven out there and checked the phone number and the site where she would pull off. She had no way of knowing that it was just a short way from where Joe had stopped for a man hitchhiking with a corpse, in September. She chose it because a car pulled just far enough off the eastbound lanes couldn't be seen from the rest area. She had bought a cellular phone. She would wait until Humphrey got out of the car and she would check it all out with binoculars that she had already bought. If he was alone she would call and tell him to walk across the median to the eastbound lanes. They could either talk in the car or drive somewhere. She wasn't afraid of Humphrey by himself. She still had the Dan Wesson revolver she had taken from the cabin, and she was confident she could use it. They would talk, and if he made the right noises, she was prepared to turn over to him a suitcase filled with a million dollars. She figured she had to give him that much, anyway, along with the prospect of more to come, in order to work out a mutually beneficial deal.

Perfect plan, except for the weather. And the phone. On the plane en route to Butte it had occurred to her that the phone at the cabin might have been disconnected. She had been away for nearly three months. She hadn't paid the phone bill. Would someone else have paid it? Would the phone company have shut it off? The minute she landed, she called U.S. West and was told that the service was still on, but the bill needed to be paid and when did she plan to pay it? She drove immediately to the phone company's local office and paid the bill.

The main point of the plan, however, was that she needn't

even go out to the cabin. She knew this answering machine. It was a new and fancy one that Joe had purchased not long before he took his last "go-go" jaunt. She could call the machine and retrieve the message. It didn't even matter if the machine had been turned off; this machine could be turned on remotely, by tapping a code number into any touch-tone phone.

As soon as she had checked into the War Bonnet Inn motel she called the number. To her delight the machine answered on the fourth ring, which meant there were no messages. It must have been left on the "Auto" setting. Joe's voice said, "Hi. You found me. After the long tone you have two minutes to leave your message. I'll get back to you as soon as I can." It was a little eerie. She tapped in the code number anyway and, as indicated, there were no messages. Good. There was even a procedure for listening to the room with this machine. She punched the "6" button and listened for thirty seconds. Nothing. Silent as a tomb. Also good. She hung up and went out to eat. It wasn't even noon. She spent a couple of hours shopping for the binoculars and phone, as well as some good boots and a warm coat and gloves. She felt prepared.

But by darkfall things began to go wrong. A storm blew in. The chances were that Humphrey would not be able to land. Helen didn't want to hang around in Butte, not knowing if the police were looking for her. Beyond that, if this proved to be a terrible blizzard, it would complicate her plan to meet Humphrey, even if he made it tomorrow. She was too anxious to just sit around and wait. Hell, she had to admit it, she was scared to death. Before, when she and Joe had done Carmine, Joe had been there to make the plans, to coach her, to calm her. It had been exhilarating. But now she could hardly bear to think about Joe. It was his fault she was here, stuck in this rathole town, sitting in some crummy motel waiting to hear from Humphrey.

Joe, of course, was well taken care of, she thought. He would be lying in a quiet, orderly hospital room, surrounded by attentive nurses. And she was paying for it! She was paying a lot for it. She knew it was the least she owed him, but she wished to hell she had never heard of the son of a bitch.

The motel had a bar and she went there after dinner. She hadn't even been able to have a decent dinner, fearing to be seen uptown in the better restaurants. She drove to a lousy fast-food joint and took out a burger and fries to eat in her room. That was when she learned how awful it was outside. The streets were nearly empty, the wind howling and snow drifting fast.

The bar was empty except for herself and a friendly guy who wanted to buy her drinks. He was a local fellow, and he said it might not be as bad as it looked. "These mountain storms can blow in and out in a matter of hours. It could be calm and clear by ten o'clock." She let him buy her a drink. He was nice, but he left a little after nine. He was back in a few moments, saying with a grin of self-congratulation, "What'd I tell ya? Stars are out! No snow. A little windy, still, but it'll drop." While his car warmed up he tossed down a parting shot of whiskey and paid for another for Helen before leaving.

The bartender sniffed, "I wouldn't pay too much attention to what Tim says. It'll blow back in as fast as it cleared. This'll just be a break in the action."

Sure enough, three men came in ten minutes later, stamping their feet and brushing snow off their overcoats. "Kicking up out there?" the bartender asked, cocking an eye at Helen.

"Sheet man, eets a focking bleezzard," one of them exclaimed. "Geev me sometheeng strong." He leaned over the bar, staring at the back bar. "Tequila. That's eet. Vetch," he called to one of the other men, "he's got tequila. Hokay?"

"Si," the one called Vetch replied, "*un grande.*"

They were all very handsome, very young. Helen was glad to see them, so comical with their funny accents. Mexicans, she thought. Rich ones. "Did you just get in?" she asked.

Vetch bowed gallantly to her and said, in nearly accentless English, "Just in the neck of time." He made a swooping gesture with his hand, as of an airplane.

"Nick," Helen said.

"As you say. Nick," Vetch said. He offered to buy her a drink. He had not expected to see such a striking woman in a burg like Butte. She was dressed in black slacks stuffed into the tall black boots, and a black sweater. Her pale face, made paler by her bright red lipstick and half-hidden by her full black hair with its silver stripe, floated alluringly in this ebony setting. "I had not expected to find such beautiful women in Butte, Montana," he said.

"I'm not from Butte," she said quickly.

"Where are you from?" Vetch asked. He sat down next to her.

"Seattle. I'm temporarily stranded," she said, "until the planes fly again."

"And where are you going?"

"New Orleans."

"Oh yes? Well, I may be going to New Orleans. Perhaps I could give you a lift."

"You have a plane?" Helen said. "Your own plane?"

"Of course," Vetch said. He pointed to one of the young men. "That is my pilot. He is a marvelous pilot. He has just landed us when the officials did not advise it. But it was no problem for Hernan. He has been flying since he was twelve years old."

"What kind of plane is it?" Helen asked.

"I don't know. Hernan," he called out, "what is the name of your airplane?"

Hernan smiled. "Carmencita," he said.

"No, you idiot." Vetch laughed. "What is the kind? The typi— the type?"

"Oh, a jet. A Jet Commander."

Helen was impressed. But then alarmed. Three Mexicans flying around in a jet? In Butte. She managed to hold her smile. "And just the three of you in a big jet?" she asked.

"Oh no, no, no, you lovely lady," Vetch said, laughing. "What do you think? This is not a—what do you say?—a passenger jet. At least, it is a passenger jet, but not one of these"—he gestured broadly with his arms—"these big jets. It is a personal jet."

"An executive jet," the bartender supplied.

"Yes," Vetch said, "thank you. It is an executive jet. Plenty of room, even sleeping room, but for just a few people. Executives."

"And you are executives?" Helen asked.

"Of course," Vetch replied with a simple toss of his head.

"Just the three of you, though?"

"Yes. So there is plenty of room for you, when you fly to New Orleans with us. Tomorrow, perhaps, after we have finished our business here. Free of charge. I promise! And champagne!"

"Champagne? Well, I can't miss that, can I?"

"You would be crazy to miss that," he assured her. "You can cash in your ticket and fly with us. Are you staying here?"

"Perhaps," Helen said. She was beginning to think that she might be paranoid. Perhaps these Mexicans were not so sinister, after all. She wanted to believe it. She was so tense, so exhausted.

"Perhaps? More drinks," Vetch demanded. "Hernan, we have a coy lady. Very beautiful, but coy." He liked the word "coy," and repeated it. "Do we have champagne? Yes?" He looked at the champagne the bartender dragged out of the cooler, then shook his head and said, sadly, "No. That is not champagne. Do you have some different kind, some different type?" The next bottle was grudgingly admitted to be champagne, more or less. The bartender opened it and poured into wide glasses, of which Vetch did not approve but which he accepted. He proposed a toast to New Orleans.

"You probably aren't going to New Orleans," Helen said, sipping the champagne. She grimaced and set it aside.

"You are right," Vetch said, responding to her gesture. "This is not good champagne. Do we have any other?"

The bartender shook his head. "The package store might have some. Want me to look?"

"Yes, look," Vetch said, "but give us first some of that cognac, that Hennessey's. That is good cognac, I think." When they had been served and the bartender had left, he said to Helen, "Of course, we are going to New Orleans. Hernan! Are we not going to New Orleans?"

"If you like," Hernan said.

"But you have business," Helen said. "I would probably find myself stuck here for days while you do your business. I don't want to hang around Butte. What is your business, anyway?"

"Our business?" Vetch shrugged. He turned to the bartender who had reentered, triumphantly holding up two bottles of French champagne. "What is the business in Butte, Montana? Yes, that looks wonderful. Open one bottle. We will have both bottles, but just open one for now."

Busying himself with untwisting the wire on the cork, the bartender said, "Butte's business is mining. Used to be, anyway."

"Mining? What kind of mines?" Vetch asked. "Gold mines?"

"Oh, there's gold here, all right. Butte started as a gold camp. Then it was copper. But there's plenty of gold still down there, you bet. Ah." The cork popped off nicely and the bartender set up fresh glasses.

"We are gold miners," Vetch said. "To gold!" He hoisted his glass and the others followed.

"Yes, gold!" Hernan exclaimed. "Colombian gold."

Helen caught Vetch's frown and Hernan's instant reaction. Drug dealers, she thought. Who would have thought that Butte would have drug dealers?

"Any kind of gold," Hernan said, quickly. "We collect gold."

"Oh, you're collectors, then," she said.

"Please, that is enough of business," Vetch said with a grimace of mock boredom. "I am tired of business. Tonight we will drink champagne. Tomorrow, we will have time for business and then on to New Orleans, where it will be much warmer, I am certain. Is there any good restaurants?"

"Well, there's Lydia's," the bartender said, glancing at his watch. "Great Italian food." He said "eye-talian." "But you better call. I bet they're closing, if they haven't already."

There was no way that Helen was going to an Italian restaurant, not if there was any chance that Humphrey was in town, but she quickly said, "What's the number? I'll call."

The bartender fished a telephone book out of a drawer and looked. He went to the end of the bar and reached around to pick up a telephone. "No, I'll call," Helen said, jumping up and moving quickly down to the end of the bar. "They'll just tell you no, but I can talk them into it. What's the number?"

The telephone was on the wall, next to a swinging door that led to a backroom. She made the bartender repeat the number and then she quickly tapped out the number of the cabin. The number rang once . . . twice . . . three times, and on four the machine answered: There were no messages. Helen quickly tapped in the code and after a long beep she punched the number "6" and listened to the room.

At first she didn't hear anything, but then she thought she heard a crackling sound. What could it be? A fire? This was followed by something that sounded for all the world like someone snoring. And then she was sure she heard a faint creaking noise. The hair rose on her neck. A beep signaled the end of thirty seconds. She depressed the hang-up device on the base unit without taking the receiver from her ear. For a long moment she stood and stared at the phone. Had she actually heard anything? It must have been her imagination. She peeked around the corner. The three men were talking and laughing. Without hesitation she redialed the number. After the first ring, the receiver was lifted and a low woman's voice said, "Hello?"

"Hello?" Helen replied, shocked. She recovered quickly. "Who is this?" she asked.

After a pause, the woman said, "Who is this? You called me."

"Is this ———," and Helen recited the number.

"Yes," the woman said, tentatively, "who is this?"

For the first time it occurred to Helen that Joe might have recovered, that he might have left the hospital and be convalescing at the cabin. Presumably, he wasn't being held by the police, although she couldn't imagine the circumstances under which this might happen. But then she thought, They never found the body! They have no reason to hold Joe. This must be a nurse. But why hadn't they answered when she called earlier? They must have been busy, in the bathroom, perhaps.

Quickly, she asked, "Is Joe there?"

After another pause, the woman said, "Yes, Mr. Service is here."

"Oh good." Helen waited, then she said, "Well, can I talk to him?"

"At this hour? I'm afraid he's asleep."

"Is this the nurse?"

"Yes," Heather said.

"Can't you wake him? It's very important."

"I'm afraid he's taken some pills, some sedatives," Heather said. "I can't wake him now. You'll have to call back in the morning." And she hung up.

Helen went back to the bar, a little dazed. The three men looked at her with expectant smiles. "That was a long conversation," Vetch said. "You must have convinced them. Shall we go? We'll take the champagne."

"What? Oh, no," Helen said. "I tried to talk them into staying open, but they . . . they already closed. The cooks have gone home. Sorry."

"Oh, too bad," Vetch said. "Oh well, we must make the best of it. At least we have champagne. And cognac! Come, sit down."

Helen sat down and drank cognac, followed by champagne. She felt drunk. She shook her head to clear it. Amazing, she thought, Joe is recovered. Or recovering, anyway. He's home! It was difficult to comprehend. Why hadn't she thought of this eventuality? Plans, indeed. What was the use of even making plans? But, she thought, Joe could help. She had gotten so used to being without him, to cursing him, in fact, that she had never considered what to do if he recovered. Now she would have to rethink everything, all of her stupid plans. She felt compelled to leave, immediately. Get rid of these crazy Mexicans and get back to her room so that she could think. But first she must be congenial. She took another sip of cognac and smiled at Vetch.

"Do you know," she said, "I am getting the most terrific headache. I—" But the telephone had rung, and now the bartender called out a name.

"Mr. Etcheverry?"

"Echeverria," Vetch corrected. "Excuse me, lovely lady," he said to Helen, and went to the phone.

Helen paid little attention. A singular notion had just struck her. The woman, the nurse, had said, "Mr. Service."

She got up quickly, saying, "Excuse me, I have to use the powder room," to Hernan, and she snatched her purse and walked out.

The blizzard was back. It was bitter cold as she raced across the parking lot, leaping through knee-deep drifts to reach her room. She was glad for the boots she had purchased earlier. She quickly gathered everything into her suitcase and donned the warm coat. Then she hauled the suitcases out and threw them into the backseat of the car she had rented. In the swirling snow she saw the three Mexicans come out of the bar, raising the collars of their overcoats and looking around. They were looking for her, she knew it. She slumped down in the seat of the car. The windows were iced and nearly opaque. She was able to watch them over the sill of the driver's side window as they stumbled and minced through the deep snow, the wind lashing the tails of their coats about them. When they disappeared around the side of the building, evidently searching for their rooms, she quickly started the car and frantically turned up the heat and the defroster fan. She waited tensely while the car warmed up and a little semicircle of defrosted windshield appeared, watching to see if the men reappeared.

After a long couple of minutes, she decided that they had gone to their rooms, and she put the automatic transmission into reverse. The car, a new Mercury, rolled smoothly backward and then bogged down in a drift. She wished to hell she had her little four-wheel-drive pickup. She'd be able to move through this stuff with ease. She moved the gear selector and went forward, turning. The car responded and gradually, shifting back and forth, she was able to turn around and head out the parking-lot exit, toward Harrison Avenue, the large main thoroughfare. She switched on her headlights. What she saw was not encouraging. There were almost no vehicles on the street, which was filled with deep snow, with a couple of wheel-marked lanes that were fast filling in with drifting snow. No sensible person would willingly be out in this mess. But she had to be out. Butte was not a safe place.

She wheeled to the left, the heavy car battering through the drifted ruts. She drove south a short distance and turned onto the entrance ramp to the interstate highway. There was no traffic, but large trucks had been through and the lanes were passable. In places the winds had even swept the pavement bare. At thirty-five miles per hour she was soon on the outskirts of Butte, headed west. She had no idea where she was going, just that she was getting out of town. She wasn't sure how far it was to Missoula; the large overhead sign had been plastered with snow and unreadable. Two minutes later, the question was moot.

The car traveled swiftly through a bare spot and then smacked into a particularly hard, wind-packed drift that caused it to swerve left. Helen overcorrected and the car spun right. Finally it ran straight, wallowing through deep snow until it stopped dead on the right shoulder. She sat for a long moment, recovering her wits. She switched on the radio and listened to, of all things, a jazz program from Detroit that was being rebroadcast on a local station. The disc jockey was Ed Love. She actually knew Ed Love, had met him anyway, at a party in Southfield. He was talking about Kenny Burrell, the Detroit guitarist, in his precise manner, a kind of restrained enthusiasm. It was strangely encouraging to hear Ed Love while sitting in a rented car, stuck in a snowbank outside Butte, Montana. Once again, however, she longed for the yellow Toyota pickup that Joe had bought for her present.

She tried backing the car, and while it would move, it wouldn't move far. And each time she went forward, it seemed to slip farther off the roadway. She had a tantalizing notion that it might be possible, given time, to rock the vehicle out of this jam; it might also be drifting deeper and deeper into immurement. Suddenly, the night was ablaze with flickering blue and red lights. "Oh no," she sighed, and shifted to "park."

A highway patrolman appeared next to the window. He was bundled up in an insulated coat and a hat with flaps. The flaps were not down. She rolled down the window.

"You'll never get out of there," he said, nearly shouting in the wind. "Where are you headed?"

"Missoula," she yelled.

"Even if you got out, you'd have a tough time making it," he told her. "If you want, I can take you back to Butte. You got friends?"

"No," she said. "Couldn't you give me a push?"

He shook his head, then buried it in his hunched shoulders. "You better come with me."

She gave up then, or would have, but another vehicle pulled

up alongside. It was a four-wheel-drive rig with big wheels. On the door was a silver shield inscribed BUTTE–SILVER BOW SHERIFF. A deputy leaned across and rolled down a window. He yelled at the state cop, "Carl, whatta you doing? Try'na pick up girls again?" He laughed and rolled up the window, then pulled the vehicle forward several feet and got out. He waved his hand at Helen to stay in her car while he opened the back door of his rig and hauled out a heavy chain. With the help of the highway patrolman, he pushed away enough snow to get down on his knees and hook the chain to the towing loop under the front of the Mercury. The state cop hooked the other end to the sheriff's Blazer while the deputy got back in. The cop stood and waved Helen forward as she gunned the engine, and the deputy's vehicle methodically ground forward. Within seconds the Mercury was safely standing on the windswept pavement. A minute later the cop had unhooked the chain and thrown it in the back of the sheriff's vehicle. He went to talk to him for a moment, then the deputy drove off. The cop came back to Helen.

"Thank you so much," she told him.

"No problemo," he said, "but you better not take a chance, going on. You take this next exit here"—he pointed up the road, into the swirling snow—"it's not five hundred yards. It'll take you right back into Butte. The deputy said a plow was just through there, so you shouldn't have any problem."

"Thank you, officer." Helen drove into the gloom and took the exit. She drove slowly and soon discovered that the cop had not followed her. As promised, the road into Butte was relatively open, though already drifting badly. She soon came to a moderately cleared major street, Montana Avenue. Down to her right, toward the interstate, she saw a county snowplow. She turned and went after it. When it turned onto the interstate she followed. It headed east. By hanging well back she could keep the rotating yellow light on the plow's cab in sight, despite the fact that the vehicle was enveloped in a cloud of snow. She followed the plow right on up and over the summit at Homestake Pass.

East of the summit the intensity of the snow dropped off considerably, and by the time she reached the first exit, it had stopped. The wind still blew, but the roads weren't bad. She took the exit and headed south, toward Tinstar.

Who was up at the cabin who knew Joe's real name? She wasn't sure, but the fact that it was a woman was encouraging, she felt. It must be a nurse. Joe must have told her his name. He must be there. She wondered if Humphrey had called. If Joe was there at the time, no message would have been recorded, and anyway, if Joe was really there, it was a whole new ballgame.

She could, of course, be rushing to her doom. Humphrey could be sitting there in the cabin with some bimbo and a brace of gunmen. In a situation like that, she had no doubt that Humphrey would throw her to the dogs. She wouldn't have a chance.

Nah, she thought, Joe's there. It'll be all right. And anyway, I can take care of myself. Besides, she had no place else to go.

20
Lock and Load

Humphrey was sound asleep when the phone rang distantly. At first he didn't know where he was, then he saw the snow in the lighted window and heard the wind buffeting the house. He was in Butte. He shuddered. The phone did not ring again. He snuggled under the down quilt and reveled in the warmth. He fell back asleep.

Fifteen minutes later he awoke to a knock on the bedroom door. "Who is it?" he grumbled. It was Rossamani. He said it was important. Humphrey switched on the bedside light. It was after eleven, according to his watch, which he had laid out on the doily under the lamp. "All right," he said.

Rossamani was still fully dressed. "Boss, we got a line on the broad," he said.

Humphrey sat up. He wore blue silk pajamas. He yawned. "So, she finally called back," he said.

"No, it was some of Smokey's boys," Rossamani said. "They think they might have a lead on where she's hanging out. You want me and Tino to go check it out?"

This was not an accurate account of the situation. Earlier, after Humphrey had gone to bed, Rossamani had called Vetch at the War Bonnet Inn, as arranged, and in the course of conversation, they had talked about Helen, of course. Vetch had no idea what the woman looked like, and when Rossamani described her as a small woman, the Basque quickly said, "Black hair with a silver stripe?"

Rossamani couldn't believe it. It was too good to be true. But then, Butte wasn't exactly a huge metropolis, and the War Bonnet was a convenient motel for air travelers. Rossamani told Vetch to grab the woman and call him back. Unfortunately, the call had not come for some time and then it wasn't gratifying. Obviously, the woman had tumbled to who Vetch was and had fled. The question was, Where would Helen go if she ran? Especially on a night like this. Another motel? Maybe, but she might just go to the place she'd shared with Service. At this point, Rossamani had turned to Smokey.

Stover knew nothing about Joe Service's cabin, but he thought Heather might know. Rossamani had tried to contact her earlier, just to see how she was getting along with Joe, but no luck. Now he sent Tino and one of Smokey's guys to Cateyo's house. They soon reported back that there were no lights on and nobody answered the door. Should they enter the house? Rossamani told them no, to come on back. Smokey said the Yoder woman was a nurse at the hospital. He called the hospital and, after laying out a farcical story about an uncle who had come to town only to find his favorite niece not home, he learned that she had taken the patient Joe Service to his home. Because of the storm, she had called in to tell them she and the patient were staying overnight. The hospital didn't know the exact location of the cabin, but it was in the Tinstar area. They gave him the phone number. The same number that Helen had given Humphrey.

Rossamani's account to Humphrey left out all reference to Vetch and his friends, of course. Otherwise, it was accurate.

"Very interesting," Humphrey said. "You've done good, Rossie. The trouble is, it don't make sense."

"Why is that, Boss?"

"Well, it sounds like our little Helen is still working with Joe. But if she's working with Joe, why did she contact me in the first place? Joe would know what to do with the money, and he sure as hell wouldn't want her talking to me. No, something else is going on, but you might be right: She might have gone to meet Joe at their old hideout. Smokey doesn't know where it is?"

"Not exactly," Rossamani said, "but this Tinstar isn't a big place, Humphrey. We oughta be able to find it." He nodded toward the windows. "It's hell out there, though. Maybe we oughta just call. Heather's there. She oughta be in control of the situation." This was a less than candid proposal, a strawman, and Rossamani was pleased to hear Humphrey demolish it.

"No, no," Humphrey said, waving away the suggestion impatiently. "Hell, for all we know, Joe has already heard the message I left on his machine and he knows I'm in town. He'll be on the lookout for sure. And this Heather . . . who knows if she's on top of it? If Joe is well enough to go out on day trips, he's probably popped her by now. No, you and Tino better go out there. But leave Smokey here—he knows enough about our business already, and the more he knows the more it costs us. Take one of his guys, someone who knows the territory. When you find the place, don't do anything, just call me and keep an eye on the joint. Or maybe you could send Smokey's guy back. We can figure out what to do from there."

This was precisely as Rossamani preferred it, except for the idea of not doing anything once they found out where Joe and Helen were holed up. And, of course, Vetch and his hands would ride along. Why, if you looked at it that way, Rossamani told himself, it was like a goddamn posse. He was especially hoping the broad, Helen, would be there. This could be fun if she and Joe didn't want to talk.

Mulheisen was dead tired and cold. He couldn't remember when he'd been so cold. He had worn normal winter clothes on leaving Detroit—a hat, an overcoat, a scarf. There was no snow on the ground in Detroit, although the temperature had been hovering around freezing ever since Thanksgiving. Salt Lake had been a little colder, but he wasn't aware of it since he'd never left the terminal. But just walking to the bus in Helena, and what he'd seen out the windows of the bus en route to Butte, had frankly scared him. Walking to Jacky's Blazer at the airport and sitting huddled in the vehicle while it warmed up had been enough to convince him that nothing would happen tonight. He would go directly to the Finlen Hotel and get a good night's sleep and then, in the morning, they could go out and round up the crooks. That was his plan.

Jacky Lee had a different plan. He too had thought that nothing would happen on such a brutal night, but then he had monitored a radio broadcast from another sheriff's deputy, concerning a woman in a rented Mercury stuck on the westbound Interstate 90. A highway patrolman had overheard Jacky's subsequent query and responded with the information that the woman had returned to Butte. From his description, the woman was Helen. But if she had returned to Butte, where was she? Jacky put out a bulletin to all law enforcement and emergency vehicles on the Mercury, whose license number the highway patrolman had dutifully logged. Soon enough, a plow driver, who had stopped at the rest area on Homestake Pass, reported that a woman in a Mercury had followed him into the rest area and had then gone on eastbound on I-90. Why the woman had been westbound in the first place wasn't at all clear, but if she was now eastbound, she was at least headed in the general direction of Tinstar.

When Mulheisen heard all this, he asked, "Did Service return from his jaunt to the cabin?"

They quickly learned that he had not. They visited Smokey's Corner. It was nearly empty, except for a couple of hardy drinkers. The barmaid said Smokey was at home, but one of the drinkers, whom Jacky knew from high school, said that Smokey's day barman had been in a while earlier, with two strangers in overcoats. "City boys," the drinker said. "They were going somewhere, in a real hurry. I tol'em, 'Ain't a fit night out for man nor beast.'"

"Amen to that," said the other drinker. "A man'd be crazy . . . a man'd have to be some kinda nut . . ." The man babbled on, hoisting a glass of beer.

The other one broke in, "Jacky? Jacky? Cal was pickin' up the Suburban."

The night bartender conceded that she had given the keys to Smokey's Chevy Suburban—a four-wheel-drive vehicle that Smokey usually kept parked at the bar, to transport beer and booze and other items—to Cal, the day man. Smokey had called to say it was all right. No, they didn't say where they were going.

"Well, we know where they're going," Jacky said to Mulheisen when they were back in the car. "Your guy, DiEbola, is in town with his heavies, and he must have found out that Joe was up at the cabin. I guess Helen's gone up there, too."

Mulheisen had to agree with this assessment. The problem was, what should they do about it?

Jacky shrugged. "We gotta go up there," he said, flatly.

Mulheisen sighed. "Yeah. Okay. But not like this."

"Right," Jacky said. "I'll get you some warm gear. And, of course, we'll have to tell the undersheriff. We'll need help, Mul. You got Service"—he ticked them off on his fingers—"Helen, at least two shooters from out of town . . ."

"Jacky, no sieges," Mulheisen said. "That's a surefire way to get people killed. No SWAT teams."

"The undersheriff has to know what's going on, Mul," Jacky said. "He'll call the DEA, the FBI . . ."

"No, Jacky," Mulheisen shook his head.

"How 'bout," Jacky considered, "you, me, Conlin—that's the resident patrol down there. It's almost impossible to keep radio contact on the other side of the pass. We can contact Conlin when we get over the top."

"Is he a good man?"

"She's very good," Jacky said. "But Mul, we gotta tell the undersheriff something. The sheriff's out of town, and this guy figures on running against him in the next election. He'd never forgive me if I cut him out of it. He won't be able to get the Feds down there before morning, anyway. We could say we're going down to keep an eye on the situation, monitor it . . . make sure nobody tries to leave."

They discussed it further while they drove to the station, refining their scheme. As predicted, the undersheriff wanted to mount an all-out assault team. He was severely hampered, however, by the hour and the weather. After much argument, he agreed to send Jacky and another deputy, Steve Minervini, and they could pick up Carrie Conlin in Tinstar. He would get to work on alerting the rest of the team. With any luck, they could be in place by dawn, which was only a few hours away.

"But if there's any shooting," the undersheriff warned, ". . . well, there better not be any shooting. If they want to leave, let them leave, but follow them." He shook his head. "This weather's no good for a chopper, but maybe it'll break by dawn."

Joe Service brought the cane down on Heather's head with every ounce of strength he could muster. The cane splintered, but she fell like an ox. He hobbled to the fireplace as fast as he could, merely glancing at the lusciously naked Cateyo, sprawled oblivious on the couch, as he passed. Oh my, he thought. He snatched up the heavy iron poker and hurried back to finish the job, but his rage had dissipated and he couldn't bring himself to use the poker. Perhaps it was the sight of Cateyo that had blunted his fury. He stood and trembled for a moment, then tossed the poker aside. He had never experienced such rage, he thought. The doctor had warned him that he might be subject to such quirks of emotion. People who had suffered brain injury often developed strange shifts of emotion and behavior. But it had gone as quickly as it had come. He was thankful that it had come, for he wasn't certain that he could have mustered the force to act, otherwise.

But now he had work to do. He had no idea what Helen was up to, nor the Fat Man, but he had an overwhelming drive to get the hell out of there. He tried to rouse Cateyo, but she was sluggish and wouldn't come awake. At last, he went to the kitchen and fetched a glass of water, which he tossed full in her face. That got her. She spluttered and sat up.

"Paul! Paul, what is . . . my clothes! What is going on?"

"Get up, babe," Joe snapped, "and quit calling me Paul, for chrissake! Listen, we've got to get out of here."

Cateyo staggered to her feet, her arms crossed on her breasts. Then she saw Heather. "Good heavens!" she cried. "What happened?" She darted to the fallen woman's side and gingerly touched her bloodied head. She looked around wildly and spied the fractured cane. "Pau— Joe! What have you done?"

Joe had hobbled to the bedroom and returned with some clothes, which he flung at Cateyo. "Had to do it, babe," he said, more calmly than he felt. "We've got to get out of here. Get dressed."

Cateyo yanked on a sweater and jeans, all the while talking at Joe. "We've got to help her, Joe. She's hurt."

"She was about to hurt us," Joe said, pulling on a coat. "Help me with these boots."

Cateyo came to assist him, still asking, still demanding answers. Joe ignored her, telling her to get some warm clothes on. He went to the kitchen and rummaged about in drawers, frantically, until he came up with a roll of duct tape. "This'll have to do." While Cateyo finished dressing he knelt and bound Heather's wrists behind her with the tape, then did the same for her ankles. "She'll be all right," he snarled over his shoulder. "Get dressed! We've got to get out!"

And then he was pushing her out into the screaming wind and shocking cold. "Jesus," he yelled, "this is even worse than I thought!

Get the car started." He pushed her toward the car, which had been pulled into the shed. He realized he would need a flashlight. When he went back into the cabin to get the big dry-cell light he kept near the door, he saw that Heather had moved. She groaned. Joe gave her a kick in the head and she fell silent. Then he limped out, slamming the door behind him. He seemed to be having a little trouble moving his right leg. He could see that Cateyo had gotten the car started, the exhaust torn away by the furious wind. She got out of the car, and he yelled for her to come with him.

Together they slogged through the snow drifts, into the biting wind, up the trail behind the house until they came to the old mine. He kicked around in the snow until he found the rock and retrieved the key. While Cateyo held the light, he fumbled the key into the lock and let them into the vault. It wasn't exactly warm inside, but it was out of the weather. Cool and dry. There was a peculiar odor, not strong, but insistent. Joe sniffed. He shook his head, dismissing it.

"Joe, what are we doing here?" Cateyo demanded. "I have to know. Are we in danger?"

"Yes," he snapped. "We're up to our asses in it, babe. Here, help me with these boxes." And then he saw the corpse. It was the same guy, the hitchhiker out on the highway, just before the curtain came down. His hat was askew on his disheveled head, his feet splayed out before him. Joe couldn't see the man's face, but he knew it. He reeled, a horde of images crowding in on him.

With incredible control he turned, blocking Cateyo's view. She had not seen the corpse, or if she had, she must have thought it was just a pile of old clothes and gear. Joe thrust a cardboard box of money at her and snatched the light from her hand, directing the beam toward the door.

"Here," he gasped, "take this down to the car. Wait there for me. I'll be down in a moment. Can you find your way without the light? Just follow the tracks. Hurry!" He pushed her out of the doorway.

When she had gone, stumbling through the drifting snow, he returned to the mine. He peered at the corpse. The face was withered and drawn, dried out. Joe couldn't repress the thought that here was a man who, if not exactly risen from the grave, seemed remarkably well-preserved. A mummy actually. He couldn't begin to speculate on how it had come about. Dry air? Cool temperature? He must have lost all or most of his blood soon after death. And damned mobile for a corpse, too.

But he had no time for this. He turned to his task. There was another whole box of money here, but there were also some guns. He couldn't carry both. Which was more valuable, at the moment? He decided on the guns. He was rummaging among them, trying to make a selection, when he heard a noise. He turned to the door, fearing that Cateyo had disobeyed him and returned.

Heather stood in the door. She lunged at Joe. They fell to the floor together, tussling. Heather's powerful hands locked on Joe's throat. They were icy cold, the grim grip of death. "Die, you little freak!" she grunted.

Joe was on the verge of blacking out. He lashed out with the lantern. It caught Heather on the side of the head and she tumbled sideways, into the lap of the corpse. She looked around and then screamed as the light fell on the dead man's face. Joe bashed her again. The lantern flickered and went out as Heather slumped.

Joe disentangled his legs from her's—or were they the dead man's?—and crawled on his hands and knees toward the door, which was little more than a glimmer of lighter darkness. When he was outside, back in the howling blizzard, he slammed the door shut and floundered down the snowy path.

He was almost to the cabin when he stumbled over Cateyo. She lay in a heap in the snow. Joe struggled to arouse her. She had been choked into unconsciousness and then idly tossed aside, but she wasn't dead. With enormous effort Joe got her to her feet and they managed to stagger to the cabin. Joe poured a glass of brandy and made her drink some. She spluttered and pushed the glass away.

When she had recovered somewhat she began to wildly recount what had happened. "My god, Joe, she tried to strangle me! I thought I was dead! What's wrong with her? Has she gone insane? She kept asking where you had gone. I wouldn't tell her and then I just . . . I just . . ."

"That's all right, babe," Joe assured her. "You did okay."

"Where is she?" Cateyo suddenly panicked. "She'll find us!"

"She's out there, looking for us," Joe said. "We've got to get the hell out of here." Cateyo was eager to fly. He told her to back the car out of the shed, he'd be right behind her. As soon as she was out the door he hobbled to the little closet off the kitchen. He slid back the concealed panel and looked at the array of switches. He sighed. He'd known when he had installed this apparatus that one day he would have to activate it. He hated the thought. He'd loved this place. But he'd always known he couldn't have it forever.

Some day the killers would come. They had come at a bad time. That's the way it always happens, he supposed. He hadn't been here to deal with them and when he did get here, he wasn't functioning very well. Well, he was a prudent man. Some might call him paranoid, but that was not the way he saw it. Be prepared. He hoped his preparations were adequate. Now he had to concentrate to remember the exact activating sequence. But it was confusing. He was blocked. He just couldn't get going with it. Long, long seconds flowed by, swept by. He almost screamed in frustration. It just wouldn't come to him.

And then he smiled and stepped back. Don't think about it, he told himself. Just do it; it'll come. He reached out . . . and his fingers did what was necessary. They flipped this switch, pressed that button, threw another switch, and that was that. He slid the panel closed and went out.

The wind was still roaring but there didn't seem to be as much snow and the car was out of the shed, turned around, and aimed down the road. He huffed up the trail and found the box that Cateyo had been lugging. He carried it down to the car. Cateyo was behind the wheel, anxiously craning around, looking for Heather. Joe put the box in the rear seat and climbed in next to her. "Let's go, babe," he said. Cateyo needed no urging. She powered forward. It was so lovely and warm inside, Joe almost fainted with gratitude. But he roused himself and kept a lookout as Cateyo steered the car slowly down the mountainside, busting through the occasional drifts. The wind had swept the road relatively clear. They made the highway with no great difficulty.

"Which way?" Cateyo said, as they bumped across the Garland Ranch cattle guard.

"Right," Joe said. And they turned toward the Ruby Valley and Salt Lake City.

After a while, when they were both sufficiently warmed and calm, Cateyo said, peering into the flying snow, "Do you think she'll be all right?"

"She'll be fine," Joe said. "She'll be back in the house, by now, drinking wine and wondering how she's going to get home."

But Heather wasn't in the house. She was in the pitch-black tomb with a dead man. She was cold, but not freezing. There were blankets and warm gear. But the door, when she found it, would not open. It had locked when Joe slammed it shut. She lunged against it with her shoulder, time and again, but it was solid, gave no hint of yielding. She told herself not to panic, to take her time. She would investigate this tomb. There would be something in here that she could use to attack the door. Just don't panic.

Outside, the tracks in the snow soon drifted over.

Joe glanced at the backseat. The box sat there, safely. He smiled and slumped back. In a little while, perhaps minutes, perhaps hours, someone would come to the cabin and they'd begin to tear it apart. Soon enough, they would find the security panel in the utility closet and a couple of red lights would convince them it was on, that there was an alarm system. He was confident that they would throw the On-Off switch. They might even throw it back on. It didn't matter. If the system wasn't armed, as he had just done, it wouldn't make a difference, nothing would happen. But when it *was* armed, unless you punched in the disarming code, an internal switch would open a little valve on the propane line just a couple of feet from where it passed through the concrete foundation, and the odorless gas would seep into the sealed crawl space under the house. Because the gas was heavier than air it would begin to pool. After a time a short circuit would occur in a section of the wiring that provided power to the electric hot-water heater. This would cause the insulation of the wiring to smolder and ignite some noxious chemicals. Fumes would issue upward. This was a kind of early warning device, a humane device in Joe Service's mind. It would alert the intruders; it should, in fact, drive them out of the house. He sincerely hoped so. He hoped nobody would be in the house when the spluttering line finally burned through and fell into the pooling propane. The explosion would be very destructive. It would also mask another, simultaneous explosion up on the ridge above the old mine. Several tons of rocks would shift down the hill, forever masking the mine entrance. The house and any evidence about Joe Service would be completely destroyed, aided by a few judicious incendiary devices here and there. Joe was fairly confident that only the shrewdest arson investigator would ever figure it out, except to say, "Aha! Leaky propane line, faulty wiring. Case closed."

At least he didn't have to worry about Helen fussing with the panel. He'd tried to explain it to her once, but she'd only rolled her eyes and said, "You and your security. I wouldn't touch it with a ten-foot pole."

* * *

"Joe," Cateyo said as they reached Interstate 15 and turned south, the road clear and stars shining overhead, "what happened back there?"

"Honey, I'm dead," Joe said. "Why don't you drive until you get tired, then wake me up. I think I can drive this thing and I'll tell you all about it when I wake."

"No," Cateyo said. She pulled over to the side of the road and stopped. It was clearing, no longer snowing. The car trembled from the buffeting gusts of wind. The stars were brilliant. They had stopped very high up in the valley and all about them lay vast sweeps of rising land. Only an occasional ranch light gleamed. "Joe," she said, "I can't do this. I can't just drive away. You have to tell me. What happened and where are we going?"

Joe liked that. He smiled. She couldn't do this, but she wanted to know where they were going. "Okay," he said, "just keep driving and I'll tell you." He looked out the window at the beautiful wind-swept snow, the mountain range beyond. It looked like wolf country to him.

"We're going to a new life, babe. You and me. The new man and the new woman. Salt Lake City. The land of the dead . . . or where they keep the names of the dead, anyway. I'll tell you all about it."

"Will we get married?" Cateyo asked suddenly. It was a bold question. She didn't dare glance at him, but looked straight down the road.

"Married? Hmmm. I hadn't thought about it. Do you want to get married?"

"Oh, I don't know," Cateyo said. "Maybe."

"What an idea. We'll have to think about it."

21
Heat

Helen was surprised to find tire tracks on the road to the cabin. Actually, not so much tracks as places where a car had broken through drifts, and fairly recently. The drifts were nearly filled in again, but it still made it easier for her to get up the hill. She couldn't imagine what would have driven Joe out of the cabin, but it occurred to her that the nurse might simply have decided to take her patient back to town. Perhaps he'd had a turn for the worse. Well, she would soon find out. Both the gates were open and the yard was empty when she arrived. She slipped the Dan Wesson into her pocket, along with some spare cartridges.

Warily, she entered the cabin. Lights were on and it was quite warm, the electric heaters having adequately compensated for a fire that had dwindled to embers in the fireplace. No one was home, although the cabin was in some disorder. It was a mystery. They had left in a hurry.

Helen didn't care. She was dog tired. She was just as glad that Joe had gone back to the hospital, taking his grouchy nurse with him. She needed rest. She built up the fire and poured herself a hefty shot of scotch whiskey. There were no messages on the machine, she no-

ticed. She also noticed, with distaste, that Joe and his nurse had left
without making the bed. And—she picked up one of her flannel
nightgowns, left crumpled on the bed, holding it at arm's length on a
fingertip—the bitch had worn her nightgown!

Why, that lousy prick, she thought. He screwed that nurse. In
her bed! No wonder they bolted. Joe must have figured out she was
coming up here, and he couldn't face her. So he couldn't be wakened,
eh? If she hadn't been so angry, she would have laughed. But there
was also a little pang of jealousy.

A flicker of light caught her eye. Headlights on the road. Humphrey! In a panic she grabbed her coat and gloves and raced into the
bedroom. The sliding glass door that opened onto the back deck was
frozen shut. She yanked and strained, almost in tears. There was no
way she was going to be caught in this cabin by Humphrey and his
goons. Just when she was about to give up, the door cracked free and
slid open. She quickly slipped out and into the storm. She stumbled
through the snow, up behind the house until she reached the trees.
Then she stopped and looked back.

A large four-wheel-drive vehicle entered the yard and parked
directly behind her rented Mercury. Three men, none of whom she
recognized, got out and cautiously approached the house. They had
guns in their hands. One of them split away and started around the
side, toward the back. With a sinking heart she realized that he would
see her tracks and follow her up into the trees. She drew back farther
into the trees, prepared to run. But where? It was so cold, the wind so
cruel.

The mine! Yes, she thought, she could hide in the cache, safe
out of the bitter howling wind. She hurried up the path and had almost reached the mine when she stopped cold: a hovering thought
had finally struck home. There was a dead man in there.

Helen was not a superstitious woman, nor was she squeamish.
She'd been through too much in the past months—hell, in the past

hours—to be anything other than tough and determined, but the thought of sharing a cold crypt with a corpse was daunting.

On the other hand, the cold was beginning to penetrate her boots, and her legs were chilled. She had to move. She considered that there were only three men; if she moved quickly she might elude them. And if not, well, she was armed. She could shoot, she was on her own turf, she could hide, she could pick them off, perhaps, one by one. For that matter, she thought, if I could take out just one of them the other two would probably bolt. She crept back down the path, clutching the Dan Wesson .357, in her pocket. She was at least momentarily, if grudgingly, grateful to Joe for teaching her to shoot.

But when she reached a point where she could view the cabin and the yard, she was startled to see another vehicle suddenly pull into the yard and stop behind the first. Three men got out, these in overcoats, and she recognized Vetch and his friends. Apparently, the first party had withdrawn to the house; they certainly weren't visible. But one of them came back out to greet the newcomers. "Gone!" he yelled. The four men stood in the yard, hunched into their coats and looking about into the storm. Vetch gestured at her rental car and the man from the first party waved his arm up toward the trees where she huddled. Then they all went inside.

What could this mean? But she soon understood. They were just regrouping. They weren't dressed for a hunt, they were cold. They would get warm, find some gear, flashlights, and plan their strategy. They'd either track her now, or wait until daybreak. But she doubted that they would take a chance that she might hike out to, say, the Garland ranch, where she could find comfort and safety. For one thing, the storm could well obliterate her tracks, and soon, which would make it difficult to track her.

She took a moment to weigh her prospects. Run for the Garland ranch? Or hide in the mine, a dead man for company or no? It was a long cold way to Garland's, she decided, and tramped back up the path to the mine. When she got there she pawed about in the snow for the rock. She finally found it and turned it over. There was no key.

She was stunned. What could have happened? Could someone have been here? Joe? Wasn't he too ill, too infirm to hike up here in a blizzard? Well, not too lame to screw his nurse, anyway, she thought bitterly. But there was no way of knowing, and she couldn't waste time pondering. She stood up and looked wistfully at the half-hidden entry. She stepped closer, through the tangles of brush, and to her relief saw that the key was still in the lock. So that was it. In her haste, weeks earlier, she must have left the key in the lock. It seemed to her that she had replaced it under the rock, but evidently not. She turned the key and opened the door.

Out of the yawning blackness of the tomb a horrifying monster rushed upon her. Helen fell back, crashing through the brush, her fall broken by the drifted snow. The monster was on top of her, immediately, its fingers clawing at her face. It snarled and roared, enraged. It was the dead man, impossible as it was. The musty smell of the grave was on its flapping cloak.

The two figures floundered and scrabbled on the rocky hillside, but Helen was the more lithe, more driven by horror and fear. She writhed away from the grasping hands of the hideous monster. She scurried up the slope on all fours, gasping and desperately clawing for safety, her tears freezing in the bitter wind. She regained the path and turned to run, but the monster, now croaking and panting, was close behind her. A powerful hand clutched at her boot. Helen stumbled and fell against the open door to the mine. Above her the great beast loomed, for all the world like one's worst nightmare of hell. Helen snatched the gun from her pocket and fired. The blast was nearly swallowed in the howling gale, but the monster was hit. It spun sideways, slamming against the door jamb and then tumbling backward, into the black entry.

Helen was up and running. She didn't look back to see the

beast dragging itself into the shelter of the mine, back into the mouth of hell. She ran down the path until she saw men come out of the house and look up her way. No doubt they had heard the shot. She turned onto the path to the hot springs and sprinted up the hill.

Here the trees had sheltered the path from the snow and wind, and not only was it easy going but obviously she would leave few tracks. It would be a different thing once she reached the meadow and headed down toward the ditch road and the ranch. Out there the wind and cold could well kill her. But she would consider that when she got to it.

What she got to was the hot springs. Here it was surprisingly warm, the steam billowing invitingly. She circled the springs, desperately looking for a cave, any kind of hole in which she could hide. In a cave she could hold her own, even if they found her. If she could just last until daylight.

But there was no cave. There really was nothing for it. She would have to leave the springs and set out across the meadow. But it was hard to leave this warm and sheltered place, this sacred place as she thought of it, for the exposed meadow. She had a momentary vision of herself floundering through arctic drifts, freezing as the killers closed in behind her.

She stared at the steaming water regretfully. It was so warm here, so inviting. The billowing steam was as thick as a Detroit River fog, one moment swept away by a stray breeze that huffed down from the roaring and pitching tree tops, then just as quickly reforming into a dense fog. She glanced back up the path. She could see lights, bobbing and flickering through the trees up on the ridge.

Without hesitation she took off only her coat, bundled it in her arms and waded into the steaming pool. Her boots filled with warm water and her pants soaked as she waded to the back wall of the pool, the wonderfully hot water rising to her waist. Best of all, the shifting, swirling steam shut out everything beyond arm's reach. She packed the coat into a crevice nearby and laid the gun next to it. She felt her spirits rise, even as she sank down to shoulder depth, leaning her back against the rugged, mossy face of the dripping rock wall.

The heat penetrated her entirely and she tried to order her racing mind. The confusion and horror of the attack at the mine was inexplicable. There was no way she could approach it, not at this moment. Perhaps in some future time she could get a handle on it, but for now it was quite like a nightmare from which one has been saved by an alarm clock. It was vivid, shocking, but incomprehensible. And as with the nightmare that is soon swept from the waking mind by the pressing events of reality, she shunted it aside as she could hear the men approaching poolside, their flashlights flickering out before them. Here was a real and present danger, but at least one more familiar.

She sank down until only her chin rose above the warm, embracing water. It was so lovely, so fine, and she was so tired, she almost felt drowsy.

Now, she thought, come and find me. With her pitch-black hair, it would be very difficult to see her here, even if they thought to look. She arranged her hair so that it masked her pale face.

She hadn't long to wait. She found that when she looked straight up she could see scattered stars. The wind still howled, tossing the tops of the ponderosas, but the only snow that fell was that blown off the boughs, sifting down into the fluctuating billows of steam. The night sky was clearing rapidly.

Four men gathered at the foot of the pool, not sixty feet away. From moment to moment the mist would part, clearly revealing them, but except for occasionally flashing a light into the mist, they never looked her way. They were bundled into a variety of jackets, taken from the house, all of them much too small for these large men. They were obviously cold, stamping their feet—none of them wore boots. They tucked their hands into their armpits, guns poking out from underarms—Uzis, revolvers. They swore a lot. She could hear them quite clearly, despite the continued roar of the wind in the treetops. It occurred to her that she could probably shoot one or even two of them before they scattered. It wouldn't be enough.

Two of them had powerful flashlights, which they played about the area incessantly. They were afraid, she was pleased to hear. One of them told the others, "You gotta watch out for this fucking bitch. She blew Carmine to rags, with a fucking sawed-off shotgun." They all craned into the darkness.

"What the fuck was she shooting at up there, anyway?" one asked, and another replied, "Probably a bear." They laughed nervously.

One of the lights played across the rock face and Helen lowered her head quickly into the water. When she could hold her breath no longer she raised her head again and took a cautious gulp of air. The light had moved on and they had seen nothing.

"She must of gone down into the field, there," one of them said. "There must be a ranch or something down there." He pointed at one of the ubiquitous sodium-vapor lights that lit up nearly every ranch yard in the country; they came on automatically at nightfall.

"Well." Another one sighed and swore bitterly. "Let's get down there." And they all set off.

But, of course, Helen realized, they will soon see that there are no tracks in the snow. They'll be back.

It didn't take long. The men returned, walking briskly, the lights bouncing. They were hunched against the cold, clearly having lost any taste for a prolonged search for a crazy armed woman in this bitter weather, a woman who had seemingly disappeared and who, anyway, had little chance of survival. They didn't even pause at the springs but hiked straight on by, breathing hoarsely, not talking, and disappeared up the trail. She had little urge to move. She lay back against the rocks, trying to find a relatively smooth spot to recline.

Whooee, she thought, little girl, you've had a long, hard day.

But she couldn't relax for long. It was one thing to lie luxuriously in one's sacred pool, emptying one's mind of troubles when there were not, in fact, any serious troubles; and another to crouch in a violated pool, conscious of the nearby presence of men who wanted to kill you. The simple fact was that she had to get moving, no doubt the sooner the better. With a sigh she stood but was immediately conscious of the incredible weight of her garments. The water poured off her, and even in the steamy heat just above the surface, she could feel the material stiffening as it began to freeze. This was no good. Even with a dry coat, by the time she was halfway to the meadow her clothes would turn to ice. The cowboys would find her come spring, standing frozen in half-stride. She almost laughed. Then she methodically began to strip. It was the only thing to do. She could wring out much of the moisture; the clothes wouldn't dry any time soon, but there was a chance that they wouldn't be quite so encumbering. It looked like it was clearing; perhaps there would be sun. She'd lie in the pool till the sun came out, letting her clothes dry at least a little on the rocks. The gunmen wouldn't be back, she told herself, wishfully. They'd be out of here before dawn. She might even be able to get back into the cabin, into warm clothes.

She had almost finished wringing out her clothes and stashing them in crevices close to the water when yet another light flickered up the trail from below. "Oh, no," she moaned and sank back into her place.

A man dressed in what looked like an old air force parka, the hood closed up to just a slit, came trudging up the trail carrying a light in one mittened hand and an automatic shotgun in the other. He was followed by another man, similarly armed and also carrying a light. They cut their lights as they approached the springs and began to walk more slowly, more carefully. They paused just above her, and she could hear the telltale "hush" of some kind of electronic transmitter.

"Carrie?" the man whispered into the device. "We're at the springs now. We're going up to take a look. We saw some lights earlier, but I don't think they saw us. There are tracks here, so obviously they're out looking around. Don't broadcast unless you absolutely have to. You can hear this damned thing even in this wind. Out." The two men trudged on.

Helen felt weak with relief. Cops! What had brought them here she didn't know and didn't care. Obviously, they had the cabin surrounded. Now more than ever she had to get out of here and down the mountain. Suddenly the pool seemed even more deliciously warm, but there was no help for it: she had to get out of the water into subzero cold and dress. And there was the hike across the meadow, with more cops waiting, cops who would have to be eluded. Cops meant immediate safety, but ultimately they meant arrest and incarceration with a murder trial.

She laid her frosted hair against the steaming rocks and wept. She would sit here in this damned hot springs until she turned into a prune, a bleached prune. And when spring came she would climb out and go back to the cabin. But at last she summoned the courage to rise up and collect her gear. It was better to take the chance. She might get off the mountain, and she might make it across the meadow, and she might elude the cops . . . No! She *would* get to the Garland place and, if need be, take a vehicle there and escape. Or die trying.

But she had not reached the edge of the pond when she saw a light coming back down the trail. She groaned. Was there no end to this? She waded back to her hiding spot and restashed her gear as one of the parkaed cops arrived. He stopped by the edge of the pool, where the killers had stopped earlier. He lifted the walkie-talkie to his mouth and said, "Carrie? This is Mulheisen. Jacky's still up there, watching. Far as we can tell they're all back in the cabin and bunkered in, I'm afraid. All we can do is wait for daybreak. Over."

A woman's voice came over the speaker. "Mul, I hate to tell you this, but the undersheriff is just pulling up, and it looks like he's got a whole division of marines or something with him. Hang on, he wants to talk to you."

A man's voice crackled out. Helen could hear it clearly in the crisp air. "Mulheisen? Crowley here. I've got my team. What's the situation?"

Mulheisen sighed and explained that he and Deputy Lee had gotten close enough to the cabin to determine that six well-armed men were inside. There was no sign of Humann or the nurse, nor of Helen Sedlacek, although her rental car was still in the yard. The nurse's car was gone. Possibly Helen had fled with Humann and the nurse before the men had arrived. He recognized some of the men as Detroit hoods. He urged the undersheriff not to do anything precipitous. Surround the house, keep under cover, and wait until daylight. It would be a lot easier then to deal with the situation, and possibly they could induce the men to come out. After all, these men hardly faced any charge more serious than breaking and entering, if that.

"Looks like this weather's clearing off," Crowley said. "We could get a chopper up here, kinda give us an overview, make sure nobody slips out."

Mulheisen didn't think that was a good idea, an unnecessary expense. The undersheriff seemed annoyed, but he didn't object to Mulheisen's analysis of the situation. He said he would send some men up that way to reinforce Mulheisen and Jacky. The others would disperse around the front gate and the cabin, to make sure no one got away.

Mulheisen had to acquiesce to this, but he repeated that no one should make a move, no shooting, no reacting to shots unless it was necessary for personal safety. It was agreed. Mulheisen switched off, once again with a sigh. He had a bad feeling. A lot of armed men, cold weather, nervousness, eagerness . . . it all presaged disaster.

Through a shift in the mist Helen watched as Mulheisen stood and gazed up at the stars. He had thrown back the hood of the parka to talk on the walkie-talkie and she could make out his face, palely glimmering in the starlight as he gazed upward. "Oh my," he suddenly

breathed, and at the same moment she saw what had drawn this ex-
clamation from him. Sheets of light spread across the night sky. She
thought they were colored, she would always tell people that they
were like vast curtains of shimmering red, blue, and green light. But
in fact, they weren't colored. They were white, fading in and out,
moving mysteriously. And they didn't crackle, either, although she
would also tell others that they did. She rose upright in the water,
dripping, her face turned to the brilliant winter sky.

Then the light caught her in the face and Mulheisen said,
"You better stay put for now, Helen. I don't have anything to keep
you from freezing, but the others will have something. You have the
right to remain silent, you have the right . . ."

He paused as she turned her naked back to him and began to
collect her gear, bundling it under her arm. Then she turned and
waded toward him, her slim white body gleaming in the light. "Get
out of my way, Mul," she said. She gestured with the heavy revolver.

Mulheisen smiled, his teeth glittering wolfishly. "I don't think
so," he said.

"I'll kill you," she said. "You know I will."

He glanced upward. "Under this magnificent dome?" he said
and laughed, a low, chilling laugh.

Helen could feel the cool breeze on her buttocks, blowing between her dripping thighs. Her body temperature was still high, but
she couldn't stand here forever. She was suddenly sick of men, always
talking, always insisting on their way. "Get out of my way, you fool,"
she said.

Now Mulheisen did not laugh. His eyes narrowed and he said,
"Give me the gun, Helen. You don't have a way, not anymore."

"You can't stop me," she said. She was very angry, he could see.

"Oh, I can stop you. I can't let you go. You'll have to shoot me,
and I don't think you want to do that. Give me the gun." He held out
his hand.

"Take the goddamn gun," she cried and threw it at him. The gun hit him in the chest and bounced away and she ran past him, flinging her clothes in his face.

He reeled from the impact of the gun and then tore angrily at the clothing, stumbling against a tree. He wrenched a pair of damp panties off his face and lumbered after her in his heavy gear, soon falling well back. She ran easily and well, her body feeling supple and lean, feeling almost exhilarated as she sprinted down the path. She felt like she could run forever. She felt warm. She would run across the wind-hardened crust of the snow and she would run, run, run like the gingerbread man until she left all these men and all her problems far behind.

In fact, her first several strides across the drifts carried her on the crust, but then a naked foot broke through and she sank thigh deep into the snow. Mulheisen caught her there, both of them tumbling. It was like trying to hold a skinned cat. She writhed and clawed and fought.

Suddenly the muffled sound of a helicopter reached them. They paused in their struggle to look up. Within seconds the helicopter swept overhead, blinding lights searching. "That son of a bitch," Mulheisen snarled, "he already had them on the way."

Jacky was hunkered in the snow, behind the cabin. Inside, he could hear the sound of men hell-bent on finding something. Nails screeched as boards were torn away, sounds of glass breaking. What the hell, he wondered. He slipped closer, crouching next to the propane tank. When he stood up he could see into the kitchen. At least three of the men were visible. They were peering into the utility closet. They were completely engrossed, gesturing and talking. For a moment he contemplated the possibility of a brilliant coup: he would slip in the back door and catch them all unaware. Perhaps a couple of shotgun blasts would get their attention. He'd have them all. He even edged closer, to test the sliding door that led into the bedroom. It was not locked. It could be done. The temptation was great. But then he thought, Nah, Mulheisen's right. Somebody could get killed. It was infinitely wiser to wait until dawn. With regret he edged back from the house, up the slope to a position where he could see all but the front of the house.

And then the chopper swept over. Jacky blessed himself, and Mulheisen, for his prudence. He would probably have been halfway into his brilliant coup when those inside were alerted by the chopper. He wouldn't have had a chance.

Now what, he thought. The sounds of the search in the cabin had instantly ceased. The men were armed and ready. What would they be thinking? It was difficult to assess. The intruders weren't guilty of anything but breaking and entering, possibly burglary, malicious damage, similar charges. Would they be likely to resist? Were there drugs, which might make a breakout seem like a worthwhile risk? He didn't know.

In the midst of these thoughts Jacky was suddenly aware that something new was happening. One of the men came to the sliding door of the bedroom, opened it, and cautiously slipped out onto the little deck. Obviously he was concerned about the helicopter, which he could only have interpreted as a police presence, but something else seemed to concern him more. He crept along the back of the house, past the propane tank, and he seemed to be sniffing and looking up at the roof. He seemed to be looking for something. He quickly returned to the deck and seemed on the verge of re-entering when others began to exit, coughing and holding cloths to their faces. Now Jacky could see faint smoke in the house and he realized that something had started a fire. Jacky counted only four men. Perhaps the others were attempting to put out the fire. For obvious reasons, these men were unwilling to go very far from the house. They milled about irresolutely on the little back deck.

A moment later something very peculiar happened. Before the

shock wave threw him back into the snow, Jacky saw a kind of white pulse, then the entire roof lifted clear of the log walls, the walls spilled outward from the interlocking corners, the logs splintering and separating. The men on the back deck never had a chance.

Jacky never really heard the explosion, although he thought he heard an explosion and a roar behind him, up the hill, the earth shaking. For a moment he irrationally thought that there had been an earthquake, perhaps even the emergence of a volcano. But that was absurd. No doubt it was the column of fire and light that shot straight up into the sky, hoisting the intact roof and briefly lighting up the surrounding trees, that had suggested it.

Then the hovering roof whomped down like a candle snuffer and all the lights went out. But almost at once the light returned with another, smaller explosion and flames hissed, curling around the edges of the roof, like a gas range burner when it first goes on under a pot.

There were no screams, nobody running. Just a muffled blast, then the wind shrieking down into the clearing and the flames burning brighter and brighter. By the time Jacky picked himself up and ran down to the front, into the yard, the undersheriff and his men were arriving. They all stared in awe as the house went up in a screaming crescendo of flames. The heat was intense, and they fell back toward the shed. Jacky noted the scorching heat on his face and the freezing cold at his back. Like the others, he simply stared at the instant inferno before him. It was then that he spotted the crumpled figure of a man lying in the front yard, smoking; that is, what was left of his clothing was smoking. With the help of another deputy Jacky was able to crawl close enough to grab the man's arms and draw him further away, although he noticed with dismay that some of the man's skin was left on the scorched pine needles.

In a surprisingly short period of time the house was essentially consumed. Mulheisen arrived, carrying Helen, wrapped in her coat.

He put her in the back of the sheriff's Blazer, which someone had finally brought up to the scene.

The story didn't make the morning edition of the *Standard*, but the following day, while waiting for Helen's extradition papers, Mulheisen was able to read how no less than six alleged drug traffickers had been cornered by the intrepid Silver Bow Sheriff's Department. At least three of the drug runners were believed to be South American aliens—"notorious drug lords." Only one of the criminals had survived a spectacular explosion and fire at the remote cabin of a mysterious Californian named Joseph Humann. The survivor, bearing a Colombian passport in the name of Victor Echeverria, was in critical condition at St. James Hospital, with severe burns. Evidently, he had left the house by the front door just prior to the explosion and was blown away from the fire. The others, except for one man believed to be trapped inside the house, were killed when the house collapsed on them at the rear of the building. Echeverria was expected to survive but as yet was unable to talk to investigators. Arson investigators were on the case, but it was believed that the criminals had caused the inferno themselves, perhaps with explosives that they had brought in with them. Undersheriff Paul Crowley revealed that he, along with drug enforcement agents and the FBI, had seized a private jet airplane at Butte airport, which was believed to belong to the drug dealers.

"Bullshit," Jacky said, sitting down heavily next to Mulheisen outside Johnny Antoni's office. "I'll tell you, though, when that chopper came over I was nearly in the door. I'm just glad I didn't do it. My grease would be congealing with theirs, right now."

Mulheisen smiled. "Well, I'm glad you didn't go in," he said.

"I'm sorry you didn't get your man," Jacky said. "We put a kidnap bulletin out on him and Cateyo, but nothing has come in. I doubt

that kidnap would hold up, anyway. He couldn't have kidnapped anyone." He laughed. "Maybe she kidnapped him."

Mulheisen smiled and shrugged. "It doesn't make much difference," he said. "I got Helen, anyway, and I'll get Service, one of these
days. At least now I know who I'm looking for." He looked at Jacky
closely. "You ever get that feeling?" he asked. "Now you know. It may
not be tomorrow, maybe not this year, but now the guy is running and
the net is closing."

Jacky Lee almost smiled. "Yeah, I know. Oh, by the way, Sally
called. She was trying to get hold of you."

"Oh yes?" Mulheisen said. "What did she want?"

Jacky eyed him blankly. "Nothing special, I guess," he said.
"She wanted to know if you were all right. Said you should call." He
handed Mulheisen a slip of paper with her name on it and a phone
number. "See ya next time," he said and left.

Antoni was bubbling. "This is great, Mul. Great. Definite
proof that the mob is moving into the Northwest. This'll give the
Northern Tier a boost. You'll see. I'll have you out here running the
whole show."

Mulheisen said they'd have to wait and see. Maybe it was on,
maybe not. For now he just wanted to pick up his prisoner and get
home.

"Ah, about the extradition," Johnny said, "I'm afraid there'll
be a delay."

"What's the deal?" Mulheisen said. "I thought everything was
all set."

"Well, you know, Ms. Sedlacek is still in the hospital," Johnny
said. "She seems to be okay, physically, the doctors say, but mentally . . ." He shook his head. "She's babbling about ghosts, monsters,
dead men. She has asked for counsel and she's retained the best lawyer in the state, and he says they'll fight the extradition. She's got
plenty of money, apparently, and someone already seems to be working on her behalf back in Michigan. Hey, you know what'd be a great

idea, Mul? How 'bout you 'n' me and the kid, we run over to the Salmon River for a day or two, catch some steelhead? You ever catch a steelhead on a fly line? It's fantastic!"

Mulheisen couldn't believe his ears. The part about Helen flipping out and at the same time starting to build a defense sounded about par for the course, but stand in a freezing river, fly-fishing? In this weather? Antoni assured him they would be toasty in their insulated waders.

Mulheisen thought about a red-haired woman with a frank, honest face and hearty laugh, to say nothing of an interesting physique, and replied, "If I'm getting into any Montana water in the next few days, it'll be hot water, my friend," and he went out to call the number Jacky had given him.